Praise for *Beyond the Tides*

"*Beyond the Tides* by Liz Johnson is an amazing contemporary novel. . . . Johnson took me on a beautiful journey of forgiveness, love, loss, grief, and healing."

Urban Lit Magazine

"An emotional and witty story, featuring flawed characters who must learn to reconcile their own shortcomings, *Beyond the Tides* is highly recommended."

Midwest Book Reviews

"Johnson returns to PEI in her new series, and fans will not be disappointed!"

Write-Read-Life

"Readers will love this romantic return to Prince Edward Island, compliments of an author who knows how to design a love story that will linger sweetly in the memories of all those who read it."

Interviews & Reviews

"Johnson kicks off her Prince Edward Island Shores series with this heartwarming romance. . . . Johnson's fans will eagerly anticipate the next installment of this promising series."

Publishers Weekly

Praise for The Last Way Home

"Johnson's sweet, small-town romance filled with strong emotion continues her Prince Edward Island Shores series."

Booklist

"Love going back to PEI and meeting new characters mixed with those readers have already grown to love!"

Write-Read-Life

"*The Last Way Home* is a transcendental experience of lost relationships, heartfelt pain, sorrow, and true unconditional love."

Romance Junkies

"This testament to the power of family and God's forgiveness will have readers eager to see what Johnson does next."

Publishers Weekly

Summer in the Spotlight

Books by Liz Johnson

PRINCE EDWARD ISLAND DREAMS

The Red Door Inn

Where Two Hearts Meet

On Love's Gentle Shore

GEORGIA COAST ROMANCE

A Sparkle of Silver

A Glitter of Gold

A Dazzle of Diamonds

PRINCE EDWARD ISLAND SHORES

Beyond the Tides

The Last Way Home

Summer in the Spotlight

PRINCE EDWARD ISLAND SHORES • 3

Summer in the Spotlight

LIZ JOHNSON

Revell

a division of Baker Publishing Group
Grand Rapids, Michigan

© 2023 by Elizabeth Johnson

Published by Revell
a division of Baker Publishing Group
Grand Rapids, Michigan
www.revellbooks.com

Printed in the United States of America

Library of Congress Cataloging-in-Publication Data
Names: Johnson, Liz, 1981– author.
Title: Summer in the spotlight / Liz Johnson.
Description: Grand Rapids, Michigan : Revell, a division of Baker Publishing
    Group, [2023] | Series: Prince Edward Island shores ; 3
Identifiers: LCCN 2022053180 | ISBN 9780800737399 (paperback) | ISBN
    9780800744625 (casebound) | ISBN 9781493441341 (ebook)
Subjects: LCGFT: Romance fiction. | Christian fiction. | Novels.
Classification: LCC PS3610.O3633 S86 2023 | DDC 813/.6—dc23/eng/20221219
LC record available at https://lccn.loc.gov/2022053180

Scripture quotations are from THE HOLY BIBLE, NEW INTERNATIONAL VERSION®, NIV® Copyright © 1973, 1978, 1984, 2011 by Biblica, Inc.® Used by permission. All rights reserved worldwide.

Published in association with Books & Such Literary Management, www.books
andsuch.com.

Baker Publishing Group publications use paper produced from sustainable forestry practices and post-consumer waste whenever possible.

23   24   25   26   27   28   29   7   6   5   4   3   2   1

To you, dear reader.
Thank you for traveling back to
the island for another story.
And for falling in love with PEI all over again.

And to the people of Prince Edward Island,
who have weathered terrible storms but remain
stalwart and strong. You inspire me.

The mouth of the righteous is a fountain of life,
but the mouth of the wicked conceals
violence.

Proverbs 10:11

one

Meteorologists could not be trusted. At least as far as Levi Ross was concerned. Last winter the guy on the news in Charlottetown had forecasted a light dusting of precipitation. The snow had reached his knees.

So Levi could be forgiven if he didn't believe the perky blond weather girl who warned Prince Edward Island that an especially early hurricane was on its way. He seemed to be the only person on the south shore who hadn't heeded the advice, ransacked grocery store shelves, and burrowed in at home. Most evenings he saw—and successfully avoided—at least one or two teachers lingering over a test to be graded or a lesson plan to be finalized. Tonight the halls of the regional high school were empty, nothing but shadows to keep him company.

Just as he liked it.

He usually shared this time with the big orange sun, but the overcast day had given way to a gray sunset. The wide windows of the school's front hallway lacked their typical glow as he pushed a round blue trash bin across the white-tiled hallway. One of the wheels squeaked, and he made a mental note to fix it for Amos, the usual janitor. Amos had called to say he was staying home because of the hurricane.

Levi didn't mind picking up a few extra hours—or the reflection of that on his paycheck. The house he'd dreamed of, the one he'd put an offer on, was gone. Sold to another buyer. Then again, the down payment he'd saved for was gone too. It had been used to rescue his eldest brother, Eli.

Levi barely missed the money. Especially since his brother was back in town to stay. Besides, he could always make more money. And there would be other houses—like the pretty gray two-story Victorian outside of town and right on the water's edge that had just sprouted a FOR SALE sign in the yard. So, yeah, he didn't mind putting in some overtime.

He glanced out the window again. Through the dim light he could just make out the trees lining the entrance, their arms bending and swaying to a song he couldn't hear. Maybe it was better he was at the school anyway, just in case there was trouble. Not that he expected any.

At least if he got stuck at the school, he'd be stuck on his own. Eli would be with their mom and Violet. Eli was always with Violet these days. And Oliver and Meg would be hunkered down in front of the fire in their bungalow.

Levi smirked to himself as he flung open the door to the first classroom on his left. Crooked rows of desks greeted him, crumpled papers a littered path weaving between the metal legs. He stooped to pick up the trash before shooting it across the room into the bin he'd parked at the far wall.

"Three points for the win."

Levi froze, his hand still suspended above his head, his fingers following the arc the paper had taken. He'd recognize that sweet voice anywhere. He should. He'd heard her perform every single summer at the community theatre. From Maria in *The Sound of Music* to Beatrice in *Much Ado About Nothing*, she'd starred in them all. Shone in them all.

Even in the shadow of the doorway—a kilometer from center stage—Kelsey Ahern very nearly glowed.

He couldn't be any more awkward if he tried as he lowered his hands and offered a shrug and a half smile by way of greeting.

"I thought I had the place to myself," she said and flashed him her straight white teeth. She'd had braces for all of junior high and most of high school, and they'd been worth every minute.

With a nod to the waste bin by Mr. Sullivan's desk, he shrugged again.

Brilliant. He sounded like an imbecile. Or, rather, *didn't* sound like a well-read individual with an operational tongue.

Kelsey nodded as though he'd managed to get out a full thought. "Just ignore me," she chirped as she slipped toward the metal cabinet at the back of the room. "Mike said he had some extra copies of *The Count*." After flinging open the double doors, she practically disappeared into the closet, rummaged around, and reappeared with a short stack of paperbacks. Waving the top one at him, she smiled.

The Count of Monte Cristo. Sword fights and duels. Lost treasure and prison escapes. Betrayal and revenge. Levi had read it at least half a dozen times, and it only got better. Her class was in for a treat.

She glanced down at the stack of books now tucked under her arm, her eyebrows pinching together. "I was going to have them read *The Three Musketeers* over the summer, but the tenth years will be studying Napoleon in their history class. It's the perfect tie-in, but I don't have enough books for everyone in my class. And I'm having to change all my lesson plans, but I think it's worth it. Do you think so?" She looked up, hope in her eyes.

Levi blinked at her, not sure if she was looking for confirmation or for someone to tell her to go back to her original plan. He wanted to tell her he thought it was a great idea, that he'd read a biography of Napoleon after reading *The Count* the first time, when he was just a few years older than her students would be when they started back to school in September.

He wanted to tell her that she couldn't go wrong. That all she had to do was show her students she cared about them.

He wanted to tell her that her smile lit the hallways— long after the students went home for the day. That he looked forward to seeing her, hoped every evening that he'd stumble upon her singing to herself in the drama room.

But since he'd managed to say exactly five words to her since the start of the school year nine months before, he settled for lifting a single shoulder and picking up the trash can he'd come to empty.

"I'm sorry." She shook her head but didn't make a move toward the door. "I'm sure you have better things to think about than my lesson plans. It's just that I doubt Mrs. Davis ever second-guessed herself when we were in school. I don't want to fail these kids—I mean, do the wrong thing for them. Not that I want any of them to fail my class either." Her cheeks turned a pretty shade of pink as she scratched at the little mole on the edge of her left cheek, and she rolled her eyes—likely at herself. "I know. I know. I'm sure it's just second-year jitters." She readjusted the books in her arms, her shoulders rising and falling like she was letting out a deep breath.

But the sound of her sigh was drowned out by a rush of wind that shrieked past the building. Windows rattled and the floor shook. In that instant, rain hammered against the roof, angry and sullen.

Kelsey's eyes flashed wide, and she hugged her books to her chest. "I guess maybe the weather girl was right," she whispered, as though raising her voice might incite the wind again. "Should have gone home early today."

Levi nodded, tearing his gaze from her and watching the torrents against the windows. The sky had been merely gray only a few minutes before. Now it was black, sinister. He couldn't see to the parking lot beyond. He couldn't even see to the trees he'd planted a few meters from the building three years ago.

A gust rattled the windows again like the storm wanted to be inside too.

His gut twisted. He took three cautious steps backward.

Kelsey let out a little peep, a sound of uncertainty mingled with something like fear. But when he turned to look at her, she was wrestling her features into something that he called *teacher face*. No nonsense. In charge. Unflappable.

Every teacher at the school had one. Hers just happened to make his skin tingle and his breath catch.

"Well." She nodded toward the hallway and her classroom beyond. "I guess I better—"

"You're not leaving." He blurted it out like a command, not the question he'd intended. He didn't know which of them was more surprised that he'd spoken.

Kelsey blinked quickly, her mouth opening and closing, but nothing came out.

He wanted to clarify. It wasn't safe. She could be injured. The roads could be flooding, her car swept away. The best thing they could do was wait out the storm. Right here. Together.

Well, together-ish.

But now that he'd actually spoken—and so poorly at that—he wanted to disappear into his work and pretend she'd never walked into this classroom.

She blinked those big blue eyes again—slowly, thoughtfully, as though trying to pick from the glut of words she could unleash on him. Finally she said, "No." She paused, then added, "I won't. I'm going to go back to my classroom now."

She left him to his trash bins and litter and enough self-chastising to rival the downpour outside.

Kelsey had read the same paragraph four times, and the sentences still didn't make sense. Probably because the letters quivered and ran together, blurring words and sentences into a collage of lines that made absolutely no sense.

She rubbed the heels of her hands against her eyes and then blinked hard. It didn't help.

Maybe the rain was too distracting. It had bypassed a simple pitter-patter and instead snapped and popped like an angry fire. Just when she thought it might let up, the wind whipped through the courtyard on the other side of the windows to her back, roaring its displeasure.

She looked behind her into the darkness beyond. There wasn't much but the reflection of the classroom lights in the window, nothing but midnight blue on the other side. She pulled her sweater tighter around her shoulders, a shiver snaking its way down her spine.

But it wasn't the weather keeping her from the book in her hands. This was perfect reading weather—even if she wasn't curled up in front of a fire with her favorite Shakespearean-insults mug filled to the brim with hot cocoa. She couldn't blame her lack of concentration on the time either, although a quick glance at the clock above the whiteboard confirmed that it was well past her pajama hour.

The words on the page weren't making any sense because every time she tried to read them, three little words echoed louder.

"You're not leaving."

Levi Ross hadn't said so many words to her in a row since they were kids. And certainly never with such conviction. His voice was deeper than she'd remembered, more resonant.

If only he could teach a few guys in her drama class to project so well. But that would require him to speak. Publicly.

Maybe he did speak—privately. But that begged the whole if-a-tree-falls-in-the-forest question.

She was supposed to be working on vocab and comprehension questions from *The Count* for next term's grade tens. She was not supposed to be daydreaming about Levi and his soft smile and deep dimples and rich voice. She had more important—

Her world exploded with a crash of shattering glass. There was no time to investigate before something shoved her to the floor, pressing her face against the icy tiles and pinning her arms beneath her. She gasped for air and only managed to choke on the water pelting her. Whatever had pinned her snagged her cotton sweater as she tried to wiggle free. But she stopped on a scream as something cold and sharp sliced into her back.

"Help." She gasped and sputtered and tried again. "Help me." But she couldn't make her voice any louder. Not without air.

Breathe. Just catch her breath. That was all she needed. Then she'd be able to get up.

She tried to capture a full breath, but an elephant had taken a seat on her back.

All right. She'd get up, then she'd breathe.

Pressing her palms flat against the floor, she pushed with everything inside her. Every muscle, every cell in her body trembled. Hopeless.

The classroom lights flickered high above. Once. Twice. Then everything went black.

There was nothing except the unending pinpricks of rain as they bit into her legs and the painful shriek of the wind rustling leaves. Right next to her ear.

All the pieces rushed together then. The tree outside her classroom had come down and crashed through the window. That was what had pinned her down. Was still pinning her down.

She was in a fight with a tree.

She was pretty sure one of her drama professors had made her act out this exact scenario in an improv class. The tree had definitely not weighed this much. And her legs hadn't gone numb, which they most definitely were at the moment. Probably from the cold. Maybe from paralysis.

That was ridiculous. She was not paralyzed. She was—as her mom had once said—imaginative.

A sudden rush of footfalls echoed down the hall outside her classroom, and she tried to call out.

"Ms. Ahern? Are you still here?"

Six words. In a row.

She'd never heard anything sweeter.

"Help." It wasn't more than a strangled whisper, but a beam of light immediately broke the darkness, sweeping across the floor. Blinking against its brilliance, she tried to wave at Levi but couldn't get her arm free.

It didn't matter. He was there in a moment, coaxing the elephant off her back until she could gather a whole breath. Sweet oxygen. Sweet air. Sweet life.

Levi grunted, and she twisted just enough to see that he was still holding the tree above her. She should crawl free. As long as she wasn't paralyzed.

A few quick scoots confirmed that she had full use of her chilled extremities, and she untangled herself from the twigs and branches. The tree collapsed behind her, and then suddenly she was scooped up, held against his chest, surrounded by his warmth. Levi Ross was better than a heater, and she shivered as she curled beneath his chin.

In a blink she was being set down on the sofa in the teachers' lounge, carefully deposited in an upright position. Two electric lanterns magically appeared, bathing them in a soft glow. Levi flipped his wet hair out of his face as he squatted before her, his bright eyes filled with worry.

"Blank-ket?" She couldn't keep her teeth from chattering.

He nodded quickly and disappeared outside the circle of light, then returned moments later with a throw that looked scratchy but warm. When he squatted again to tuck it around her legs, she stopped him with a hand on his forearm. "I want to wrap up in it."

The muscles of his face twitched, and he shook his head slowly, pressing a hand to the outside of her left shoulder. Maybe it was his heat that made pain shoot down her back, but she wasn't holding out hope. A twist and a glance confirmed her doubts. A jagged piece of glass jutted out from her shoulder, a red smear slashed across it.

So, she was impaled and bleeding. And she was probably going to pass out.

Perfect.

A tree with a nefarious agenda? She'd survived.

Possible paralysis? She'd figure it out.

A single drop of blood? Nope. Just nope.

She squeezed her eyes closed and sagged into Levi's shoulder. His flannel shirt was soft against her forehead and smelled like rain and wood shavings.

"Ms. Ahern?" He spoke in a quiet tone, his voice flush with concern but still calm, as he slipped an arm around her side to hold her up.

Her head spun, her stomach on a roller coaster without end.

This was going to get embarrassing. Fast.

two

Levi jostled the woman who had collapsed against him. She didn't respond. "Ms. Ahern?" Still nothing. "Kelsey?" Her name tasted like licorice, a long-lost treat on his lips. But he couldn't afford to start calling her by her first name. Not again. He wasn't the boy he'd been all those years ago. And her pigtails were gone, her knee-high socks too. But her freckles remained, a liberal dusting over the bridge of her nose, across her cheeks, and down her neck. Once, he'd thought about how he'd count every single one of them.

He wasn't that ridiculous anymore.

Levi shook her again, careful not to shift the glass shard in her back. Her head lolled to the side and the corners of her lips pinched, accentuating the little mole tucked into the line of her cheek. The shallow expanding and contracting of her rib cage within his embrace continued. That and the sweet coconut scent of her hair beneath his nose.

Her forehead fell against his shoulder, and she let out a thin cry.

"Ms. Ahern." *Come on. Wake up.* He just needed her to help him out.

But wishing didn't make it so. Her body, limp and unmanageable, seemed to have lost its bone structure. Lowering her to her side, he cushioned her cheek with his palm until she rested against the twill of the sofa and let out a soft snore.

He couldn't help the grin that tugged at the corners of his mouth. If it weren't for the blood on her back and the fact that she'd very clearly passed out, she'd be about perfect.

He skimmed his fingers across the satin skin of her chin and leaned away. Just then she tried to roll onto her back. Grabbing her narrow waist, he held her in place, his breath suddenly coming nearly as fast as the accelerated rate of his heart.

All right, keeping her on her side wasn't going to work. At least as long as she was unconscious.

The school board–mandated first aid training hadn't exactly covered being gouged by glass. Pencil stabbings and slipping on ice had been at the top of that curriculum. Still, he'd read more than a dozen books that dealt with medicine. To be fair, they were novels about a medical detective. But even a novelist had to do some research, right? And Detective Alec Blodger, MD, said never to remove the item used to stab a victim. Often the object was keeping the injured person from bleeding out.

But if he didn't remove it carefully—and Blodger would say to put pressure on the wound immediately—she was going to roll over and dislodge it on her own. Or worse, push it deeper.

His stomach lurched. He had to help her.

No need to look through the window. The black clouds

and pelting rain hadn't relented. No one was coming to help—no one knew they needed help. He plucked his phone out of his pocket to check again. Still no service. The storm had toppled more than trees.

They could be stuck there all night. And he wasn't going to let her lie there with a piece of glass sticking out of her back. Not if he could help it.

Blodger would expect no less.

Levi jumped up, raced toward the white metal cabinet secured to the wall behind the door, and flung the latch open. It clanged against the cinder blocks as he surveyed the first aid instruments. They weren't of the caliber that Blodger carried around in his antiquated medical bag, but Levi wasn't in a position to be picky. He loaded up his arms with the full box of gauze, a flutter of bandages, a half-size bottle of antiseptic spray, and a string of alcohol wipe packets long enough to trail all the way across the dingy tile floor. But there were no latex gloves. The empty box was still there, but he'd cleaned up the contents blown into balloons in the science lab the week before.

He dumped his treasures onto the couch beside his patient, ripped open a wipe, and rubbed it across his palms and up and down each finger. It didn't change the fact that there was dirt under two of his fingernails—or that he'd emptied a dozen trash cans that evening. He could afford another wipe.

"You ready?" he asked his patient. "Yeah, me neither." He sighed as he knelt next to Kelsey and brushed her damp hair from her face. She took a deep breath, completely unaware of what was coming. He wanted to reassure her, but he'd never performed surgery, minor or otherwise.

Grabbing the shard with a gauze pad, he tested the edges of her skin and the depth of the wound. She gasped, her cute little snore replaced with a telling grunt of annoyance.

Noted.

With a deep breath and a firm hand, he gave the glass a quick tug. It immediately popped loose. And the crater left behind filled with blood.

Shoot. Shoot. Shoot.

Blodger would have been prepared.

Levi scrambled for a clean piece of gauze, mopping up the oozing blood. It smelled sharp. Metallic. Quickly overwhelming the scent of clean rain that still clung to Kelsey. His stomach flipped.

Keep it together, man.

They could only afford for one of them to lose it at the sight of blood. Kelsey had called dibs.

Forcing steel somewhere near the vicinity of his spine, he swallowed the bitterness at the back of his throat and lifted the cotton pad. The white was stained red, but the crater was much less so. In fact, without the blood in the way, he could see that the wound wasn't much more than a scratch. Maybe a gash. But certainly not life-threatening.

After he'd applied pressure for another minute, the bleeding had almost stopped, so he picked up the antiseptic spray and gave the wound three quick shots.

He almost missed the movement of her arm but couldn't miss the ringing in his ear as her fist connected with the side of his head. "Owwwww!" she bellowed like a cow with indigestion.

Not that she was a cow. Or anything like one. At all.

She took a shaky breath before her eyelids fluttered,

only teasing him with the sapphire depths of her eyes. On a tight breath, she whispered, "Was that entirely necessary?"

In that moment Levi wanted more than anything to have the words to explain. But his tongue was numb, his brain frozen. He managed only a choked cough.

It was apparently enough to shake off her sleep. Eyes flying open wide, she tried to sit up. But he placed his hand on her shoulder, keeping her firmly on the couch.

"I fainted, didn't I? You must think I'm such a ninny. I'm not. I promise. I just don't like bl—"

He shook his head quickly, but he couldn't fight the tug at the corners of his lips. She'd gone from zero to sixty in two seconds flat. Despite her discomfort.

And somehow she still managed to look prettier than a sunflower while doing it.

She had hit him. Her knuckles still stung from the impact. Nearly as much as whatever was on the back of her shoulder, which still burned like Levi had used a blowtorch on it.

She didn't dare glance back lest there be blood. She did not need to make herself into even more of a ridiculous fool.

"I'm sorry," she finally whispered into the scratchy brown fabric of the couch. She'd sat on it dozens of times, grading papers there after her desk chair had succeeded in putting her backside to sleep. But she'd never sprawled across it with quite so little care. And she'd never noticed the musty smell of its cushions until she'd pressed her nose so firmly against them.

Twisting her neck to face him, she waited for Levi to

unload his annoyance and anger. But they weren't there. He seemed to be fighting a smile instead.

"Did I hurt you?"

He shook his head, then ducked his chin into his shoulder.

"Are you sure?"

After a long moment, his gaze swung back to meet hers, and he held up a bandage. A quick nod at her shoulder, and she understood.

"Thank you," she mumbled as he pressed the bandage in place, his fingers warm and firm against her back.

He moved with such care that the sharp pain almost eased at his touch. Then he sat back on his heels, pressing his hands to his thighs.

Risking a glance at her back, she saw the white gauze tidily taped to her skin where the glass had been before. "So what's the prognosis, Doc?"

His chuckle reverberated somewhere deep in her own chest, and she immediately knew it meant "You'll survive."

"Thank you. I don't know what I would have done if you hadn't been here. There's . . . Is there even anyone else in the building?"

A quick shake of his head confirmed her suspicions, and she wanted to throw her arms around his neck and give him a rave review in the local newspaper. His picture on the front page, his smile charming the whole town. He the hero. She the damsel in distress.

Only, she didn't think he'd appreciate that very much.

He wasn't playing a role, and this definitely wasn't part of some script they'd memorized. Levi Ross wanted attention about as much as a lobster wanted to end up on someone's dinner plate.

So, maybe a no to the front-page story. But the minute she told her best friend Meg—who also happened to be Levi's sister-in-law—all of Victoria by the Sea was going to know he'd rescued her. It couldn't be helped.

The whole town was also going to know that they'd been stuck in the school alone during the hurricane. Good thing she wasn't one of those frontier teachers from a century and a half ago. This didn't violate her contract, and she wasn't going to be forced to marry him.

Kelsey choked on her own breath. She didn't know where that thought had come from, and she wasn't interested in dwelling on it.

"Have you eaten?" She spit the words out in an effort to displace her own wayward musings. It didn't exactly help, but it did make Levi jump into action.

He raced to the refrigerator in the far corner and ducked into the darkness, then appeared again with a single sandwich in hand. With the lift of one shoulder, he asked if that was okay but didn't wait for a response before loping back across the room.

After helping her sit up, he perched on the edge of the couch beside her and handed her the baggie, the crinkling of the plastic cutting through the unending torrent against the windows.

"Is this your dinner?" she asked.

His smile turned a little bit guilty, his gaze darting toward the arm of the sofa to his left.

She'd take that as a no. But the turkey with white cheese on a roll wasn't going to survive the weekend in a refrigerator without power. Even if Levi could fix the problem at the school—and she knew he could—she suspected that all of Victoria by the Sea was without power tonight. And if Charlottetown and Summerside had been hit by the hurricane too, their little hamlet wouldn't be where the power company started their repairs. Besides, maybe her fellow teacher—whoever had brought in this meal—would take pity on her and Levi.

That was an awful lot of rationalizing just to eat a turkey sandwich that was going to end up in the trash next week anyway.

Tearing it in a messy half, she held the bigger portion out to him as crumbs coated the cushion between them. With a laugh she brushed them on the floor with the back of her hand, but her chuckle died on her lips the moment she realized that he and his crew would have to clean up the mess.

"I'm sorry. I didn't mean to . . . to make more work for your team. You all do such a great job, and I mean, you're . . . well, I'm pretty sure this building would fall down without you. Well, I mean, it would have fallen down sooner. Without the tree. But that wasn't your fault. Who could have known . . . except maybe the weather forecasters." Her cheeks burned, and she prayed that the dim shadows kept the pink of her blush hidden. "I just meant that you're so important to this school. And I didn't mean to . . ."

"It's okay."

She wasn't sure if it was the depth of his voice or the warmth of his hand on her own that made her heart skip a beat. Either way, she let out a strained breath and sank into his side as he took the half sandwich from her still outstretched hand. They sat in companionable silence as she stared at her lap. Though she wouldn't look to confirm, she suspected that he was staring at her.

Long after she'd swallowed her last bite, Levi took a deep breath, which shifted her enough to make her realize just how far she'd leaned against his arm. She tried to sit up to give him space.

"Are you comfortable?"

"Yes." She couldn't help responding before he'd even finished his question. She just didn't know if it was an invitation to stay snuggled up against him.

Levi cleared his throat. "I mean, how is your shoulder?"

"My shoulder?" Right. Her injury. The part of her that had bled enough to cause a full-on faint. Not that it took that much. She gave it a small stretch and winced.

He moved as though to stand.

"No." Her word was sharper than she meant it to be. But she couldn't help it. He was warm all over. Her blouse and skirt had turned the blanket damp, so it did little to ward off the chills that still made her arms break out in gooseflesh. "Stay. Please." Risking a glance into his face, she watched for any indication that she'd scared him off.

No, that wasn't quite right. Levi was quiet and soft-spoken, but he didn't frighten easily. There had been a rod of steel down his spine when he'd thrown that tree off her.

"I've had worse dates," she said.

His eyes flashed with something hot then cold, a flame immediately put out by the downpour.

She clapped a hand over her mouth, shaking her head furiously. She needed a script tonight, and instead she had slightly foggy, recently fainted brain. Not good.

"I'm sorry. I just meant . . ." What had she meant? "Not that this was a date. It's not a date. Obviously."

Had she wanted it to be?

That was a silly question. Because it wasn't. Period. End of the essay. Additional paragraphs of support not needed.

He wasn't interested. And she hadn't thought of Levi in those terms since . . . well, that didn't really matter.

"Now I've gone and made this terribly awkward when you rescued me," she said. "I don't suppose we could just blame my unhinged tongue on my injury? Maybe the tree hit my head? Yeah, I'm sure that's what it was. That must have been why I passed out. And why I can't seem to shut up."

He cocked his head to the side, but a grin appeared in the crinkles at the corners of his eyes.

"I'm making this worse, aren't I? I'm sorry. You're just so easy to talk to, and my brain isn't braining very well. I think I need to lie back down." She didn't give him time to get up again, pulling her legs up on the sofa and resting her head on his knee.

Levi froze for a moment. She could feel every muscle in his thigh tense. Then he let out a soft breath, relaxing into this new position.

"Is this all right? Do you mind if I take a little nap?"

He didn't say anything, but leaning over her, he tucked the blanket tighter around her. She took it as permission and stopped fighting her drooping eyelids.

If she'd been playing Laura Ingalls, this would not have gone over well with the school board—a dark night alone with a single man. Good thing she wasn't, because she liked the weight of his hand on her arm and the warmth of his internal heater a little too much.

Giving in to one more shiver, she let out a sigh and fell into the darkness.

three

I assume you've seen the theatre."

Kelsey could only nod mutely. She'd seen it. She couldn't stop seeing it. Every time she closed her eyes, she saw its gray-shingled roof ripped open wide, the rear entrance door hanging by a single bolt, and half the stage sunken and almost unrecognizable.

Sylvia Tremblay, lipstick enthusiast and longtime high school principal, cringed before adjusting her features into a more neutral expression. "The hurricane did more damage than anyone expected."

Kelsey nodded again, pressing a hand to the back of her shoulder where her injury was well on the path to healing. She barely needed a Band-Aid to cover it anymore, and the doctor had been very impressed with Levi's handiwork.

"I'm sorry." Sylvia sighed. "I suppose you know that more than most of us. How are you feeling?"

Kelsey bit her bottom lip, hoping it would script the perfect lines to explain the last three days. Waking up on the couch in the teachers' lounge. Being forced to put the last week of school on hold until the building could be reopened. Seeing her beloved theatre brought so low.

No amount of chewing on her lip helped, so she went with her standard. "My shoulder is feeling fine. Thank you."

Sylvia smiled brightly, folding her hands and leaning on the only available spot on her desk.

Kelsey had a strong suspicion that Sylvia hadn't called her into this den of file folders and paper stacks just to ask about her injury. Not when the only other people in the building were construction workers. And probably Levi. Somewhere in the maze of broken windows and drenched ceiling tiles, he was conducting it all like an orchestra. Probably silently. But no less competently.

She hadn't seen him since she'd woken up, her head still on his knee.

He'd been awake too, his eyes fixed on the leveled trees beyond the window, his dark brows pinched together. She was pretty sure he would have insisted on taking her to the doctor—if he'd opened his mouth. But she'd rolled her shoulder without even a wince and told him to take care of the school. She was fine.

The injury on her shoulder had left very little evidence behind. The hurricane, not so much.

Ripping her thoughts from Levi and that night, Kelsey forced a smile in place. Perhaps this summons was about her still unsigned contract for the next school year. After all, school business had to go on.

"Are you ready for me to sign my new contract?" she asked.

When the corners of Sylvia's too-pink lips dipped, Kelsey's stomach did a barrel roll.

"So, this isn't about that?"

Letting out a slow breath between clenched teeth, the older woman bounced her hands against the desktop exactly three times. When she looked up, her pale eyes were filled with painful resolve. "I'm afraid I can't offer you a contract for next year."

Kelsey gasped on a breath that caught in her throat. "No, but—we talked about . . ."

Sylvia shook her head.

Kelsey couldn't keep her mouth shut. "Is this about changing the summer reading syllabus? I can change it back. I thought my students would have a lively discussion about *The Count of Monte Cristo*, and Mike Sullivan offered me his extra copies. But if you want me to change it back, I will. It's not really a big deal."

Sylvia's chin jerked side to side only once. "Kelsey, I'm sorry. I know this is difficult."

"But I moved back to the island for this job. And I think I've done a good—"

"There's no question about your work. You've been an excellent first-year teacher."

Kelsey sat up a little straighter. "I don't understand the problem. I'm doing my job. My students seem to like me, and the school drama department put on its first independent production in decades. Is there something else I should be doing?"

"No. This is not about you."

"I don't understand. How can it not be about me? You're firing me."

Something fierce flashed in Sylvia's eyes, and Kelsey slammed her mouth closed.

"I am most certainly not firing you. You'll finish out your current contract. I just can't offer you one for next year."

"That's basically the same thing. And it makes no sense. You have no one else to lead the drama program. Unless . . ." Her tongue sputtered to keep up with her thoughts. "Are you going to hire Mike? I mean, he's a great English teacher, but he doesn't have any stage—"

Sylvia swiped her hand through the air. "If you'd stop talking for a second, I'll tell you why."

"Sorry." Kelsey sat on her hands and pressed her lips together.

With a deep breath and an indulgent tilt of her head, Sylvia said, "We're not replacing you. The school board has decided to cut the drama program."

She couldn't be serious. Kelsey couldn't help the way her chin dropped, her mouth hanging open. The school board had been thrilled when she pitched the drama program to them. She'd left Toronto's thriving theatre scene almost a year ago to return to Victoria for this opportunity to make a difference in the lives of her hometown students. To teach them about the joys of the stage and the skills of being part of a production. And even if she'd had other reasons for leaving Toronto—unspoken reasons—she'd made good on her promise to the school and its students.

And all for what? To have them change their minds?

"This doesn't make sense. I don't understand. You just said that I've done a good job."

Sylvia bent her chin over her folded hands and flicked a long pink fingernail against her lip for several seconds. "We couldn't have foreseen the hurricane."

"Is this about money? The cost of fixing the high school?"

"No. This is about the money it will take to fix the theatre." As Sylvia lifted her gaze, her eyes turned watery.

Kelsey blinked quickly, her stomach leaking toward her toes even as a knot formed in her throat.

"I'm sorry. I know it means a lot to you, but the foundation that runs the theatre has decided to close it."

Kelsey gulped in air that was suddenly too thin.

"Without the Victoria Playhouse to feed into, the school board has decided there's not enough reason to continue the drama department."

"No, that's not true." Kelsey almost launched herself out of her chair, but at the wide-eyed look on Sylvia's face, she slowly lowered herself back into her seat. "There are so many benefits to the drama department. Art and theatre teach so much more than just how to memorize a script. Being in a production teaches self-confidence and teamwork. It teaches perseverance and gives a community—"

With a short wave of her hand, Sylvia cut her off. "I understand all of that. But we're a small region with a small school. Without the community theatre, we have no stage to host a production. And these kids won't have much opportunity to continue after graduation." With a sigh and a shake of her head that made her neck wobble, she said, "The school board had to make some tough budget decisions. This is one of them."

"But you're willing to bring in Eli Ross to coach the hockey team next year." Crossing her arms as though she were the petulant child she felt like, she spit out, "I bet that was cheap."

Beneath her pale powder, Sylvia's cheeks pinked.

Yes, news had gotten out. It wasn't official yet. The

school board hadn't sent out a press release or anything. But the town knew.

All right, that might not be entirely true. But at least part of the town knew, including her best friend Meg— Eli's sister-in-law. The school board was plunking down a pretty penny to hire the former New York Rangers' center to coach the boys' team—when he wasn't coaching the Victoria Stars girls' team.

To her credit, Sylvia didn't try to deny the fact. "Hockey is a staple on this island."

Sliding to the edge of her chair until it nearly tipped forward on two legs, Kelsey whispered through gritted teeth, "And so is theatre. You know it is. That building is packed every summer. Tourists. Locals. Kids. Pensioners. Everyone in between. That theatre is the h-heart of this community." Her voice broke, and she gulped against the emotion that made her throat burn and her nose run.

"Honey." Sylvia's features softened as she reached her hand out.

Kelsey pulled back before her boss could give her a condescending pat on the arm. She'd been enduring those since she'd returned to the island. Condolences that ran about as deep as the creek that had trickled through her parents' backyard. Back when they'd lived on the island. Back before they'd decided she wasn't worth sticking around for.

"Please. You can't give up on the drama program." She heaved a silent sigh. "You can't give up on the *theatre*. Not now. Not yet. It's only been a few days."

With a shake of her white curls, Sylvia said, "If it were up to me . . ." Her voice trailed off.

"What?" Kelsey jumped at any sign of hope, remote as it was. "What would you do?"

Sylvia's lips formed a perfectly pink *O*, her eyebrows knitting a single row of despair. "I don't know. But there's nothing I can do. There's nothing anyone can do."

"That can't be true. Someone made this decision. It stands to reason that they can unmake it, right?"

"Sweetie." With that word, Sylvia's face softened. "It wasn't some*one*. It was the whole board. Unanimous. And you know it's extreme when Mable Jean Huxley votes the same way as Henry Deering."

The knot in her stomach grew tighter with each word, no matter how hard Kelsey pressed her hand to it.

Not only was the school board taking her job, but the playhouse foundation was also taking away her theatre. They were trying to tear down her memories. Every note that had been sung, every spin that had been taken on that stage—they wanted to forget those and the people who had performed them. And they were going to steal the opportunity to know that feeling, to stand in that spotlight, from a new generation.

Kelsey stood up so fast that her chair toppled over. She righted it before staring hard at the principal. "Well, maybe Mable Jean Huxley needs a reminder of why she thinks Henry Deering is a softheaded nincompoop."

Sylvia snorted a laugh as Kelsey spun toward the hall, catching her foot on the chair and tumbling through the doorway.

Perhaps not the powerful exit she'd imagined, but it was definitely memorable. And in reviews, memorable was always better than technically perfect.

Levi knew the voice rising from Mrs. Tremblay's office. He just didn't expect its owner to come flying through the door at the exact moment he wheeled a tool cart through the administration offices.

Kelsey fell against him hard enough to shove him into his cart, sending wrenches, winches, and the Mike Myers book on Canada that he'd been reading over lunch flying across the tile floor. The tools' shrieks and screams bounced and echoed through the empty offices.

"Are you all right?" Mrs. Tremblay called from behind her desk.

Kelsey shook her head against his shoulder, but Levi offered an affirmative grunt, pushing the office door closed with the toe of his boot. The principal didn't get up to investigate further, so Levi ignored the mess, immediately wrapping his arms around the trembling woman leaning into him.

We have to stop meeting this way.

He smiled into the crown of her coppery hair. She smelled the same as she had that night—only without the scent of rain and wind and tree. Ducking his head, he tried to look into her eyes, but they were pinched closed, her face redder than a cooked lobster.

Okay, his communication options were limited if she wouldn't look at him. With a gentle squeeze around her shoulders, he tried to release her, but her fists tucked into the front of his tan Henley, twisting the soft fabric in her vise grip.

Something in his gut churned just as hard.

"Kelsey?" He whispered her name, his voice gravelly, out of practice. He couldn't remember if he'd spoken since their last encounter.

"They're not renewing my contract. They're closing the drama program. They—they're—" She finally opened her eyes, the brilliant blue clouded by shimmering waves. "They're closing the playhouse."

"What?" The word popped out before he could think about it. There was no other response to such a ludicrous statement. The Victoria Playhouse was the pillar of their small community. It was a tourist draw and elevated the whole town. No one would dare close it.

"It was—was damaged." Her voice wavered under an unseen pressure. "By the storm."

Yes, he'd figured that much out. But that wasn't a reason to close it. Damages could be fixed. They weren't razing the high school just because a few windows had been shattered and the ceiling had acquired a leak or two. Surely the theatre could be fixed too.

Shaking his head hard, he conveyed that there had to be a misunderstanding. But she still refused to look at him.

"Kelsey." Her name tasted like fresh summer strawberries on his tongue, but he tried not to think about that as he gave her shoulders a small shake. Enough to get her to look at him, for her to see the furrow so deep between his eyebrows that he could physically feel it.

Her lower lip, full and usually turned up in a smile, trembled. "I'm going to lose my job. I'm going to lose . . ."

No. He wasn't going to let that happen. Not that he had a grand plan or anything. But he could do *something*. He hoped.

Just as he began to squeeze her forearm, his entire back vibrated, the epicenter his back pocket. Out of habit, he snatched his phone from his jeans and held it over Kelsey's head. Alice Arcona's name flashed across the screen. His stomach dropped for the second time that morning.

Kelsey let go of his shirt and swiped the heels of her hands across her eyes, leaving a trail of black makeup in their wake. "You should take that."

He gave both her and Alice a firm shake of his head. Alice should know better than to call him. He didn't answer on the best days. He sure wasn't going to now, when Kelsey was having a breakdown—he glanced down to the damp spot on his shirt—on the middle of his chest.

Slipping his phone back into his pocket, he tried to tell Kelsey that he wasn't going anywhere, that she had his whole focus. Instead, he brushed his thumb across her temple over the smudged line.

"I'm a mess, aren't I?" She covered her face with both hands, her long red hair swinging over her shoulders.

Never. Well, maybe a little bit. But less than the last time they'd met.

With a mirthless giggle, she revealed her eyes. "I'm sorry. You keep finding me at my worst, Levi Ross."

The way she used his first and last name felt like a punch in the gut. In a good way. If that were possible.

Her gaze dipped as her eyebrows pinched together. "Only, I don't think you can save me this time." Pressing her shoulders back and forcing her chin up, she said, "I'm going to have to do it myself," as she marched toward the exit.

He opened his mouth to stop her, but he couldn't get a

word out, so he let her go fight her own battle. As Mama Potts would say, God bless whoever she was going to track down.

In his back pocket, his phone vibrated again, then quickly stopped. It was probably Alice's follow-up. Her short-lived stint as his realtor should have taught her that he didn't answer his phone. Period.

He stooped to pick up the tools and his lunch reading that had gone flying.

But what if it was Mama Potts? Or Eli? What if Eli had finally proposed to Violet, and Levi was going to miss out on the celebration because he didn't answer his phone?

Then again, celebrations weren't confined to a single day.

He pushed his cart toward the assistant principal's office, but his brain refused to stop filling in possibilities.

What if Oliver or Meg had been injured? Or there had been another fire? Or . . .

Levi nearly ripped his pocket getting his phone out to check the text. From Alice.

> I'm trying to call you. Answer your phone.

Unlikely.

Just then, another text.

> I'm serious, Levi. You'll want to hear this.

He frowned. The last interaction they'd had hadn't ended well. More accurately, it had ended with her crumpling up an offer for the green house on the shore and throwing it at his head.

You don't have to say a word. Just answer.

With a sigh, he texted back a simple thumbs-up emoji. No need to waste words.

Immediately his phone buzzed angrily. He pressed it to his ear and held his breath.

She didn't bother with niceties. "The new owners are selling the green house."

He managed only a questioning grunt in response. Already? They'd bought it less than a year before. After he'd had to walk away from the storybook cottage. After he'd had to rescind his offer.

"I know what you're thinking, but it wasn't damaged by the storm. The owners had started the process to put it on the market even before the hurricane. I guess they couldn't handle the snow."

Levi snorted. Figured. People who came from away to visit in the summers conveniently forgot about the winters. Islanders knew how to deal with them. Knew how to prepare. Knew that suffering the bitter cold, biting wind, and massive snowfalls a few months a year were worth the view and the smell of salt in the air. They were worth the brilliant yellow canola fields and lavender lupin growing taller than his head.

"So, do you want to put in an offer? The market is hot right now, so we can't dillydally."

Yes. Yes! He wanted to put in an offer. He wanted to call that home his own and drink his coffee from an Adirondack on the porch overlooking the shoreline. He wanted to tear down the wall between the kitchen and the living room and add a breakfast nook. He wanted to turn the gabled attic into a playroom for the nieces and nephews that his brothers and their wives were sure to give him.

Yes. He wanted that house.

But wanting didn't fill empty bank accounts. He'd given nearly every penny of his savings to pay off his brother's debts.

A soft sigh into the phone was all Alice needed to hear.

"Isn't there any chance?" Her voice lost its normally crisp cadence. "Is there someone who could—"

He grunted to cut her off. There was no one he could ask. Not when Mama Potts's Red Clay Shoppe was still finding its footing after the fire last summer. Oliver and Meg's capital was tied up in their new fishing tour business. And even with Eli's new coaching job, his every extra penny was going to save up for an engagement ring for Violet. Not that Eli had officially announced his intentions. But even if Levi hadn't spied his brother shopping on ring websites, he'd have to be in full-on ostrich mode to miss the way Violet bloomed in Eli's presence.

Levi smiled to himself as he pressed the bottom of his foot against the wall at his back, sinking against the cinder blocks. His down payment had made that possible, had kept Eli and Violet together. And he'd do it all over again.

Which would put him in exactly the same spot.

He cleared his throat. "No."

Alice took an audible breath as though she was preparing for verbal battle, and every muscle inside him tensed. Pinching his lips together, he prayed for an escape.

"Levi, listen to me. I've known you since you were knee-high to a grasshopper. I taught your Sunday school class before you could even pick up a book—Lord knows you were probably reading before that though. I've seen you quietly care for your family. I've seen you head off to work at the school, diligently, faithfully. I've seen you reading a thousand books and silently slipping into the library to stock up on even more."

He held his breath, unsure where she was going with all this, somehow craving the validation and terrified of the recognition at the same time.

"But I've never seen you get as excited about anything as I did when we toured the green house. The way your face lit up . . . well, I could almost see your plans for that place in your eyes. It was made for you."

four

'm sorry, Miss Ahern. It's just not our decision."

Kelsey wanted to stamp her foot in the middle of Carrie's bustling café, and only the etiquette Grandma Coletta had forced her to practice as a child kept her feet firmly on the ground and her hands folded primly in front of her as she stood beside Mable Jean Huxley's table. But there wasn't a thing she could do about making her voice match her appearance. "Of course it is."

Mable Jean pursed her lips as she glanced around at her fellow diners. "I know this is disappointing. Trust me." She kept her voice low, her tone even. But her nostrils flared as her eyes rolled toward the restaurant's ceiling. "And the good Lord knows I don't appreciate being put in a position where I have to agree with Henry Deering. But the theatre board has made their decision. And without the playhouse, we can't justify the drama program."

Mable Jean was one of Victoria's most notable matrons. Head of the Victoria Stars hockey team boosters. Married to the senior deacon at Grace Community Church. Longest continuous member of the local school board.

Kelsey eyed the empty chair at the table. Mable Jean's gaze also dipped toward the seat, but she pushed herself gracefully to her feet before Kelsey could claim it. "This isn't what anyone wants, least of all me." She pressed a hand to Kelsey's upper arm as Mr. Huxley strolled across the lively dining room toward them.

"So, you don't want to get rid of the theatre program at the high school?" Kelsey asked.

"That's what I've been saying."

Something in her chest snapped like a rubber band pulled too tight, and she blurted out the only thing she could think. "So you're saying if the Victoria Playhouse reopens, you'll keep the program?"

Mable Jean's eyes flashed with something that looked a lot like hope. "I'd say that would at least give you a fighting chance."

Mable Jean and her husband disappeared through the front door with a wave at one of the waitresses who Kelsey vaguely recognized as a student from the high school. But she couldn't get her feet to follow them. She knew she had to be drawing the curious stares of others in the dining room, but she held herself as still as possible, her gaze focused on a wooden ceiling beam as she tried to wrap her head around what Mable Jean had just said.

If she could save the theatre, she could save her program. And her job.

It sounded so simple. An equation even she could solve.

Only . . . how on earth could she save the Victoria Playhouse when the board had already decided to close it?

The back of her throat burned, and she pinched her eyes against the flames licking at her temples.

This wasn't over. She just needed a plan. And maybe a little bit of help.

She knew what it took to make a stage come alive. She just had no idea what it took to actually make a stage. Or the walls surrounding it.

But she knew someone who did.

Running for the door, she nearly trampled the busboy coming to clear the Huxleys' table. With a quick apology and an expert-level spin, she darted out the door and into the sunshine. She raced down the green wooden stairs and threw herself behind the wheel of her ten-year-old Ford compact. Gravel flew as she swerved to miss a wooden barrier.

"Lord, let him be at the school," she whispered as she barreled down the two-lane road. She felt a little guilty about adding a prayer that Kevin would be at home enjoying a leisurely lunch instead of on patrol, while she stretched the speed limit. But some things couldn't be helped. Every moment that she let the board of the playhouse settle into the idea that they'd made the right decision would make it even harder to change their minds.

After skidding into the empty school parking lot, she threw her car into Park and prayed that Levi's truck was in the back. By the time she flung open the school's front door, her breathing was coming in heaving waves, her ears ringing. She was going to have to work in some cardio before her next musical.

But there wasn't time to dwell on that as she raced toward the wing where she'd last seen the contractors working on the roof. As she whipped around a corner, she pulled up short, stopping a centimeter before plowing into Levi. Again.

Immediately his face contorted with concern. His lips remained in a tight line, but his blue eyes asked a million questions.

Kelsey opened her mouth to answer them, but the only sound that came out was a gasp—and then three more. Her lungs ached, and her pulse pounded behind her eyes.

More cardio was definitely in order. More cardio and less stress. And maybe a little less melting inside whenever she ran into Levi Ross. The man made her heart do a running leap, which did not help her wheezing.

Leaning on her knees, she gulped in air until her pulse was fast but steady. Then she looked up at Levi through one open eye. "I'm okay."

He nodded, the worry still written across every wrinkle of his forehead.

"Really." She snatched another deep breath before opening her other eye and pushing herself upright. Hands on her hips and back straight, she said, "I need your help."

He responded with a quick nod.

Her smile came just as quickly. "But I haven't told you what I need."

He lifted a single shoulder under the white Henley that hugged him in all the right places, showing off his sturdy shoulders and narrow waist.

Like warm maple syrup coating a pancake, his trust flowed through her, easing the constriction around her lungs and somehow making everything right.

"I . . ." Suddenly she couldn't ask him. He'd already rescued her from under a tree, removed the glass from her shoulder, kept her calm during a raging storm. She owed him everything. He owed her nothing.

With a small shake of her head, she sighed, her gaze dropping to the scuffed floor tiles. "Never mind. I can't ask you for another favor."

"Why not?"

Sometimes she forgot how deep and smooth his voice was, how it wrapped around her, filling her senses. She thought it would feel like a weighted blanket on a cold winter night.

Forcing herself to focus on his two simple words and not the way he spoke them, she tried for a smile that didn't quite stick. "Because you're . . ."

His eyes narrowed and filled with something she couldn't quite define. It wasn't anger, but it was dark. Pained.

"You're so busy," she rushed to continue. "And I owe you way more than I can repay. And . . . the theatre is my thing. I can't ask you to drop your work." Hanging her head, she sighed. This had been a stupid idea. "I'm sorry for wasting your time."

She hadn't even gotten halfway turned around when his hand caught her wrist. His fingers were long and firm, roughened by work yet just as gentle as he'd been the night of the storm. She froze at his touch, her gaze landing at the point where they connected, where her skin felt like it glowed. She looked up at him, and his eyes were trained on the same spot.

"What if I want you to?"

She swallowed. "Waste your time?"

The corner of his mouth rose into a tiny smirk, but he nodded.

"You want to help me save the theatre?"

His eyes flashed bright, and she realized that only then had she revealed why she was there. But the light in his face couldn't be mistaken, though he said nothing else.

"I . . . I'm going to figure out a way to keep the playhouse open. But I don't know what kind of damage was done or what it would take to fix it. I thought you might . . ."

He didn't need to say a single word. A small dip of his chin communicated it all.

He was in.

Levi probably should have taken a look at the theatre before committing to help Kelsey the day before. Repairs on the school would be done in short order, but he was going to need to pick up a second job over the summer if he wanted to make another offer on the green house. And that would not leave much time to help with the disaster before him.

But the minute Kelsey had suggested she shouldn't have asked him for a favor, Levi had imagined her going to someone else. Asking another man.

A fire in his belly like he'd eaten an entire kettle of Mama Potts's chili consumed him. He didn't want her going to someone else. He wanted her to *want* to ask him.

The fact that she'd trust him to help her save the thing she loved the most made his pulse beat a little harder. Which didn't make any sense.

Some things couldn't be overanalyzed.

Now he stood on a half-destroyed stage that smelled of mold and warped wood and stared at the cerulean blue sky through a gaping hole in the roof of the playhouse. The front of the hall hadn't sustained much damage. But like the school, the stage side had taken a direct hit from an uprooted tree. He could almost feel the rain still pouring through the hole, pooling on the stage, soaking the insulation in the walls.

This building didn't require a patch job. It needed to be torn down to the studs from the first row of red-velvet seats all the way to the last dressing room backstage.

"Didn't expect to see you today, Levi."

He turned at the voice of Patrick Macon, who had managed the old building for as long as Levi had been alive, and probably for years before that. A friend of his dad's—from before—Patrick had helped Levi get the job at the school and taught him pretty much everything he knew about keeping a building standing. Things his dad might have taught him if he'd been around.

Levi grabbed Patrick's outstretched hand and shook it by way of response.

"How's your mom?" The corners of Patrick's eyes crinkled, the gray flashing so bright it matched the hair at his temples.

With a nod and a smile, Levi confirmed that Mama Potts was doing well. Better than well, actually. Her Red Clay Shoppe was recovering from the fire last year, and sales were nearly double what they'd been the year before. Maybe having all three of her sons back on the island agreed with her.

Not that Levi was going to share all of that with the older man.

"So what brings you by today?"

"I'm sorry I'm late!" Out of breath and face glowing, Kelsey jogged down the center aisle. The little hairs around her face curled sweetly as she swiped her hand over her upper lip and pressed a finger to the mole tucked into the smile line of her cheek.

Patrick looked down the aisle, grinned, and gave Levi a knowing nudge with his elbow. "Enough said," he grunted under his breath.

It wasn't like that. Well, at least not from where Kelsey stood.

"Why, Kelsey Ahern, what a sight for sore eyes. I haven't seen you since your last show here. What was that . . . three—"

"Four."

"—four years ago." With a shake of his head, Patrick corrected himself as he pulled Kelsey in for a hug. "*Annie*, was it?"

"Yep."

Levi ducked his head, fighting the heat at his neck and praying that the color didn't reach his ears. He'd seen that show four times, always from the shadows of the back row. He knew he wasn't supposed to root for Miss Hannigan, but Kelsey had played her with so much heart that he'd seen right through her stringy wig and wicked sneer.

"You should have played the title role," Patrick said, tugging on the tip of her red ponytail.

"Yeah, right." She laughed a sweet melody. "I was a little too old for that. Besides, Miss Hannigan is a much more fun role."

"You were perfect." Levi wanted to clamp his hand over his mouth. He rarely let anything out without due consideration. But Kelsey had him doing all sorts of surprising things lately. And if her wide blue eyes and the high arch of her eyebrows were any indication, he'd surprised her too.

Patrick didn't bother feigning surprise. Instead, he offered a knowing chuckle.

Levi shot him a look he hoped told Patrick to cut it out. The message was clearly received and ignored.

Even in the dim lights, Kelsey's cheeks had turned rosy. "I didn't know you . . . I don't remember you in the foyer after the show."

Because he'd bolted before the curtain was halfway down. Because someone would have noticed him there. Because foyers were a cesspool of small talk.

And now they were talking about him. The only thing worse than talking in public was being talked about in public.

Tilting his head toward the hole in the ceiling, he tried to change the subject.

Kelsey followed along, her teeth immediately sinking into her lower lip. "It's bad, isn't it?"

"I don't think *bad* is the right word," Patrick said as he crossed his arms and arched his back to get a better view of the exposed ceiling beams. "Catastrophic. That's the word you're looking for."

"But it's just a hole. Can't it be patched?"

Levi knew the answer. Patrick spoke it. "It's not just patching a hole. At least half the roof will have to be fixed. And I suspect that when a roofer gets up there, we'll discover the whole thing needs to be replaced."

"How much would that be?"

"Twenty or thirty thousand. At least."

Kelsey's gaze darted toward Levi, clearly asking him to disagree, but he could only nod. Patrick was right. Actually, his estimate might be on the low end.

Her shoulders sank. "And the stage? It'll have to be replaced too?"

Levi nodded again.

"And there's no way to . . . to put on a show here?"

Patrick gave a humorless chuckle. "I know this is tough news. Nobody wants to close the playhouse. But the board of directors doesn't have the budget to make the repairs. And without those, there's no way to host a production. The building is just going to sit and rot, a pock on the town."

"But if it closes, the whole town is going to be hurt. What about all of the tourists who come to see a show? They won't rent rooms at the B and B. They won't get a meal at Carrie's. They won't shop at Mama Potts's." Kelsey had let everything out in one breath and sucked in more air before speaking again. "Are we just going to let the whole community crumble?"

"You're not the only one this affects," Patrick said. "I'm losing my job too."

Levi jerked back with the force of the realization.

Patrick shrugged. "I figured it was the good Lord's way of telling me it's time to retire."

He couldn't be much past sixty. He was about the same age as Mama Potts, and she wasn't going to give up her shop and studio anytime soon.

Kelsey pressed her fingers to her lips, but Levi could still see the quiver of her chin. "Oh, Pat. I didn't know. I'm so sorry. Here I am going on . . . I must sound so selfish."

Patrick's big paw clamped on her shoulder as his eyes darted toward the worst of the damage. "There's plenty of heartbreak to go around, I suppose. We all have lots of memories in this building. There's just nothing to be done about it."

Kelsey's shoulder drooped, seemingly no longer able to support the weight of Patrick's hand. The other shoulder quickly followed. She was crumbling before them.

Sweeping his arm behind her, Levi ushered Kelsey toward the still-standing side of the stage. He wrapped his hands around her waist and gave her a boost until she sat on the edge, her bright green sneakers dangling above the floor. She offered him a soft smile of thanks.

Anytime. At least that was what he tried to convey with a subtle tilt of his head.

Kelsey's eyes glittered like a gemstone, and he couldn't look away.

Until Patrick cleared his throat louder than necessary. "Well then. I guess I'll let you kids look around a little more. I've got a meeting with the executive director—or, the soon-to-be former director."

"Thank you," Kelsey said, her voice small, her back hunched over.

"Wish I could have done more," Patrick said.

Levi held out his hand, which Patrick took in a solid shake.

"Say hi to your mom for me." With a sly grin and a quick wave, he strolled down the center aisle and disappeared into the front of the playhouse.

Suddenly alone with Kelsey, Levi felt the weight of silence more keenly than usual. He couldn't remember the last time he'd wanted to drown out the rustling leaves or fill a vacancy. But somehow he couldn't keep from staring at her. And even he knew that staring silently at a pretty girl was a little bit creepy.

Since he had no words adequate for the moment, he hopped onto the stage to sit beside her, the heels of his work boots bouncing an unsteady rhythm against the wood finishing. *Boom. Pop, pop.* The sounds repeated over and over, the rhythm offering a sad apology. *I'm sor-ry. I'm sor-ry.*

The wind through the roof swept the sounds away, mingling them with twittering birdsong until he couldn't tell where the echoes began and ended.

"I had an idea."

Levi glanced at Kelsey out of the corner of his eye to see her chewing on her thumbnail.

"But now that we're here . . . I guess it was a silly idea all along."

"Doubt it."

five

The hand Kelsey had been leaning on flew off the boards, and she nearly tumbled off the stage at Levi's words. She wasn't sure what was more surprising—what he'd said or *that* he'd said it.

Either way, his "Doubt it" had set her heart thundering. Or maybe it was the way she'd nearly planted herself on the ground. Probably the latter. Definitely that.

Levi reached for her but stopped before his hand could cup her elbow. The question in his raised eyebrows was all too familiar—the one she got every time she stumbled.

Well, she wasn't going to answer it this time. Instead, she said, "How do you know it's not a silly idea? You haven't even heard it. I don't even have it fleshed out. It's more like three-quarters of an idea—or maybe two-thirds. I've literally told no one else, and now it's all a moot—"

He cleared his throat, and she bit her tongue, which wanted to keep flapping. She was doing that thing again where she filled the silence. That was so much easier than just sitting in the quiet.

Levi didn't seem afflicted with the same. Nor did he seem to mind when she rambled on.

Except his low "ahem" was loaded. He didn't want to silence her. He wanted to hear her idea. Her ridiculous idea. And she had a strong suspicion that he was going to keep staring at her until she told him what it was.

"Fine." She swung her legs and bumped the stage with her heels. "I had this idea that the island really loves this theatre and maybe they would—I don't know—come out for a benefit show. We could raise enough with ticket sales and donations to fix the theatre and keep it open. Just saying it out loud sounds selfish. But honestly, I'd want to help keep the theatre open even if my job wasn't on the line." Her breath came out on a stutter as she hung her chin. "But I can't put on a show by myself. Even a small production would take a dozen cast and crew members. And even if I could round up enough people willing to donate their time . . ." She swung her hand toward the gaping hole in the roof as though that was enough to complete her thought.

Chancing a glance in Levi's direction, she waited for his laughter. But he wasn't chuckling. He wasn't even smiling. He was plucking at his chin and staring at the front row of seats like it might hold the key to all of his future happiness.

"I mean, the whole idea is flawed. You can't hold a benefit at the place that needs to be fixed up."

Levi's black hair shifted, reflecting the sunlight from a new angle as he tilted his head. A low hum in the back of his throat made her lean in as though it might be the precursor to something brilliant. But he didn't speak. He didn't even look in her direction.

"I'm sorry I wasted your afternoon. Like I said, it was a silly idea. I didn't realize just how badly this old building was damaged." With a hand on either side of her, she pushed herself off the stage and turned to face him.

Levi hadn't agreed with her verdict, and he still wasn't looking at her.

"Should we . . ." She motioned toward the exit, taking a step down the aisle.

"It's not silly. It's a good idea."

Despite the earnest gravel in his voice, she laughed. "Thank you for trying to cheer me up, but no. I'm fully aware of my own irrationalities. Sometimes I just let myself get carried away by a dream. By a memory. I forget that I live in the real world, not in my own daydreams. I can't just snap my fingers and make this happen."

His feet thumped on the damp carpet when he hopped down to join her. "Who said it has to take place here?"

"Well, we don't have another stage in town."

Summerside's theatre was the closest on the south shore, but it was already booked from May through September. And most of the performances would be completely sold out. They couldn't fit another show into their season.

Levi nodded but added a strange dip to his chin, a subtle invitation to keep thinking it through. She wanted to poke his shoulder until he spoke again, to get him to tell her what he was thinking. To use all his words. But he only left her to her own trail of thoughts, to work out whatever he'd thought could build on her idea.

"You think a show would work?"

He nodded.

"But where? The playhouse is out. Summerside is

booked." She bit her lip and stared at a patch of flooring beside his feet. "Charlottetown is for the professional
shows. But maybe . . . like a community hall?" She quickly
dismissed that with a shake of her head. "They're too small.
We need to be able to seat more than that."

Even with old church pews lining the walls and folding chairs filling every corner of the Stanley Bridge Hall,
it wouldn't be big enough. It could fit only a few hundred—if the fire marshal from Charlottetown didn't shut
them down. To save the Victoria Playhouse, they needed
enough space to host the whole island. Or at least friends
from every corner. They had to look beyond their own
community.

With a quick nod toward the aisle and a subtle sweep
of his hand toward the foyer, Levi seemed to be inviting
her to take a walk with him. She had a feeling that was the
only way she was going to learn what he wasn't saying.

Falling into step together, they strolled through the foyer
draped in ruby-red curtains and plush carpeting. As they
walked into the bright summer sun, Levi lifted his face to
its warmth, and Kelsey couldn't help raising her own to
watch him. A muscle in his jaw jumped, and he stretched
his neck, showing off the strength there.

By the time she tore her gaze away from the cords at his
throat, they were halfway to the shore, the empty fishing
harbor off to their right, the lighthouse museum straight
ahead. The cement dock held a few cars, most likely diners
at the Lobster Barn, the gray-shingled building at the end
of the pier. Although lobster boats around the rest of the
island—those that hadn't been damaged by the storm—
were out en masse, Victoria lobstermen wouldn't set their

traps until August. Most local boats had been taken up from the harbor for the winter and wouldn't set out again for a few more weeks.

At the intersection, she began to stroll toward the dock, but Levi plucked at her sleeve, nodding toward the lighthouse. It wasn't very tall as island lighthouses went, but its four white walls and traditional red trim had all the hallmarks of a classic. She didn't know a single local who had visited it, but after a quick traffic check, Levi led her across the street.

"The lighthouse?" She couldn't keep the skepticism from her voice. Whatever she'd thought he was going to show her, this wasn't it. "I've seen it before." Like every day of her growing-up years.

Levi rolled his eyes, then caught her gaze and held it for a full second before spreading his arms wide, palms up.

She blinked, following his movement, trying to see what he did.

The lawn of the park spread out far beyond the lighthouse. Green and lush, it reached all the way to the red shoreline, where the waves frolicked along the pebble-covered beach. It made her want to slip off her shoes and wiggle her toes into the earth.

She shrugged. "It's beautiful. But I don't understand."

His throat contracted as he swallowed, then he let out a little breath between the firm line of his lips. "It could be an outdoor show."

"Here?" Of course he meant here.

With a slow spin, she took a better look at their surroundings. The lawn stretched for meters and meters, as though it had been planted for a Sunday afternoon picnic. A gentle breeze carried the scent of earth and water, sunshine and life.

Suddenly she could see it. Bright blankets dotting the green. Moms and dads and kids in lawn chairs. Baskets of food unpacked with joy and laughter. And beside the lighthouse, a stage.

"We'll put the platform over here," she announced, her hands stretching wide to show him her vision. "And we'll build a frame to hold the curtain." She paused and blinked at him. "Well, I can't build that. I don't know how to build anything, but . . ."

Levi chuckled and nodded.

"So you're in this with me? You'll help me out?"

If he thought about it, he didn't take long. With another nod, he was all in.

Kelsey flung her arms around his neck. He hesitated for a moment, then wrapped his arms about her waist, holding her close enough to steal her breath.

Or maybe that was the excitement of their plan. It was going to work. It had to. Not just for her job but for the memories the playhouse held.

If Central Park could host Shakespeare outdoors every summer, then Victoria could host a show or two by the shore. And they could save the playhouse.

———

"Levi Michael Ross."

Levi froze on the couch, mid turn of the page. He was almost done with Mike Meyers's book—basically a love letter to Canada—and he'd been hoping to finish it in peace. Violet's greeting suggested he wasn't going to get his wish.

The brunette stomped through the kitchen and into Mama Potts's living room. She stopped right before him, her fists on her hips. If he didn't know her better, he'd think she was upset. But he could read the verve in her eyes.

"Mable Jean Huxley told Eli she saw you in a *romantic embrace*"—she punctuated the last two words with air quotes—"at the lighthouse earlier today."

Levi rolled his eyes and tried to go back to his book. He wouldn't have minded Violet asking him—she was more sister than friend. But he wasn't inclined to respond to gossip coming from Mable Jean Huxley and the other town biddies.

Besides, it hadn't been a *romantic embrace*. That sounded like something that happened only in books that featured Fabio on the cover.

So what if his heart had hammered a little harder than usual when Kelsey launched herself at him? He'd had only half a second to brace for impact, and he was thankful at least for that. If he was lucky, she hadn't felt him sway or noticed the half step back he'd needed to keep them both steady. Or the hesitancy in his return hug.

"Le-vi." Violet plopped down a little closer than necessary, hip to hip, and her shoulder pressed against his arm. "Who was it? Are you seeing someone? And you didn't even tell me?"

With a sigh, he closed his book. Meeting her gaze straight on, he said, "No."

"No, what? No, you didn't tell me? Or no, you aren't seeing anyone?"

Most of the time it was easy to pick and choose when he wanted to speak—to decide when he had something worth adding. He just let others carry the conversation. That was harder to do when Violet pestered him with direct questions.

Squeezing his forearm between her hands, she leaned in so close that he couldn't have seen the page of his book even if he'd tried. "Levi." She smiled big and blinked her long black lashes at him. "Please."

He snorted a laugh. "Go try that on my brother."

She chuckled too. "Have you told *him* who you're seeing?"

"Nope."

"Then what's the use?" With a giggle she sat back on the blue sofa and crossed her arms over a lumpy gray throw pillow.

"Done flirting with Eli already?"

The kitchen door slammed closed, and his eldest brother's voice carried through the whole first floor. "Who's flirting with me?"

"I am," Violet called, shooting Levi a wink.

"Good." Eli appeared, his hockey sweater pulled off over his head but still on one arm, revealing the red Victoria Stars T-shirt beneath. He leaned over the arm of the couch and pressed his lips to Violet's.

That was common practice these days. Had been for almost a year. But it still made Levi look away.

There hadn't been much love in their childhood home by the time Levi arrived. In fact, he couldn't remember his dad kissing Mama Potts—ever—before he left when Levi was fifteen. Maybe his older brothers had different memories, but Levi hadn't been used to seeing much affection until Oliver met Meg—or, rather, re-met her.

Now love seemed to be everywhere he turned. It was a nice change.

Eli finally looked up from his girlfriend's smile and slapped him on the back. "Hey, Levi. She trying to get you to talk again?"

"Pretty much always," Violet said.

Eli tugged off the rest of his sweater and stretched his neck and shoulders like his workout with the Stars was on par with his time with the Rangers. "About anything in particular?"

Violet's smile could have relit the sun. "You know what Mab—"

Levi gave her knee a shove and shot her a serious side-eye. But the damage was already done.

"Mable Jean was right?" Eli's eyebrows shot up. "Were you making out with someone by the lighthouse?"

"Who's making out by the lighthouse?"

Perfect. Oliver had stopped by. The man had his own home and a pretty, pregnant wife in it. Why wasn't he there?

"No one," Levi grumbled at the same time Violet sang, "Levi!"

"No way." Oliver dropped into the armchair across from the sofa, tossing his ankle over the opposite knee. "You finally get up the nerve to ask a girl out?"

That hit like a cheap shot. Entirely accurate, but still a low blow.

"Apparently," Eli responded. "Mable Jean saw him in a torrid embrace by the lighthouse."

"Not torrid. *Romantic.*"

Oliver and Eli shot him big-brother smirks, and Levi immediately regretted correcting Eli.

"Leave me alone. I'm reading."

Technically his book was closed. Still, he was attempting to read. He *would* be reading if the majority of the Ross family hadn't invaded his space and time. Then again, he couldn't blame anyone but himself. They were a family again—an actual, fully formed family—since he'd gone and given Eli his down payment on the green house. Because he'd wanted Eli to stick around. So this was what he got.

He couldn't help the grin that tugged at the corners of his lips.

"Seriously, man," Violet said, her voice dripping with maple syrup. "Tell us what's going on. Who's the girl? Anyone we know?"

Oliver snorted. As though they wouldn't know her.

Levi started to shake his head, but he knew better than that when Eli pinned him with a hard stare. Pigheaded. Stubborn. Didn't know how to quit. That was how Eli had made it to the NHL. And apparently it was how he was going to force his brother to open up.

"Kelsey."

"Ahern?" Oliver choked on his own tongue. "Meg's friend?"

Levi shrugged, but Violet waved her someday brother-in-law silent. "You were making out with Kelsey Ahern?"

"No." Levi spoke slow and clearly. There was no room for rumors in a town that couldn't even fill the local community theatre. "We were *not* kissing."

Eli leaned closer, elbows resting on his knees, eyes flashing the same bright blue Levi saw in the mirror. "Then what were you doing?"

Scrubbing a hand down his face, Levi had to physically hold himself back from throwing his hardback at his brother. He just didn't know which one of them he wanted on the receiving end of it.

"There was no kissing. There was nothing. We were just talking." His voice dropped to barely above a whisper. "She may have hugged me."

Violet squealed and clapped her hands twice. "I knew it! You do have a girlfriend."

He exploded to his feet. "I do not have a girlfriend. I wasn't kissing anyone, and there's nothing happening between me and Kelsey." He hoped his tone didn't carry the flash of disappointment that rushed through him at his words. Taking a deep breath through his nose, he pointed at Eli. "You need to end those rumors. I don't care what you tell Mable Jean, just fix this. Kelsey didn't do anything wrong, and she doesn't deserve to have the gossips using her for fodder. She's had a hard enough week as it is. I don't care if they talk about me, but Kelsey deserves better. She's trying to do something good for this community, and they don't even know it yet."

Violet's eyes were as big as a doe's, her mouth hanging open as she tugged on his arm.

Levi dropped back into his seat, his hands shaking and his lungs contracting. He hadn't spoken that many words in a row in a long time. Maybe ever. Definitely not since he was fifteen.

Pressing a cool hand on his forearm, Violet offered a soft smile. "What is Kelsey doing?"

He bit his bottom lip and pinched the bridge of his nose. Maybe Kelsey wasn't ready to talk about the idea. It was hers, and she should be the one to tell the town about it.

As far as he knew, the pool of people who knew she had lost her job was confined to the school, the theatre, and him. But he couldn't exactly say as much as he had and leave his still gaping brothers hanging.

"It's a . . . the playhouse . . ."

He was silent long enough that Oliver chimed in. "I drove by it on my way to the dock today. It looks pretty beat up. Are they going to have to cancel a show or two?"

"Not a show. The season. And every one after that."

"They can't close the playhouse," Violet said, glancing at Eli like she was looking for confirmation that she'd misunderstood. "Why would they do that?"

"It's bad." Levi felt his face folding in distaste. "The foundation decided it couldn't afford to keep it open."

Oliver grunted. His carefree pose had turned rigid. "What does that have to do with Kelsey?"

"She's going to try to save it," Violet supplied. With a glance at Levi, she raised an eyebrow to confirm.

He shrugged his agreement.

"And you're going to help?" she continued.

He nodded.

"So, what's she going to do?" Maybe Violet could read the hesitation on his face. Or maybe she could read his mind. Either way, she gave Eli and Oliver each a pointed look. "We won't say a word."

Both of them knew better than to cross her.

Levi sighed. "A show in the park beside the lighthouse."

"A benefit?" Her eyes lit up, her whole body nearly buzzing with joy. "Oh, that's perfect! And you're going to help with the stage."

He nodded.

"And the set?"

Probably. His shrug was all Violet needed to keep going.

"And you're going to help pack the park."

He frowned.

Violet's mouth turned down to match his. "You're going to need more than Victoria to raise enough to fix the playhouse, aren't you?"

Kelsey had said the same thing.

Oliver covered a snort with back of his knuckles. "Sure. Put Levi on TV inviting the whole island to attend. That's going to work well."

"Oh, be quiet, you." Violet tugged off her glaze-splattered shoe and feigned chucking it at him. "There are lots of ways that Levi can help spread the word."

Except, he couldn't think of one.

He squeezed the book he was still holding until his knuckles were white. But his mind was still blank.

He could help Kelsey build an outdoor stage, complete with spotlights and sound system. He could help her create the set and practice with the cast. But he could not ask someone to show up.

He wouldn't do that. Not again.

As his brothers stared at him, Levi hunched in on himself, pinching his eyes closed and praying for Mama Potts to come home and take all the focus. After all, they hadn't come to the house to see him. No matter what curiosity Mable Jean had stirred up, he knew the truth. He wasn't the reason they were at the house. And he'd much rather not have their eyes on him while he tried to come up with a plan to help Kelsey—one that didn't involve speaking to anyone.

six

Levi rolled his shoulders and stretched his neck before putting his hands on his hips and surveying his paint job. Kelsey's classroom looked better than new. Bright. Polished. Inviting. Just like her.

Only, it wasn't going to be her classroom again. Her smile wasn't going to light it up. Her voice wasn't going to ring from it. She wasn't going to be at his school any longer.

His gut twisted.

That didn't work for him. At all.

He had to help her succeed. He had to do his part to keep her around. And somehow he had to figure out how to do that while also earning enough extra money for the down payment on the green house.

At least he had an idea where to start on one of those problems. If he wasn't too late.

Most of the farms in the area had hired their summer help already. He'd heard some of the high school students talking about their jobs even before the hurricane.

He wasn't as young as those kids. He rubbed his bicep,

which was already feeling the efforts of painting the room. But he could still do the work. If he could find a job.

After sealing the bucket and cleaning up his painting supplies, he locked his office and the big one-story building. With a glance at his truck parked up front, he dismissed it and set off at a slow stroll along the ditch.

It wasn't far to Mr. Herman's farm, and maybe the bright afternoon sun would spark a solution for his other issue. But the scent of growing alfalfa and fresh earth under the clear blue sky only lulled him into a false reprieve.

He lifted his face to the warmth and breathed in deeply. This was his home, his haven. He wanted to put down roots here, dig deep into the red clay, make his mark on the island. Not in a flashy way. Just in the way that rivers and trees changed the landscape.

Before he knew it, he'd arrived at the Herman house. The white two-story Victorian sat off the main road, down a meandering gravel drive. Beyond it, acres of green swayed in the gentle wind.

Generations of Hermans had lived here for so long that Levi remembered someone at church suggesting the town should be renamed after them. There was already a Hermanville up toward the north shore, and the next generation of Hermans had moved to Summerside and Charlottetown, so the idea had dried up.

Levi couldn't imagine Victoria without the couple though.

He knocked on the maroon door, and it flew open almost immediately.

"Levi Ross. Saw you walking up the lane," Faye Herman said, her grin so wide that she clicked her dentures twice.

The skin of her face was pale and thin, peppered with age spots and a generous dose of wrinkles. Her eyes might have been a vibrant green in her youth, but now they were pale and cloudy. Yet she moved with joy in every step.

Levi returned her smile and gave a dip of his chin in greeting.

"Bet you're here to see Mel."

Levi nodded again.

"Well, come in, come in." She stepped back and let him pass before closing the door behind him.

The living room smelled of cinnamon and sugar and a berry he couldn't name. He didn't have to know what it was for the scent to make his mouth water.

"Melvin! You have a visitor," Faye called up the stairs before turning back. "I just made some boysenberry cobbler. Would you like some? It's still warm."

Levi hesitated. Of course he wanted some. But if he got two bites in and Mr. Herman sent him packing without a summer job, he didn't know what he'd do with a half-full bowl of cobbler and no hope for the green house.

"No thank you, ma'am."

Narrowing her gaze on him, she shook her head and then stomped to the kitchen as though he'd personally offended her.

"Levi? What are you doing here, boy?" Mel Herman used the ornate banister to help him down the last few steps before shuffling across the hardwood and into the living room. Mel clapped him on the back, his hand still strong though his body was visibly diminished. "Have a seat. I'm going to."

Levi kept his hand under the older man's elbow as Mel

lowered himself to the nearby rocker. Then he sank into the sofa across from him.

"Haven't seen you in a while," Mel said.

He offered a shrugged shoulder—half apology, half acknowledgment.

"You've been busy at the school, I'd guess. That storm sure caused a mess."

Levi nodded his *Yes, sir.*

"You seen the playhouse?" Mel let out a low whistle. "It's a darn shame, is what it is. No shows, no tourists. Half the shops in town are going to close their doors. Just you watch."

Swallowing Kelsey's plan to save the theatre—and maybe the whole town—Levi scrunched up the left side of his face.

"But I don't suppose you're here to talk about the town's troubles." Mel's wrinkles cracked with his wide grin. He was clearly amused at himself. "What brings you by? Your mama doing okay? Your brothers?"

Levi offered a low-watt smile and a quick nod.

Mel intertwined his fingers and rested them across his trim midsection as he leaned back with a deep sigh. His eyelids began to droop, and he let out a low snore. Levi nearly chuckled. The old man had been this way for as long as he could remember, feigning disinterest until Levi spoke up.

This was probably a waste of time. Mel had almost certainly found guys to work for him over the summer. Guys who weren't juggling other commitments—not to mention a full-time job.

Levi could just go. He didn't have to ask. He didn't *need* the money.

But when he closed his eyes, he could see the gleaming hardwood floors of the green house. He saw dust motes dancing in the beam of light through the kitchen window and heard the rolling waves against the shore just beyond the back door.

If he held his breath, he could hear the giggles of a toddler, the pitter-patter of little feet. And he could almost see the little scamp with her mom's flaming hair and liberal sprinkle of freckles.

The daydream socked him like an ornery bull.

He had nothing to offer Kelsey—besides being handy with a hammer and nails—but he'd sure like to give her a home like the green house. And even though that was the longest of shots, there was no chance if he didn't open his mouth. Now.

"Are you looking for any help this summer?"

Opening one eye, Mel muttered, "What was that now?" But the humor on the old man's face said he'd heard exactly what Levi asked.

Old coot.

Levi cleared his throat. "Are you looking for any more help on the farm this summer?"

"Huh?" Mel cupped his hand behind his ear, still with only one eye open.

"Melvin Herman, you stop that," his wife called from the kitchen. "You heard that boy clear as day. Now give him a job."

Mel chuckled, something rattling deep in his chest. "She knows me too well."

Levi didn't know how to respond to that. He wasn't sure that anyone could be known too well.

With a wink, Mel added, "Just makes it more fun to tease her."

A blanket settled over him, part discomfort, part envy. This was too much like watching his brothers in love. It felt like he'd showed up to a party he wasn't invited to. Like he'd eavesdropped on a private moment.

They hadn't said anything particularly personal, but intimacy was in being known. And Mr. and Mrs. Herman had known each other for nearly seventy years.

Levi didn't have even a chance at that if he couldn't offer a home. And if he couldn't manage to offer more than a perfunctory response to even the simplest question.

How could Kelsey—

He literally heard a record scratch between his ears.

This wasn't about Kelsey. It wasn't about *anyone*. Well, not anyone specific. But if he wanted to be known, *someone* had to know him. He just needed to have something worth saying.

"So you're looking for some work?" Mel scratched at his chin, and his white whiskers hissed in response. "Seems like Alice might have said something about that."

The pit in his stomach opened to a chasm. He'd forgotten that his realtor was Mrs. Herman's niece. They probably already knew the whole story of how he'd put in an offer on the house and then backed out, only to decide he wanted it again a year later.

But there wasn't exactly an *again* in that scenario. He'd never *not* wanted it.

He'd also never wanted to be fodder for the town gossips.

Jumping to his feet and very thankful that he hadn't

accepted the boysenberry treat that still called to him from the kitchen, Levi moved toward the door. If he'd had a hat, it would have been in his hands. Instead, he shoved his fists into his pockets. "Thanks for your time."

"Hey now." Mel grinned sheepishly. He pushed himself up, and Levi couldn't tell if it was Mel's knees or the chair creaking at the movement. "Alice may have let it slip that you're interested in the little cottage, but it makes no difference to me. I've hired a full team to harvest the hay this summer, but I'm sure there's enough work for one more." Mel shuffled up to him and clapped him on the back. "Levi Ross, I'd hire you full-time if you needed it."

His ears burned, and he had to look down.

"And if you want to marry into the family and inherit the farm, we have some single granddaughters." This from the kitchen.

Fire flew over Levi's cheeks and reached all the way to his hairline.

Mel chuckled. "She's only half teasing."

A lump lodged in his throat.

Leaning in, Mel continued in a conspiratorial whisper. "But she's totally serious about the single granddaughters. The oldest is just a few years younger than you. Awfully pretty. She takes after Faye."

Levi blinked hard. He had so many words—of surprise, humor, gratitude. But none of them would come. Not one was worthy of joining a conversation where a man like Mel Herman invited *him* to be part of the family.

"Faye's been after our granddaughter Meredith to settle down, so if you hang around this summer, I'm sure she'll introduce you two."

Levi tried to decline the offer, but Mel waved off his refusal. "Either way, I could still use your help with the baling and showing the kids how it's done this month and in July and August. The grass is still wet from the storm, so we might have to push back our first harvest a week or two. But I'll let you know."

Levi met Mel's gaze and, giving him a firm handshake, thanked him for the job.

———

"You have to at least let me try." Kelsey swallowed the tremble in her words. "Please." She was already perched on the edge of the chair in front of Mitch Trumball's giant oak desk, but she scooted as far forward as she could without dumping herself directly on the floor.

Mitch, the playhouse's executive director, couldn't be much over forty, but the gray at his temples had started to migrate to his dark brown beard. His broad shoulders and perpetual frown always made him an imposing figure, and the flint in his gray eyes made her insides quiver more than they had when she'd entered his office fifteen minutes before.

She'd met him only a few times, and always on a performance high, giddy after a great show. He'd started the summer before she moved to Toronto just four years before, a transplant from away, and she'd never had a problem with him. Until now.

Now he grumbled like she was asking for the moon. "The board already voted. This is a nonprofit that is no longer viable."

"You can't really believe that."

"Miss Ahern—"

"Kelsey."

He nodded, his frown somehow finding the range of motion to dip even lower. "Kelsey, the insurance payout won't come close to covering the repairs. And the rest of the town was hit too. No one has extra money to pitch in for a luxury."

"But theatre isn't a luxury. Not here. It's the lifeblood of our community."

"I think some local lobstermen would disagree with you."

She cringed. That was probably true. But the theatre was so much more than a luxury. "What about the tourists? How are Mama Potts and Jenny and other artists going to keep their stores open without summer shows to draw them in?"

"This town will find a way."

She heaved a big breath, shoving her hands under her thighs. "I have an idea to raise the money you'll need to fix the hall. I just need the summer. I need you to promise me that you won't give up on the theatre."

"It's too late."

"But why? The building's still standing. I'm only asking for ten weeks."

He sighed and tapped the phone on his desk, either checking the time or hoping for an excuse. When it came up blank, he rubbed his face. "Fine. What's your idea?"

"A production. A benefit show."

He snorted. "You can't possibly pull that off in ten weeks."

"I can." Probably. Most likely. With some help. A lot of help. And the right team.

"Who are you going to get to attend this show?"

"I'm working on that." Or she would be as soon as she got Mitch to agree to give her a shot. She didn't need his permission to have a show, but it would all be for nothing if he wouldn't even consider reopening the playhouse.

"Uh-huh." He did not sound convinced. "Who would be in said production?"

She gave him her best smile. "I have students who would love to be part of it. And there are lots of townsfolk who want to participate."

"And where exactly are you going to hold this magical show that's going to solve all of our financial issues?"

"I have a plan. Well, actually, it was Levi Ross's plan."

"Levi's in on this?"

She bit her lip, not sure how much she should promise on his behalf. Or if the mention of his name would be an asset or a hurdle. Something had happened when they were younger. His dad had taken off—she knew that much. But why the rest of the town hated Mr. Ross for it, she didn't know. Her parents had been surprisingly tight-lipped about the whole thing. And Grandma Coletta had said only to be gentle with the Ross brothers. As though she could have been anything but to the deflated version of Levi that appeared at school the day after his dad left town. Oliver had been absent for another week, but he was older than her, and she'd only seen him in passing in the school halls after his return.

"He's . . . yes. He's been brainstorming with me. He said he'd help build a stage and set."

Mitch grunted.

She couldn't tell if it was a good grunt or not, but she'd

picked her line. Time to stick with it. "In fact, it was his idea to have the show in the park by the lighthouse."

Another grunt, this one decidedly unhappy.

Kelsey glanced over her shoulder at the door to the office. Maybe she should make a dash for it before she began begging and completely embarrassed herself.

"How much do you think you can make with this show?"

"Oh . . ." Well, she hadn't exactly worked that out. But it had to be enough. Patrick and Levi had said the roof could be more than thirty thousand dollars. "As much as forty thousand dollars?"

Something in his eyes glowed. Was it hope? Maybe he wanted to keep the playhouse open as much as she did. Well, almost as much.

"And costs?"

Her swallow seemed to echo to the farthest corners of his office. "Most of the work will be on a volunteer basis. We'll try to get as much of the materials donated as we can. They should be minimal . . . but I'd like to reimburse the most invested volunteers for their time." Levi's face immediately jumped to her mind even as Mitch frowned. "It would be a very small portion of what's raised. And only if we raise enough."

His fingers drummed on top of the desk as his lips pinched even tighter.

"Please," she whispered. "My grandma and I performed on that stage together for years, and more generations deserve that same chance."

"Yes, we were all very sorry to hear of your grandmother's passing." His tone was dry, his features completely impassive.

Grandma Coletta had never said anything directly, but Kelsey had always gotten the feeling that she wasn't a fan of the new executive director. Even so, Mitch was her only chance.

The lines that appeared above his nose didn't do much to distract from its size, but they did give her a bit of hope. "You really think you can do this in ten weeks?"

———

"Pick up, pick up, pick up," Kelsey whispered under her breath. But no matter how hard she stared at the phone in her hand, she couldn't will Levi into answering it. Come to think of it, she'd never actually seen him answer any call. She'd seen him ignore plenty. Apparently hers was one that he screened.

"Kelsey?"

She jumped as his low voice asked a myriad of questions. Chief among them, *What's wrong?*

His worry made her smile. "Everything's all right. I'm fine. I'm good. Great, actually."

"Eh?" His tone was a hundred pounds lighter.

"Mitch Trumball agreed to give me to the end of the summer to put on the benefit show. Can you believe it? We can do this!"

Levi grunted. She'd take it to mean he was celebrating with her.

"There's so much to do. We have to confirm the park is available, land on a date, get together a cast and crew. Then we have to build a stage—I mean, you have to build a stage because I can't be trusted not to break my own thumb with a hammer." She laughed at her own lack of skill.

Levi did not.

She gulped into the silence. Had she assumed too much in calling him? He'd said he would help, but she'd just signed him up for a whole summer.

"I'm sorry. I just assumed since you said you'd help me . . . If it's too much, I completely understand. I just need a few more volunteers. If you can't . . . that is, if you'd rather not be part of the show, I understand. Or—or if you want to only do the stage or oversee the others working on it . . . Whatever works with your schedule. I might be able to pay you a little bit too."

Silence except for his slow breathing. And the pounding of her heart at the base of her throat.

"Levi?"

"Uh-huh."

Talking to him was so much harder when she couldn't see his expression, couldn't feel the emotions that buzzed just beneath his skin. Maybe that was why he didn't talk on the phone very often. It had to be like trying to build a stage with one hand tied behind his back.

"Do you . . . can we meet up tomorrow?"

"Uh-huh."

"I'll text you."

Another grunt of agreement, and he hung up before she could say goodbye.

seven

"Levi! I'm sorry, I'm—"

Levi unfolded a camp chair next to his desk at the school and helped his sister-in-law sit in it before looking toward the door, where Kelsey had skidded to a halt, fanning her face with a small book.

"Meg," she wheezed, her eyes alight. Dodging the paint buckets and tool carts, she raced across the cement floor and kissed Meg on the cheek. "I wasn't expecting to see you today. How are you feeling?" The protective hand on Meg's round stomach left no question of what she was really asking.

Meg frowned and gave her neck a twitch, which sent her long blond ponytail dancing. "I'd be a whole lot better if Oliver would stop hovering. You'd think this was the first baby ever born in Canada. He won't even let me onto the *Pinch*."

Probably because seasickness and morning sickness didn't mesh well, and Meg tended toward severe cases of both. But Levi wasn't going to remind a woman in a delicate situation of that.

Not that Meg was delicate. She was tall and strong and regularly went nose to nose with his brother. But growing a baby didn't look like easy work. And she *had* missed more than one family lunch in favor of a nap.

"Well, you look gorgeous," Kelsey said. She wasn't lying. Meg had that maternal glow that the books talked about. It filled her eyes and eclipsed her face, better than a summer tan. She emanated life.

"I had to get out of the house, so I made Levi bring me with him." Meg's frown quickly flipped into a smile. Patting the armrest of the canvas chair, she chuckled. "And this seat is about the only comfortable place I've found, so I tote it with me everywhere I go."

Levi cleared his throat, and Meg chuckled.

"Okay, one of the Ross brothers totes it with me. And helps me get out of it."

Kelsey laughed as she plopped onto a student desk off to the side. Immediately it tilted back, and she flapped her arms, the book she'd been holding skittering across the floor.

Levi grabbed her arm, yanking her to her feet and against his chest before her scream could even leave her perfectly pink lips.

"Thanks," she breathed as she reached up to adjust the blue bandanna that kept her strawberry hair out of her face.

"Broken desk." He hadn't meant to match the volume of her voice, but his words came out lower, softer, than usual. It had absolutely nothing to do with the scent of coconut and honey that surrounded her.

"I think maybe there should be a warning sign on that." The twinkle in her eyes threatened to push him over more than the actual press of her hands against his chest did. Her warmth set off sparks at the ten points where her fingers touched him. Electrical outlets didn't have anything on her.

Ducking his chin, he glanced at Meg, who was watching them like she just needed some popcorn to complete the experience. This wasn't a show, and he certainly wasn't going to be on the stage.

Making sure that Kelsey was stable on her feet, Levi put some space between them.

There. Breathing room. Nothing for Meg to ask him about later.

Except the mischievous smile she tried to hide behind her hand told him he wasn't going to be so lucky. "So . . ." Meg said, apparently not interested in waiting until they were alone to grill him.

"No time to waste," Levi interrupted her.

Kelsey nodded and held up her empty hands before scrambling for the booklet she'd been carrying. "Earnest!" she called as she swooped onto the book.

Levi and Meg shared a confused look as Kelsey skipped back to them, waving the script. "*The Importance of Being Earnest*. It's the perfect show, don't you think?"

Levi grinned as he took the outstretched script and flipped through the familiar pages.

"Have you read it?"

Meg rolled her eyes. "No. I've seen the movie. But Mr. Library Card over here has read every book ever written."

After shooting Meg his raised eyebrows to let her know

the nickname was not necessary—nor inaccurate—he opened the script to one of his favorite scenes, where Gwendolen and Cecily were arguing about which of them Ernest had proposed to first.

"I never travel without my diary. One should always have something sensational to read in the train," he said in his best impression of the heroine.

"Do you want a part in the play?" Even Kelsey looked surprised that she'd blurted out the offer.

Meg snorted, and Levi's gut twisted into something completely unrecognizable. He put it to rest with a hard shake of his head. He could build a stage. He would not be setting foot on one.

"It was worth a try." Kelsey shrugged. "You've got some natural talent."

Meg folded her hands beneath her chin, looking back and forth between them. "And you'd have all the girls swooning."

Why did everyone seem set on finding him a girl this summer? If it was just Violet and Meg, then he could chalk it up to meddling sisters-in-law. But Mel and Faye Herman had flat-out offered him their farm if he settled down with their granddaughter. They clearly thought he was some kind of catch. They'd be better off focusing on the lobster season.

Levi couldn't meet Meg's gaze, and he wouldn't torture himself by looking at Kelsey, so he grumbled something under his breath. They weren't really words, more a request to please move on.

Whether Kelsey understood him or couldn't stand the awkwardness either, she put a hand on his shoulder. "You don't have to help this summer if you don't want to. I basically reeled you into this, and if it's too much—I know the pay is next to nothing."

"Are you kidding me?" Meg threw her hands up. "Levi hasn't stopped talking about this for days."

Levi couldn't hold back his laughter, and it mingled with the sweet notes of Kelsey's humor as she ducked her head and caught his eye. "For real?"

He nodded. He was all in—except for a few weeks of baling hay. He'd have jumped at the chance to work with her all summer even if she hadn't said she'd pay him a couple grand for his skills. But he couldn't deny that her offer put him one step closer to the down payment on the green house.

Pointing her sharp chin toward the script, she said, "What do you think? I mean, I wanted to do something island specific, but the *Anne* shows in Charlottetown have exclusive rights. And we need something in the public domain. We can't really afford to pay for rights. Will that work?"

It was perfect. The story of two silly girls in Victorian England who insisted on marrying men named Ernest, and two even more ridiculous men who pretended to be named such to win their hearts. Antics ensued, and hearts were won and lost and won again. Funny and witty, appropriate for the whole family yet smart enough for the parents to enjoy, it was a classic for a reason.

Levi hoped his smile conveyed all that, but the tight lines on either side of Kelsey's lips left him in doubt.

Swallowing a brick lodged in his throat, he tried to shut out the voice in his head that told him his opinion didn't matter, that it was better to stay silent than to risk the rejection he'd known. "They're going to love it."

Pride nearly flowed out of Kelsey as she danced on the tips of her toes. "It has a pretty small cast—only nine roles. But we have to fill them right away so people can start learning their lines."

Meg piped up. "I can send an email to the parents of students at the school." Even though she'd be missing the first month of school for maternity leave, she still had all the privileges of her position as the physics and calculus teacher at the high school.

Kelsey's shoulders fell, her breaths suddenly coming out in shallow bursts. She'd clearly just realized that she no longer had those privileges. Not without a new contract.

"Where are you going to hold auditions?" Levi asked. Better to distract her with logistics.

"Um . . ." She put her hands on her slender hips and wrinkled the tip of her pert nose, which somehow made the cute little mole on her cheek pop out more. "Here?"

He gave his office a quick survey. Its cages along each wall served their purpose, keeping chemicals and cleaners separate and behind a lock. But the narrow aisles and walls of tool-covered corkboard didn't exactly lend itself to a performance space.

"No, not *here* here. The school. The cafeteria. It's fixed, isn't it?"

"Yes."

"Can we get permission?"

Meg smiled. "I'll take care of that." She whipped out her phone from an unseen pocket somewhere beneath her belly and began typing with her thumbs. "There. That text should settle it." Not looking up from the screen, she asked, "When are you going to do the auditions?"

"As soon as we can."

"And what about getting permission to use the park? I'm sure we only need to fill out an application."

Levi raised his hand. The park had been his idea, and paperwork was not his least favorite part of any job.

Meg grinned at him, making more notes on her phone. "What about costumes and props?"

Kelsey rocked from one foot to the other, crossing her arms over her chest and gazing at the ceiling. "Maybe there's something salvageable from the theatre. I'll ask Patrick."

"There might be some vests and shirts from last year's madrigal at the church too," Meg said, her thumbs flying. "I'll ask Pastor Dell."

Before Levi knew it, it seemed that all the jobs had been assigned. Meg had even volunteered Oliver to help with the set. He was sure to appreciate that on top of preparing for the lobster season in Victoria and launching a tour business on his boat.

Levi had put his name by nearly everything that didn't require putting a voice to it.

But one unanswered question remained. How were they going to spread the word?

⌒

Levi looked over his shoulder one more time. He was the only soul in the school, and he'd locked the door behind him when he returned after dropping Meg back at home for what she promised would be a "short rest." If Oliver's laugh had meant anything, she was likely to have an epic nap spanning centuries.

Levi needed a few minutes alone. No one looking over his shoulder or questioning his words. He could do that just fine on his own, thank you very much.

With a deep breath, he turned on his work computer and opened his email. When he closed his eyes, the face of the pretty blond news anchor from Charlottetown flashed before him.

Violet and his meddling brothers had instigated this with their teasing. But he didn't need to be interviewed on the news to get the word out. He just needed to get someone to interview Kelsey. She shone in the spotlight. Always had. It was probably genetics from her grandma. Coletta Ahern had stolen every show, drawn every eye when she'd been on the boards.

He'd gladly let the Ahern magic take center stage.

Leaning his elbows on his desk and pressing his face into his palms, he groaned. Kelsey had been taking that place in his thoughts ever since the night of the storm. He just had to get her where she belonged.

Punching a few keys, he added the news anchor's email address. Then he began, each strike of his keyboard slow and measured.

Dear Ms. Hyndes,

The small community of Victoria by the Sea here on the south shore has sustained a blow. While the hurricane damaged many roofs and even our regional high school, the worst was to Victoria's beloved playhouse.

Every summer for the last four decades, the playhouse has been part of the island's rich tradition of theatre, boasting full houses in one of the smallest villages. Now the foundation that runs the playhouse is threatening to close the hall for good without the funds to fix the damaged roof and stage.

Enter local teacher Kelsey Ahern, who has long graced the Victoria stage. Intent on saving the theatre, she's producing a benefit show beneath the stars on August 11.

Would you help us spread the word? Auditions will be held at the Victoria high school this coming Saturday morning.

Sincerely,
Levi Ross

His chair creaked as he leaned back and rested his hands on his thighs. No one was going to accuse him of being a professional writer. Kelsey could have made the words sound a lot more exciting and the stakes so much higher.

His finger hovered over the delete button. This was a stupid idea. Maybe he wasn't the right person to try to convince anyone.

Only, Kelsey had too much to do already. When Meg had stopped typing on her phone, Kelsey's assignments were triple his and Meg's combined.

He couldn't ask her to take on another task. Or let her think he wasn't going to do what he'd already agreed to.

Okay, so reaching out to local news stations hadn't made it onto his to-do list. Or anyone's, for that matter. But probably only because Kelsey hadn't thought of it yet.

He could do this. He could invite them to cover this event.

His cursor hovered over the Send icon on the screen.

Unless he sounded like a complete imbecile. Which wouldn't be the first time in his life.

He shifted the cursor to the opposite side of the screen as a voice in his head seethed those oft-repeated words. *"You think you have something worth saying? You think anyone wants to hear a word that comes out of your mouth?"*

He closed his eyes, his face burning at the memory. Pressing his hands to his cheeks only fueled the fire, singeing his eyes over a fresh flame.

It didn't matter how long it had been since he'd first heard those words. They refused to be silenced. They refused to be proven wrong.

Yeah, well, he wasn't saying a single word today.

That may be splitting hairs. But at least his face wasn't on the email, and his mouth wasn't forming the syllables. And really, the idea wasn't even his. Blame it on Violet and Eli and Oliver.

Before he could talk himself out of it, he hit Send. Then he sent the same email to the other three island stations.

Kelsey hadn't experienced stage fright since her first show as a child. But standing before a room full of curious faces and wide eyes, she wished Grandma Coletta was by her side.

As she looked off to the side of the room, she found Meg's bright smile and encouraging nod. And in the very far corner of the high school's cafeteria, a head of black hair capped a handsome face nearly eclipsed by brilliant blue eyes.

Levi.

She almost mouthed his name as she steeled her shoulders.

Over the heads of nearly every citizen of Victoria—plus most of the surrounding area—his eyes flashed brighter. Just for a moment. A second of recognition.

Had her lips actually formed his name? Maybe.

Flames licked up her neck, past her cheeks, and all the way to her hairline. She scrambled to adjust the bandanna holding her hair out of her face, but there was no way to cover all of her features or hide the pink that certainly tinged her skin.

This was the perfect way to instill confidence as the director.

Lord, help me.

"H-hi," she stuttered into the low-pitched rumble of dozens of conversations.

No one stopped talking.

Yeah, this was starting off great.

Meg mouthed "Louder" from her seat just as the metal door at the side of the room slammed shut and every eye turned to stare.

"Sorry about that." The man who had just entered offered an exaggerated bow along with his apology while Kelsey tried to figure out where she knew his voice from. It was velvety and low, filled with authority yet friendly. He looked up at her, all brown eyes and charming smile. He combed long fingers through his dark brown hair, giving his head an Elvis-worthy toss in the process.

It was Gunner Raines. *The* Gunner Raines. Meteorologist extraordinaire.

If she'd listened to him, she would have gone home well before the storm hit. She would never have been attacked by a tree. And she wouldn't have passed out in front of Levi. Then again, she wouldn't have gotten to spend that night with him either.

She clearly wasn't the only one to recognize Gunner. A collective gasp swept the room, sure to be followed by an unending titter of recognition.

Kelsey jumped to fill the moment of silence. "Welcome," she said with every vocal tool she'd learned for the stage.

Eyes snapped in her direction, and she rushed to keep their attention with the speech she'd prepared about why she loved theatre so much—and why her grandmother had too. "Thank you for coming to audition for the benefit show." A few faces in the crowd remained focused on her, but many were already slipping back toward their unexpected visitor. "We're going to need all of your help to make this a success and save the playhouse!"

That caught the attention of a few more, so she rushed on to get them moving. "As the flyers said, we're going to put on *The Importance of Being Earnest*. If you know what part you'd like to audition for, please see Meg Ross to get your name on the list." Kelsey pointed, and Meg waved. A handful of the audience was already streaming in that direction. "If you don't know what part you'd like to audition for—or you don't want to be in the spotlight—see Levi Ross in the back."

Levi's chin jerked up, his eyes bright with alarm.

"Please," she whispered at him, hard enough that he could read her lips. She had meant to take care of the uncertains herself, but someone had to check on their guest.

The strange thing was that as soon as she'd said Levi's name, she'd seen Gunner perk up and follow the direction of her gaze. She was pretty sure they were both staring at Levi, who looked about as eager to be the focus of their attention as a fox was to be discovered in a henhouse.

Please, please, please. Come on, Levi.

It was too late to confirm with him as the entire back row swarmed him. He was pollen and they the bees, and he no longer had a choice.

Kelsey owed him an apology. And maybe a home-cooked meal. And probably a pay raise.

She didn't have time to give that more thought as she darted through the crowd, bumping into several familiar faces and offering little more than a wave of her hand at their greetings. She wasn't the only one headed toward the handsome weatherman, but she had to be the first.

Mable Jean Huxley beat her by two full seconds.

"Why, Gunner Raines." Mable Jean sounded like she was there to audition for *Gone with the Wind*, all Southern charm and smooth vowels.

Southern, my foot. Kelsey wanted to announce that she'd heard Mable Jean herself say she'd made it to the southern end of the Confederation Bridge in New Brunswick, and that was plenty far enough away for her.

"Never expected to see you in our little village. To what do we owe this honor?" Mable Jean purred.

Kelsey looked around for Mr. Huxley, but he was conveniently absent. Thrusting her hand out, she said, "I'm Kelsey Ahern—"

"The local teacher." His gaze swept over her. It wasn't lecherous or leering, just inquisitive, curious.

"Yes, but . . . how do you know that?"

He cocked his head to the side. "I'm in the news business."

"But what are . . . why are you here?"

With a half grin, Gunner knocked her full on her backside. "I'm here for Levi Ross."

eight

"Levi Ross?" There was no way not to sound absolutely gobsmacked. Kelsey cleared her throat and tried again. "Our Levi Ross?"

Mable Jean chuckled and tugged on Gunner's arm like there had to be a mistake. "Levi is as shy as a summer day is long. Why would he . . ." Her words petered off into silence as Gunner pulled out his phone and thumbed his way through a few screens.

"My producer told me I had to talk with"—he enlarged the words and showed them the screen—"Levi Ross."

As if someone repeating his name enough times had drawn him out of his corner, Levi appeared, his lips tight and one hand scratching at his five o'clock shadow. He kept his gaze down but his shoulders straight. "You're here because of the email?"

Gunner looked Levi up and down, his eyes assessing but not unkind. As though he didn't find Levi wanting, just outside the norm of his on-air circle. For all of Levi's introverted tendencies, the men were quite well matched. Both stood nearly two meters tall. While Gunner had slightly broader shoulders, Levi had a strength that couldn't be denied. Both had nearly black hair, though Levi's was richer and thicker. Both were handsome in nearly every regard. But Gunner's charisma and charm surrounded him, drawing everyone in his vicinity straight to him.

Kelsey had been too busy analyzing the men to consider the question Levi had asked, but when she did, she parroted him. "Because of the email? What email?"

"But I sent it to Hope Hyndes."

"The news anchor?" Mable Jean joined the questioning.

Gunner gave her a wink. "I just call her my coworker."

"Yes, yes, of course. But, Levi, why did you email her?" Mable Jean couldn't seem to put the pieces of the story together. And she wasn't the only one.

Kelsey wanted to ask for more clarification, but her tongue seemed to have stopped working. She could do nothing but stare at Levi, who met her eyes with plenty of questions in his own. But she couldn't translate them. Not with her heart pounding and her mind a muddled mess.

When Levi finally cleared his throat, Kelsey and Mable Jean held their breath. But his words were for Gunner. "I didn't think they'd actually send anyone over."

"You write a better letter than you give yourself credit for." Gunner stuck out his hand and pumped Levi's. "My producer said it's the most riveting human-interest story he's seen come across his desk in a while. And he figured I'd better get out here right away before one of the other stations heard about it and scooped the story."

"You don't usually cover human interest," Mable Jean cut in.

"You're right about that, but seeing as the whole need for

rebuilding the theatre came from a hurricane, they thought I'd be the perfect fit to interview you all about it." Gunner glanced over his shoulder to the closed double doors. "I've got a camera guy outside if you're interested."

Mable Jean stepped forward, already primping her gray curls.

Gunner quickly amended his statement. "Levi. I'm supposed to interview Levi."

A firm hand landed square on her back, and Kelsey was propelled forward right under Gunner's nose. He was warm and smelled of something pretty from a bottle.

He grinned down at her like she was a rose among thistles. Glancing above her head, he asked, "You want me to interview her instead?"

Levi must have nodded because his silence seemed enough of a response.

"Well then, Miss Ahern—it is 'Miss,' isn't it?"

"Yes," she croaked out of a suddenly dry throat.

"Shall we?"

"Go on, dear." Mable Jean sighed. "We'll keep things moving here."

She didn't move until Levi gave her another push. Gunner pressed the bar to open the door, and all of summer spilled in. The brilliant sun caressed her skin, and the smell of earth and sky and sea—always the sea—surrounded her. Whatever had caused her to be starstruck by the weatherman vanished.

"It's kind of you to come out and invite the island to get involved," she said, "but tickets aren't on sale just yet."

Waving away her concern, he motioned for his cameraman—really more of a kid, still sporting spots on his face and jeans hung so low his belt threatened to give up at any moment—to set up the shot. "Oh, this is just the first interview. This is going to be a whole summer series. I figured we'd start at the beginning and check in with you all the way to the production."

A series? About *her* show? This didn't make any sense.

Before she could begin to make heads or tails of the last fifteen minutes, Gunner sidled up next to her, a microphone already pressed to his mouth. "You ready?"

She nodded, the camera kid pointed, and Gunner was on. "I'm live today in Victoria by the Sea, home of the island's historic Victoria Playhouse. If you haven't been, you've missed one of PEI's sweetest treats. No one does small community theatre quite like the town of Victoria. But after Hurricane Adelle, the white playhouse with the red-velvet seats may never get to open again."

Kelsey had to fight to stay in the moment and not get lost in the breezy delivery of each line. If she hadn't known better, she'd have thought he had memorized his script.

Maybe he had. Maybe he'd written it in advance. Or maybe—

He shoved the mic into her face, and she plastered on the smile her grandma had taught her. Coy and secretive, it covered a multitude of sins—forgotten lines, flubbed dance steps, and even missed cues.

She'd missed her cue with Gunner, all right. But how many questions could he have asked? She'd just try to answer all of them. "Today we're at the high school here in Victoria holding first-round auditions for our production of Oscar Wilde's *The Importance of Being Earnest*. Once we have our cast and crew finalized, we'll rehearse over the summer to put on a spectacular show on August 11th right by the shore." She smiled at him, hoping she'd fully answered whatever he'd asked, but his perfectly smooth forehead broke with one crease between his full eyebrows.

So maybe she hadn't.

"And do you think I'd make a good lead in the show?" he said, clearly asking his question again.

"Yes! Of course. You'd make a great Jack." She blurted out the answer before she could consider its ramifications, but it was clearly the response he was looking for, the wrinkle disappearing instantly.

"Well, how can I say no to an invitation like that? You've got your Jack." He gave her a smile that was clearly practiced but no less charming for it.

She hadn't thought she was offering him the role on the spot, but before she could subtly suggest he audition like everyone else, he moved on with the interview.

"So tell me why saving the theatre matters so much to you."

She swallowed the immediate urge to reveal that it might save her job. Instead, she pictured her favorite memories on the now damaged stage. "My grandma Coletta taught me to love theatre. We performed nearly a dozen shows together at the Victoria Playhouse, and I want to make sure future generations have the same opportunity."

Gunner pulled the mic away slowly, his smile not quite so dazzling but somehow more genuine. "What a great gift to your community. And your grandma." He looked back at the camera and nodded toward the building behind them. "Let's go inside and see what it's going to take to make this show a success—other than casting me, of course." He laughed at his own joke, his teeth almost blinding in the midmorning sunshine.

The camera kid waved his hand, and Gunner dropped the mic to his side. "Not bad."

His shrug said she hadn't been great either. But with no warning, she'd count this as a win. Besides, she'd apparently cast an island celebrity in her show.

Now she hoped his experience in front of a camera translated to the stage.

———

So many people.

Their voices still echoed in his head, despite the empty cafeteria. No matter how hard Levi pinched his eyes closed, he could still see them, feel them. Pressing in, demanding his attention, asking for an in with the director.

He'd agreed to take down names and pass out scripts. Well, actually, he hadn't agreed to that at all. Kelsey had nodded at him, and he'd caved. Typical.

Leaning over in the hard plastic chair, he propped his elbows on his knees and pressed his hands to his face. He needed a shower, a sandwich, and a full-on hibernation from the rest of the world.

A big hand clapped his shoulder, and he knew he was going to get only two of the three. And even they were going to be delayed.

"Oliver," he said through his fingers by way of greeting.

"You gonna make it, little brother?"

"Maybe," he mumbled. He wanted to shrug his brother off, give him the usual silent treatment. But after a day of so much stimulation, he couldn't help the words. They were easier than lifting his throbbing head.

"Have you seen my wife?"

He nodded.

"Recently?"

Levi cracked one eye open above his fingers. "Bathroom?"

"Probably. Pretty much the best guess since we found out about the baby." Oliver fell into the chair beside him. "Sounds like you had an eventful day. Gunner Raines, eh?"

"I guess."

"What do you mean, you guess? The story going around town, as personally relayed by Mrs. Mable Jean Huxley, is that her favorite Ross boy—her words, not mine—single-handedly set this whole thing up to be a success."

"Not true. This is Kelsey's project. She spent the entire day auditioning talented and not-so-talented townsfolk." He raised his head, silencing the ringing still between his ears. "The rest of my job is building a stage and a set."

Oliver grunted a laugh. "Yeah, you could still mess that up."

Levi scowled and mustered the ability to bite back. "Besides, the news was your idea."

"Mine?" Oliver pressed a hand to this throat and looked like he'd been personally affronted. "I don't think so."

"You and Violet and Eli. We needed more people."

"You got the idea to reach out to the TV stations because of that one conversation?" Oliver's laugh boomed as he clapped Levi on the back. "If only people knew how smart you are. Because I promise you that not a single one of us was thinking you'd literally go public with this thing. But it was a brilliant idea."

Levi wasn't entirely convinced of his own brilliance in this scenario, especially since he hadn't had a chance to hear about Kelsey's interview yet. And he sure hadn't appreciated the way that Gunner had looked at Kelsey, like she was the prettiest girl on the south shore.

She was. But Gunner didn't need to be noticing that.

Just then, the doors at the back of the room opened with a sharp metallic click. The slap of shoes on the tile floor preceded Kelsey's and Meg's entrance by a split second.

The minute that Oliver saw his wife, he jumped from his seat and strolled over to her. Wrapping his arm around her back, he guided her to the seat he'd vacated. When she was situated, he pressed a kiss to her forehead. "How was your day?"

"Exciting." Meg's eyes caught Kelsey's, and Levi pushed himself up, nodding for Kelsey to take his seat.

With a mumble of gratitude, she sank into the chair, every bone in her body visibly liquid at this point in the day.

"So how was your interview with Gunner Raines?" Oliver used his impression of the weatherman, smooth talking and head bobbing.

"Fine. Good. I mean—" Kelsey took a deep breath, closed her eyes for a second, and then tried again. "He wants to be in the show!"

Levi's stomach shot through the floor.

"His producer wants him to run a whole series this summer about the show, and he thought that being in the cast would give him a behind-the-scenes view of the production."

Oliver's sagging jaw looked just how Levi felt. But Meg

had clearly heard about this earlier. "Well, I think that isn't the only reason he wants to join the production."

What was that supposed to mean?

The pink in Kelsey's cheeks began to explain.

Of course the man was attracted to her. He wasn't an idiot.

Even with the fine hairs around her face disheveled from a long day, her red and brown striped kerchief slightly off center, she shone. He'd thought once that she didn't need the lights on the stage. She made her own. Gunner would have to be blind not to see that.

"Oh, yeah, right." Kelsey waved off Meg's insinuation. "He's just interested in getting the scoop, and honestly, I think he'll help sell a lot more tickets. So we need him."

"But what about his job? It's in Charlottetown."

God bless Oliver and his pesky questions.

"I guess he'll be here in Victoria for rehearsals and then drive back to Charlottetown for the evening news. He said there's a team that can do most of the work during the day to, you know, track the weather. And if need be, he can do a live remote."

So they were stuck with him. Levi rubbed at his cheeks to cover his scowl.

Gunner. Famous. Smooth spoken. Self-assured. Of course he belonged on the stage. One that wasn't built yet.

"You okay there, Levi?" Oliver asked. "You look like you swallowed a toad."

"Thinking about the stage." It was partly true, at least.

"The stage?" Kelsey sat up, all evidence of her embarrassment gone.

If that didn't define the difference between Gunner and

Levi, he didn't know what could. Gunner was the type to cause a flush of pleasure at just the thought of him. Levi was so unremarkable that he made it disappear.

"What have you come up with?" she continued.

Not a thing. So he blurted out the first words that came to mind. "Hay wagons."

"Wagons? Like trailers?" Meg looked confused, but Oliver's head was already bobbing in agreement.

"Good height so everyone can see the show," he said, "plus fully portable in case the park won't let you build a more permanent structure. Besides, you probably don't want to build it outside without any covering. Another storm like Adelle, and you'd need a benefit for your benefit."

All excellent points. Ones that hadn't crossed Levi's mind yet, but he'd have gotten there. Eventually.

"I guess that could work," Kelsey said. "But what about lights and audio?"

"We'll make them mobile," Meg said. "It'll be easy enough to borrow a generator. And I can help you wire it."

His sister-in-law had been only a few classes shy of her master's in mechanical engineering—with plenty of experience in electrical engineering too—when she'd returned to the island to help care for her mom. She'd started teaching high school science and taken a short break for what she described as a miserable stint in lobster fishing. Now she left the fishing to Oliver and took care of the physics herself.

"Thanks," Levi said.

"Anytime." She winked up at him and reached to give his hand a squeeze.

Kelsey sighed. "That might work, but where are we going to get wagons and a barn to store them in?"

He had a pretty good idea where to start.

—

After church the next afternoon, Levi didn't even get his fist to the door to knock before Faye Herman swung it open.

"Twice in a week? We are lucky! Come on in, young man."

Levi stepped into the cool living room where Mel sat in his rocker, a newspaper spread across his chest. Its corners flapped in time to his low snore until Faye snuck up to his side and whispered in his ear, "You have a visitor."

Mel jumped, clamping a hand to his chest and wrinkling the newspaper in his grip. "Nearly made my ticker stop tickin' there, Mrs. Herman."

"Oh, I think you're made of sturdier stuff." She chuckled as she sashayed to the kitchen.

Mel's eyes never wavered from her as he mumbled, "That woman'll be the death of me. Guess there's worse ways to go." Without turning his head to acknowledge Levi, he said, "You haven't changed your mind about working for me, have you?"

"No, sir."

Finally Mel looked at him and lifted his bushy white brows. "Then to what do I owe this visit? Just saw you this morning at service."

"See the news last night?"

"You mean Coletta's granddaughter and the show she's puttin' on down there by the water? I did."

He tried to continue, but a lump formed in his throat, choking out his words. He should have asked Meg to come with him or waited until Oliver was free. They knew the plan, and they knew what he needed. He could have avoided looking any more the fool than he usually did. Especially in front of the man who'd hired him for the summer.

Mel stared him down, waiting, pushing for a follow-up.

Levi pinched the bridge of his nose and swallowed hard against the boulder that had settled into what felt like a permanent resting place. Clearing his throat, he forced himself to speak. "I'm part of that. We need a stage."

Mel smiled like he'd won a small victory. "Uh-huh?"

Oh, come on, Mel. He could ask a few questions and they'd get to the point. But instead, the stubborn man was insisting on making Levi work for it.

Levi didn't mind work. In fact, he enjoyed physical labor, the way his muscles ached after painting a classroom and the blisters he got from a hammer. Those were signs of a job well done. But speaking up for what he wanted, using words that hadn't been written by someone else? That was torture.

The last time Levi asked Mel for what he needed, it had been about the green house. This was about Kelsey.

No. That wasn't right. This was about the show. This was about the playhouse. This was about the future of theatre in Victoria.

Worthy causes, all.

Swiping his perspiring palms down the legs of his jeans, Levi took a soft breath. "We need a mobile stage, something we can build indoors and then deliver to the park on the day of the event."

"And what did that brain of yours come up with?"

"Hay wagons. Do you have a few to spare? Maybe some space in your barn?"

Mel's shoulders sagged as he folded up the newspaper that had still covered his chest. "The ones in working order I'll need for baling this summer."

"And the ones not in working order?"

The wrinkles around the old man's eyes made them almost disappear. "I've got a few in the old barn, but they're not safe. Axles broken, missing wheels, busted floorboards."

"I could fix them up."

"How much you gonna charge me?"

Levi bit his lips together. He wanted to ask for the moon. At least for a few thousand dollars to add to his down payment. But that wasn't fair. Not when he needed the trailers far more than Mel did.

"I'll fix them if you'll let me use them for the summer for free."

Mel grinned. "I'll send Dusty over to give you a hand."

nine

Levi shoved open the big metal barn door, and it slid along the tracks, hissing that it hadn't been used in far too long. The scent of dust and hay hit him square in the face as he walked into the darkness, guided only by the light behind him. Just beyond the illuminated square on the ground, he could make out the shapes of four flatbeds, uneven and rotted in places.

Lord, let this work.

"Mr. Ross?"

Levi jumped, looking over his shoulder for his father. Which was entirely ridiculous. His dad had been gone for a dozen years. He'd vanished in the middle of the night with pretty much anything of value from Jeffrey Druthers's fishing boat. Never to be seen again.

Except he had been seen. Eli had run into him a couple years ago in New York, down on his luck, deep in gambling debts. He'd been the same Dean Ross who had left his family broke, homeless, and alone.

But the kid behind Levi wasn't looking for Dean Ross. The kid was looking for him.

Levi crossed his arms and raised his eyebrows in question.

"I'm Dustin. Dustin Crowder. But everyone calls me Dusty. I guess that's fine." He thrust out his hand, and Levi allowed his own hand to be pumped like an old water spigot. "Mr. Herman sent me out here. He said you could use a hand with these old trailers. What are you gonna use them for? Are you working with Mr. Herman this summer too? I'm going to help bale hay. Never done it before, but my mama said I better get out of the house or she was going to send me to my dad's this summer. He lives in Boston, and he's always working, wearing suits and ties."

Dusty slapped his T-shirt, which had a prominent hole at the collar. It was stained and seasoned and just the kind of thing Levi himself had worn over the summer when he was this kid's age.

"So I told my mom I was going to help Mr. Herman, and he sent me over here. Said you needed a hand." The kid looked down at his own hands and made a face like he didn't know what they were good for while he rattled away.

Levi wasn't sure Dusty ever stopped talking, but it didn't bother him much. Better to have the kid fill the air with words than to be looked at to hold up his side of the conversation.

"What are we gonna do?"

"Find a light," Levi mumbled.

"Right here." The kid jumped to a nearby wall, and something clanged to the ground. "Oops. I'm okay."

The overhead fluorescents flickered across the central

beam. They were yellow at first, heaving and grumbling as they tried to remember their job. But even at their worst, they revealed just what Levi had hoped for. Four beauties that needed only a little bit of care. He whistled low, and Dusty stopped talking. Levi hadn't realized the kid was still chattering, so skilled was he at diving into the depths of his own mind.

"What is it? What are you looking for? These old things? Mr. Herman said you could use them for whatever you wanted. Are you going to cut 'em up into scrap wood? Sell 'em for firewood?"

Levi shook his head. "We're going to make 'em shine."

Dusty looked appalled, his face twisting in disgust beneath his messy mop of sandy blond hair. "You're kidding, right? These are gross." Reaching out with all the mettle of an unconcerned teenager, he flicked a long cobweb, which stuck to his fingers.

"Guess we've got our work cut out for us then."

Dusty did not look convinced. Levi reached out to lay a hand on the layer upon layer of dust on the six-meter flatbed. It rocked toward him, balancing on two opposite tires. When the metal frame rising from the front swayed, he pushed Dusty out of the way.

"Must be the one with a broken axle." Dusty sighed.

The big beast groaned as it rocked back and forth, and Levi made a note to put it on a jack before touching it again. "Let's start with another one."

Dusty frowned. "With what?"

"Find a broom and some rags."

As if on cue, the kid sneezed loudly, sounding more like Mr. Herman than a teenager. With a mumbled "Excuse me," he wandered into the far shadows of the building but shortly returned, holding up a push broom nearly worn to a nub and a pile of old towels almost as grimy as the trailers that needed to be cleaned.

Levi shrugged and grabbed the broom. They had to start somewhere. He gave the next trailer a solid nudge. It barely swayed, though a flat tire in the back made the whole thing lean. He jumped up on it, took a step, and promptly put his boot through the boards, all the way to his knee.

Dusty laughed but managed to ask, "You okay, Mr. Ross?"

Levi spent a few seconds wiggling his leg free, thankful he'd worn his usual work uniform—jeans and a long-sleeve Henley. His shin smarted, but if there was a bruise, it wouldn't last long. And a wiggle of his ankle confirmed that nothing was seriously damaged.

When he finally looked up, Dusty was still staring at him, dancing on his toes as though ready to dash for help if needed.

"I'm fine. And it's Levi." It wouldn't do to have the kid calling him Mr. Ross all summer. And he had a terrible feeling that they were going to be spending a good chunk of the summer together.

"My mom says I have to call everyone who works at my school 'Mr.' or 'Ms.' She told me you work there—that you run the whole place."

Levi paused and looked hard at the kid. "The high school?"

Dusty grinned. "I'll be a ninth year in August."

The kid was probably thirteen or fourteen and lonely as

all get-out if he was stuck spending the summer with the school facilities director.

"How about just when we're alone you call me Levi and I'll call you Dusty? Seems fair."

"Really?" Bright green eyes shone beneath overgrown bangs. "You won't tell my mom I was disrespectful or nothing?"

Levi's stomach cramped. Whatever had happened to this kid, he'd gotten it in his head that he wasn't worth much. For a split second, Dusty was a mirror, a reminder of that summer twelve years before.

"We're good. So long as you do as I say. And watch where you put your feet."

Dusty nodded hard. "Absolutely. Yes. I will, definitely. Only . . ." His lips pinched at the corner, and his eyes dropped to the cement floor covered in years of hay. "Do you think you could . . . would it be all right if you . . . could you call me Dustin?"

"Dustin?"

"Yeah, I just like it better."

Levi had to fight a smile. No need to get the kid thinking he was a complete softy. Silent and stern and always with a book—that was his brand, and he couldn't have a new student spreading the word that he was approachable. Heaven forbid students start looking to him for conversation. Or worse, advice.

"Get to work, Dustin."

The kid beamed, cracking the dust out of a towel before scrubbing it over the tongue and hitch of the trailer. They worked together—Levi in silence and Dustin in a steady stream of whatever came into his mind—until they could see what they were working with. Levi caught himself grinning as the kid talked about starting high school and trying out for the hockey team.

"Did you hear that Eli—Eli Ross—is coaching this year?"

Levi nodded. He had heard something about that. And he'd almost taken a right hook to his jaw when he'd asked a few months before if Eli was going to give up coaching the Victoria Stars, the all-girls bantam hockey club he'd taken to the spring season playoffs.

"The Stars are my team," Eli had said. "But a man's got to be able to provide for his family." There had been no doubt that he meant Violet.

Dustin kept chattering. "Not that I think I'll make varsity or anything, but he'll be there. Maybe even be at tryouts." He stopped. "Do you know him?"

Levi leaned into his broom, pushing it forward and then coming back to sweep the same section again. "We've met." He hoped Dustin wouldn't notice the smile in his tone. The kid had been too young to remember when Eli had left town—just a few days after their dad. He wasn't part of the gossip rings that had kept the news of the Ross family's scandal alive and well for years. And he probably couldn't be bothered to put two Rosses together to make a family. That suited Levi just fine.

"Whoa." Dustin shook a dust cloud from his rag and wheezed into it. "What's he like? Is he how everyone says? My little cousin was skating one time and nearly fell down, and Eli came up behind him and rescued him. He swears it happened, but I wasn't there."

That sounded about right.

Thankfully Dustin kept talking, so Levi didn't have to

give his full opinion on his brother—the prodigal Ross, the one he was thankful had returned. The one who had broken Mama Potts's heart. The one who had shown them how much they had longed to forgive. The one who had cost Levi the green house.

The one who had been worth it.

But that wasn't what the biddies in the back pews talked about at church on Sundays. They talked about how handsome Eli was and how he'd stolen the hearts of all their hockey girls.

They didn't know that it was Eli who had longed for their family to be restored more than anyone else. They didn't know what he'd been willing to give up. They didn't know his heart.

But Levi did.

Suddenly Dustin stopped talking, and Levi felt the additional presence in the room before he turned to see her. Kelsey.

"Whoa," the kid whispered, his eyes eclipsing his face.

The corner of Levi's mouth turned up. Smart kid.

"Levi? Are you—" She slammed on the brakes when she spotted Dustin. "Oh, hello. I'm Kelsey."

"Dustin—Dusty." His tongue sounded too big for his mouth. Levi recognized the symptom immediately. "Everyone calls me Dusty." He hadn't blinked in a full minute, so Levi jumped from the trailer and landed in front of Kelsey.

"Everything okay?"

"Yes. I just wanted to see how you were coming. These aren't our stage, are they?"

There weren't others parked out back. "They look rough,

but we"—he pointed to Dustin and then back at himself—"can make them work."

"But there's a giant hole in this one."

Dustin snorted. "Levi—I mean, Mr. Ross—almost lost his leg."

"You fell in that?" He couldn't tell what was more horrified, her voice or her eyes.

He shrugged off the worry.

"But what if one of the actors falls through during the performance? We can't—"

"We'll reinforce the flooring."

Her eyes narrowed. "And you can do that in time?"

He shrugged again.

"For rehearsals?"

He pursed his lips to the side. Okay, he hadn't quite considered that in his timing, but he didn't have an option. And he had a helper. At least he hoped Dustin wasn't a liability.

Dustin scrambled toward the door. "Sun's starting to go down. Mama hates it when I'm late for dinner. See you tomorrow, Mr. Ross."

"G'night, Dustin."

The kid beamed before racing down the lane to the main road. When Levi looked back at Kelsey, her smile asked a thousand questions, but she spoke only one. "Where'd you find him?"

Levi shrugged.

"Sure, you'll talk to him, but you don't have much for me?"

He shot her a look that reminded her she should be used to it by now but ended up matching her grin.

"You're something else, Levi. I mean, seriously. I heard you both talking all the way down the drive."

"Not both. Just him."

She gave a snort of laughter. "That tracks."

Kelsey hadn't really had a reason for stopping by the Hermans' farm. She only knew that Levi had said this was where he'd be, and it had felt strange *not* to see him.

Which made exactly no sense. Except that she was used to being part of an ensemble, and right now her crew was made up of one soft-spoken jack-of-all-trades and one very pregnant science teacher.

Oh, and a weatherman with a handsome face and a smooth voice.

Turning in a slow circle, she took in the barn. It was a single room, no loft, no bales of hay. Just tin siding and roof nailed to wooden beams and rafters. She didn't know how much life the old structure had left in it, but it had withstood the hurricane. The six-by-six beams didn't even look like they'd sustained a beating. The dust and hay and the remnants of whatever had been on the trailers before were still dry. And still very present.

She stepped toward the closest trailer to run a finger over the grain, not sure if she'd find the wood splintered or smooth.

Just before she got there, Levi called out, "Not that one."

Yanking her hand back, she looked up at him through narrowed eyes.

"Broken axle. Nearly took me and Dustin out earlier."

"Ah. Of course."

The problem was that she was left with nothing to do except keep spinning, keep trying to make this all make sense. It felt like a game of wooden blocks. Get this square piece in the square hole. But there were only round holes and lots and lots of square blocks.

On one of her slow spins, Levi hopped up on a trailer, his legs dangling and his hands cupped around the edges. He leaned forward, his gaze unwavering but not heavy.

"Okay then, Levi. I give up. What do you see here?"

He motioned for her to join him, and she tried to scramble up beside him. But her jump was too low, her legs too short, and she only managed to scrape her thigh through her jeans. When she turned to frown at him, he had already hopped down. His hands on her shoulders gave her a quick spin. Then they were on her waist, long fingers digging in just enough to hoist her to the perch.

Her hands shot to his shoulders to keep her balance. This was just like a move in a musical, except he didn't spin her. And he didn't let her go.

Even when she was firmly seated and he had to look up at her, he kept his hands on her hips. Her heart slammed against her ribs. Once. Twice. A third time.

"Okay there?" His words were low and deep and not much stronger than a sigh. Which did not explain why her breath had suddenly vanished.

She pulled a Levi, offering nothing more than a silent nod. And then one by one he released his fingers, stepped to the side, and jumped up beside her. His limbs were graceful like a cat's, his landing not even rocking the tilted seat.

"They'll interlock. Two in the front, two in the back.

That'll be about twelve meters across, a little more than four meters deep. Big enough for you?"

"Yes, plenty big, but what are you going to do with the . . ." She waved at the metal grates at the ends.

He eyed them for a long second, sucking on his front tooth. "Whatever we want to, I guess. I was thinking we could move them and use them to hold up a backdrop. Or we could keep them on the sides and use them to hold a light board. Or . . . basically whatever Meg wants to do."

Kelsey chuckled. Meg would know. She would already have a plan. "And we can keep them here in this barn? All summer? Mr. Herman won't mind?"

"Uh-huh."

"And how much is this going to cost us?"

"Just a few hours of labor."

She crossed her arms. "A few hours?"

"A few more than a few. I'll take care of it."

"But, Levi . . ." She sighed. This was too much to ask of a friend. "I know what I offered to pay you at the end of the summer. It's not enough."

He swung his leg until his heel thumped against the rubber tire beneath them. She could feel the vibrations through the entire bed. "Didn't ask you to pay me anything."

"I know, but this is going to be so much. How are you going to do all of this in time to get the sets built and rehearsals done? Plus you have a full-time job."

"I recall."

She pressed her shoulder against his, and he swayed much farther than he should have. When he dramatically righted himself, she rolled her eyes.

"If you have volunteers, I'll take the help," he said.

"I'll ask around, but for now, what can I do?" She should be organizing callbacks and thinking through scene sets, but Levi Ross was having a legitimate conversation. With her. And walking away seemed like a terribly foolish way to end it. She liked the way his voice drifted over her skin like the tides at the shore, pulling then tugging. Gentle and somehow urgent too.

"I don't have to be home for dinner." She winked at him. "So put me to work." Scooting to the edge of the seat, she glanced over. "But first, will you help me down?"

ten

watch you on the news every day. You're the only weather-man I trust."

Kelsey bit her tongue to keep from snapping at Alexia Benson, who, along with most of the other women in the school cafeteria, had surrounded Gunner Raines as soon as he arrived that morning for callbacks. Their titters echoed and swarmed, and Kelsey wasn't sure she had the patience for this today.

A sneeze caught her off guard, and she wiped her chafed nose with a tissue that promised softness and caused only more irritation. She groaned into her hand as another sneeze merely threatened, throbbing deep behind her eyes.

Stupid allergies. Stupid hay.

That's what she got for spending most of the last three days in a barn with Levi and Dusty. And more dust than a body could handle, apparently. Between the three of them, they'd stripped all four of the old trailers down to their studs, shored them up, and even replaced the broken axle. All to the sound of Dusty's cheerful prattling.

But today her head felt like it was going to explode. And the next woman to swoon over Gunner Raines—tacking a sigh on to the end of his name—was not going to get a part. Then again, she had to stop thinking of him by his full name too. Just because that was how he was introduced on television didn't mean that was what she should call him.

"Now over to Gunner Raines with the latest weather."

"Gunner Raines, the name you can trust in weather."

"I'm Gunner Raines, and that's your island weather."

He wasn't his television persona right this minute. And she prayed he hadn't brought his camera kid to the callbacks.

Kelsey bounced her pen against the table, clicking the end incessantly.

"You okay?" Meg whispered from the seat beside her, resting a hand on her forearm. Motioning to her own eyes and nose, she said, "You look a little bit red."

Then she looked exactly like she felt. With a sniffle and a cough, Kelsey pushed herself up in her seat. "Too much time with Levi."

Meg's chin dropped, and she looked up through her long brown lashes. "You getting a little up close and personal or something?"

"No. In the barn. Hay barn. Fixing the stage."

"Oh."

Kelsey couldn't tell if Meg was happy for the explanation or disappointed that she wasn't making out with Levi. Like he'd ever make a move. The man had had more than twenty years to strike up a conversation, to ask her to a dance, to ask her to sit under the stars and listen to the ocean. He'd never done a single one.

Which was probably why she was scowling.

"I've got this," Meg said. When she spoke again, she used every ounce of her teacher voice. "Ladies and gentlemen, please have a seat. Men over here on my left. Women on my right."

The group that had gathered at Gunner's entrance gave Meg a careful review, as though checking to see what she'd do if they didn't let him out of their grasps. She stared them down, just as she did every challenge from a wayward student, and slowly they shuffled toward the tables, finding chairs.

"Thanks," Kelsey whispered. Pushing herself up, she tried for a smile despite the face she knew she was presenting. "Welcome to callbacks. Congratulations." Her voice sounded as scratchy as her throat felt, but there wasn't anything to be done about it. If she talked fast, she wouldn't have to talk as long. "As you know by now, we're casting nine roles. Two main men, two main women, two mature women, and three other men. The role of Jack Worthing—our protagonist—will be played by Gunner Raines."

He stood up to take a bow as the section of ladies clapped and cheered and all but fainted at the mere mention of his name.

Dear Lord, what I have gotten myself into?

But there was no answer. Whatever she'd hoped to hear, it was too late to back out now.

When his fan club finally died down and Gunner found his seat, Kelsey managed a smile, though she was well aware that it wouldn't reach her eyes. It barely touched her lips.

"Everyone has been given a scene to read with a partner." Checking her clipboard, she quickly ticked off the partners and held up their copied script for them to retrieve. "Since we already have our Jack, he'll read opposite one of our Gwendolen Fairfaxes. Take a few minutes and run your lines together. We'll start the scenes shortly."

The young Gwendolen opposite Gunner—Charity Prince—received a few death glares from her opposition, but all in all they did as they were instructed, pairing off in various corners of the room. Kelsey meandered among them, listening to their lines, watching the way they moved and how they breathed. This was just a trial, but she'd learned early on that practicing good habits made them second nature. If these actors were using good technique now, they'd certainly be doing so on the stage.

She slipped past Willow Singer, who projected her lines for Miss Cecily Cardew like she hadn't struggled in the drama program at the beginning of the last school year. Kelsey had spent hours with Willow, helping her practice her breathing, showing her how to use her diaphragm. They'd even used an app so Willow could visualize the strength of her voice. Now she spoke like a stage veteran.

Well done, Willow. She caught her former student's eye and gave her a big grin. Willow's eyes flashed with pleasure at the praise before she went right back into character.

As Kelsey neared Charity and Gunner, she watched the young lady's hand movements. Not exactly Victorian like the play's setting. And her voice was so soft that Kelsey had to lean in to catch the end of her line. "My ideal has always been to love some one of the name of Ernest. There is something in that name that inspires absolute confidence. The moment Algernon first mentioned to me that he had a friend called Ernest, I knew I was destined to love you."

Kelsey nearly went deaf when Gunner trumpeted his response. "You really love me, Gwendolen?"

His words were flat. There was no other description for them. Loud and flat, and they squeezed her lungs under a brand-new pressure.

Meanwhile Charity continued her scene. "Passionately!"

"Darling! You don't know how happy you've made me." Gunner sounded like he'd rather be on the sharp side of a lobster's claw than fall in love with Charity's Gwendolen.

Suddenly Kelsey couldn't breathe.

No. No. No.

This couldn't be happening. She could not have cast the worst actor on the island as the lead in her show.

She stumbled back to her chair and gulped from her water bottle. Staring straight ahead, she saw nothing except her show crashing around her. Her chance to save the stage her grandma had loved so well disappearing with one rash decision.

Maybe it wasn't so bad. Maybe she'd just . . . caught him on the wrong line. Or maybe Charity had bad breath, and he wasn't keen to get close to her.

Meg leaned over and whispered, "You look like you saw a grizzly."

"I just . . . tell me everything is going to be all right."

Meg's eyebrows drew together until they were almost a single line. "Of course it is. But what makes you unsure?"

"Only . . ." She risked a glance in Gunner's direction. "Nothing. It'll be great. It has to be."

A few minutes later, they called the pairs to the stage area, and each took turns acting out their scene. Some were clearly better than others, and Kelsey quickly crossed off a few names, including several of Willow's competitors for the role of Cecily.

Gunner and Charity stepped forward. Every eye in the room was on them, and Gunner seemed to glow in the attention, his tan somehow even more golden, his dark hair glimmering more than usual.

And then he spoke.

She could see the reaction on the faces of the other men in the room, the ones who had almost certainly wanted his role. They stared without blinking. Without breathing.

Meg grabbed Kelsey's arm beneath the table, her nails digging in, saying everything that needed to be said without a word.

They could not go on with Gunner's untuned trumpet blasting words as though they had no meaning whatsoever. He spoke like the goal was to make everyone in Victoria hear the words regardless of what they meant or the person he was playing off of.

Oh, how she wanted to give him a note. Or ten. But she hadn't stopped any of the other scenes—even the poorly done ones—and she wouldn't embarrass her lead actor in front of the rest of the cast. Because everyone who would be in the final cast was also in this room.

Meg's nails dug in even further, the pain not nearly as sharp as watching this audition. Kelsey looked at her friend out of the corner of her eye, and Meg wore the same mask of horror that she felt.

When the couple finally exited the makeshift stage area,

Meg leaned over. "What are you going to do?" Her question was barely more than a breath.

At the moment, Kelsey had no idea.

The rest of the auditions went smoothly, and by early afternoon, she'd circled several actors for specific roles. Two of them she'd been in shows with at the playhouse, and Willow, of course, had been her student.

"Thank you all for coming out today. I'll be in touch with the results in the next couple days."

The actors filed by, and one of the gray-haired men—Keith Iverson, who she'd slotted to play the butler—paused at the table, his weather-worn hand resting in front of her. "Your grandma Coletta, she'd have liked to see you here today."

Her vision suddenly went blurry, her eyes burning. She wanted to blame it on her runny nose and those ridiculous allergies, but the truth was she hadn't known how much she needed to hear that. How she'd longed to be told that the woman she'd respected more than anyone else on the planet would support this cause.

The Lord knew her own parents wouldn't. They hadn't supported her shows even when they'd lived in the same village.

But Grandma Coletta had been at every one, usually on the stage right beside her. During curtain calls, it was always her grandma's high-pitched whistle that she heard. And when a role went to someone else, no matter how deserving they were, it was Grandma Coletta's hug that fixed the little part of her heart that had broken.

Kelsey blinked against the tears as she looked up at Keith. "You think so?"

Keith winked. "I know it. She never stopped talking about you. She was so pleased when you went to Toronto to pursue your dream. I remember the exact day. She swept into Carrie's Café like a queen and told everyone there."

Her lungs seized, and she couldn't find the breath to express her thanks, so she squeezed his hand and offered him a tremulous smile. With a pat on her shoulder, he shuffled away. Meg stuffed a tissue into her hand.

"Thanks," she mumbled as she pressed it to her face, mopping up her mess and stemming the flow of her runny nose.

"Do you have a moment, Kelsey?"

She looked up into Gunner's deep brown eyes as he leaned over the table. "Sure." She gulped down the rest of the words that were on the tip of her tongue.

His gaze darted pointedly at Meg. "Alone."

Meg groaned as she stood up, cradling her bump. "I need to use the ladies' room anyway."

Gunner offered an appreciative nod and quickly slipped into the vacant seat. By the time Kelsey had swung around to face him, he'd leaned all the way forward, elbows resting on his knees, hands clasped before him. "You cannot cast Charity as Gwendolen. I beg you."

She blinked slowly, trying to form a response, trying to make sense of the unexpected when what she really wanted to say was that she couldn't cast him. "Wh-what makes you say that?"

"You saw her up there." His arm swept toward the make-shift stage area as his voice rose.

Kelsey jerked her head around, her gaze darting into

every corner of the big room to make sure they were alone before she responded. "I did."

"I'll do whatever needs to be done for this show, but I just can't work with her. She has no life in her performance, and I can barely hear her."

"Thank you for your input." The words dragged out as she tried to figure out what to add to them. Finally an idea popped into her mind. "Gunner, do you want this role?"

He jerked back, her words apparently a slap in the face. "Of course. This is such a great opportunity to have as part of my story. My producer is loving it."

"Yes, but this is a huge commitment—even for an experienced actor."

"I was in the drama program back in school." His perfectly shaped lips molded into a Cheshire grin. "Of course, I'd have shown up to rehearsals more if my teacher looked like you."

She waved off his compliment as she ran a hand over her messy bun and looked down at her casual jeans. They had holes in the knees and frayed hems above the ankles of her multicolored slip-on sneakers. She wasn't exactly school appropriate. Then again, she didn't officially work for the school at the moment.

"This is a big role. I'm just . . . I'm concerned it'll be a lot for you to take on, on top of your job at the station. I can still give you backstage access for whatever features you want to make."

He waved away her concerns with a swipe of his hand. "The first segment in the series has already brought in loads of fan mail. My viewers can't wait to see me on the stage. They're going to pack out the park."

"And you're sure you have time to memorize the lines and attend all the rehearsals?"

He dismissed her again with a breezy smile. "I've got this."

But who was going to have her when their show flopped?

———

"I've done it now!"

Levi jerked up from some paperwork at his desk as Kelsey raced into his office, hands shaking and face redder than the wild knot on top of her head. She sneezed, and he pulled the clean handkerchief out of his pocket before tossing it her way. She caught it and unceremoniously blew her nose into it before stuffing it into the pocket of her jeans.

"That's reusable, you know."

She glanced down then back up, a little question mark forming above her nose.

"Can I have it back?" he asked, reaching for it.

"Oh, gross. I'll wash it for you."

He snorted. If she thought that was gross, it was a good thing she'd never had to clean up after a high school full of teenagers.

She threw herself against his desk, perching on the edge and stretching her legs out in front of her. While he appreciated the view—and he'd have to be lacking a pulse not to notice the gentle curves and sweet shape of the legs filling out those jeans—he stood and motioned for her to sit in his rolling chair. He grabbed a folding chair, flipped it open, and spun it around before sitting down across from her. His arms rested on the back of the chair as he looked at her—really looked.

Her blue eyes were watery, and her nose looked irritated like she'd been blowing it all day. He'd been there.

Leaning over, he pulled out one of the desk drawers and found a rattling white bottle. He tossed it to her and sat back as she reviewed the label, her eyes following the script back and forth.

"Do these work?" she asked.

He nodded. He took the over-the-counter antihistamine every summer day he was in the alfalfa fields and hay barns—so his face didn't feel like it was going to explode and his nose found the off switch.

"Thank you," she said, already popping the top and throwing one of the pills back. With a thick swallow she sighed. "If only all of my problems could be solved with a little white pill."

He leaned forward, inviting her to tell him more.

"Oh, Levi." Her groan made his chest ache. "He can't act. At all."

"Who?"

"Our Jack Worthing—our lead. Gunner Raines."

Levi snapped his neck back so hard that it popped.

"I know. I feel the same way. How is it even possible?" She covered her face with her hands and then dropped them so they only covered her lips, her eyes speaking volumes. "He works in the news. He has to know that the tone he uses to cover the hurricane that destroyed our playhouse shouldn't be the same as the one he uses for a blue sky and sunny summer day. Right? There's context there that informs how you speak. It's the same in acting. It should absolutely translate for him." Somehow her eyes grew even larger. "But it doesn't."

His gut twisted hard. Maybe it was a misunderstanding.

"When he interviewed me for the news, his voice was so smooth. He had great inflection, a real connection with the audience." Waving her hand toward the cafeteria where he assumed they'd just wrapped up the callback auditions, she shook her head. "He was basically yelling every line, like the words had no meaning."

"Maybe it was a hard scene?" He had no idea why he was standing up for the meteorologist, except that it might make Kelsey feel a little bit better about the predicament.

It clearly did not. "Nope. He was confessing his love to Gwendolen. You could play it a dozen ways and it would be fine. He picked the only bad choice—to yell at her that she didn't know how happy she'd made him."

Ouch. That was a good scene. The crowd was supposed to giggle, but they had to buy that Jack really did love Gwendolen enough to pretend his name was Ernest.

"What if he just needs an audience?"

"He had one. Me and Meg and everyone auditioning." She crossed her arms and then her legs for good measure.

"He's used to performing for the camera, right?"

She nodded.

"Then maybe he just needs to learn to perform for a live audience."

A small puff of air escaped between Kelsey's tight lips. "You think?"

In all his years, it had never been easy to talk with anyone. He managed with his mom because she'd always cared what he had to say. His brothers had been more difficult—usually talking for him or over him when they were younger. But ever since Meg and Violet entered the picture, ever since Eli came back, it wasn't as hard to find his words with them.

With Kelsey, it wasn't easy, but it was safe. Somehow he knew that whatever he said, she'd take and consider. Nothing would be dismissed out of hand. And when he had nothing to say, she didn't push him to fill in the silence. She filled it for him, usually. And he'd gladly listen to the melody of her voice anytime. But at this moment, he could see her uncertainty, sense her fear that she'd jumped into the bay without knowing how deep it was.

Stretching forward, he pressed a few fingers to her knee. She glanced down at it but didn't pull away, so he charged on.

"You are the best drama teacher this school has ever had."

Her cute snort interrupted him. "You're only saying that because the drama teacher before me left before you were born."

He snickered. "Okay, that's a little bit true. But hear me out. You are a very talented teacher. If you can teach a room full of indifferent teenagers who signed up for the only available elective how to make Shakespeare come alive, then you can teach anyone willing to learn."

"But what if he doesn't think he needs to learn?"

That was a level of arrogance Levi couldn't fathom. He'd been learning his whole life. From books, from mentors, even from his brothers. There was always more to discover. The world was way too big to assume he was an expert at anything. Sufficiently skilled? Perhaps. But to never have anything left to learn? That was more than he could imagine.

"I tried to get him to back out." She sighed. "But he

really wants the role, I guess. He likes being in the action, and I think it's probably good for his special series this summer. But . . ."

"You're the director. Direct. Give him notes like you would anyone else. Stand your ground. This is your show. You can make it shine."

She wrinkled the tip of her nose. "You say that like it'll be easy. Your part of the show won't fight back."

That much was true. The trailers had only given him a couple splinters and never talked back. "But I still had to strip away all that wouldn't work."

"So you think I should strip away Gunner?"

Levi nearly choked on his tongue. "No. Just his rough edges."

"And you think I can do it?"

"If he's a good man, he'll take your notes and get better."

eleven

Kelsey hadn't been able to stop thinking about her conversation three days before with Levi—or her problem performer. She also hadn't had time to connect with him, as she'd been finalizing the cast, setting up the rehearsal schedule, and passing out scripts.

As far as she knew, Levi had been busy working in the barn. Or maybe at school. She hadn't had a reason to go back there to see him since the callbacks. Either way, when Gunner called her that morning, she was more than happy to comply with his request.

"I'd like to get some B-roll of the behind-the-scenes work," he said. "How the outdoor set is coming together. That kind of thing. I'd like to get a few new faces on the screen—to show how the whole community is coming together to make this show a reality."

The idea of a trip to the barn made her smile. "We can do that."

"Perfect. We'll pick you up in about an hour."

She tried to tell herself that any extra effort she put into doing her hair—a sleek ponytail with a slight curl to the ends—was for the camera. The extra layer of mascara too. And the funky sundress that showed off her waist to its best advantage.

When the white news van with its logo plastered across the side pulled up outside her house, she hopped into the passenger seat with a bright smile.

A low whistle of approval came from the camera kid in the rear. "Excuse me, ma'am. But you look extra pretty today."

Gunner's eyes glowed with the same admiration. "Indeed."

Perfect. Just the response she was hoping to get from Levi.

When they arrived at the Hermans' farm, the van bounced hard down the lane, finding every divot from the last century and rattling her teeth. The camera kid grunted as he fell against some of the equipment.

"You okay back there, Vic?" Gunner asked as he slowed the van.

"Just fine, boss."

Gunner winked at her. "Maybe I should start calling you boss, since you call all the shots in the show."

Pretty soon they were going to see if that was true. But before she could respond, Vic appeared between them, his forearms resting on the backs of the bucket seats. "Whoa. That's old-school."

The silver building before them was exactly that, the tin siding probably state of the art when it was built. On the far side of it, a larger barn had been erected. Its red paint and white trim dwarfed the not insubstantial metal building. Mr. Herman had needed more space for new equipment over the years, and he'd added to the new barn, leaving the other building all but forgotten until Levi came along with his idea.

"Are they actually building something for the show in there?" Vic asked.

Kelsey smiled. "They sure are."

Gunner parked the van beside Levi's old truck and leaned forward, as though he might be able to see through the open sliding door into the yellow dimness beyond. "Who's in there?"

"Levi."

"The one who emailed us?"

She nodded. "And probably Dusty Crowder."

Gunner checked his hair in the visor mirror before jumping to the ground, slamming his door, and swinging the bay door open. Calling to her on the other side, he asked, "Who's Dusty?"

"A local community member helping out."

After Vic and Gunner collected their equipment, Kelsey led them inside, where the overhead lights couldn't compete with the morning sun. She blinked against the black spots in her vision until she could make out Dusty's skinny arms lifting a board onto one of the flatbeds before he scrambled up after it.

Off to her right, Levi was hunched over a two-by-four stretched between a couple sawhorses, his hands spreading a bright yellow tape measure. He reached up to pull a faded blue pencil from behind his ear, sleeves rolled up to his elbows and shoulders stretching the green plaid of his flannel shirt. She imagined in a couple hours the afternoon heat would make him tie his flannel around his waist, leaving just the V-neck T-shirt beneath.

Suddenly her mouth went dry, her throat completely packed with cotton. No amount of swallowing was going to loosen that up.

Perhaps it was their shadow that alerted Levi to his visitors, because he popped the pencil between his teeth and glanced over his shoulder before Dusty called out, "Hey, Miss Ahern. We weren't looking for you here today."

Her gaze met Levi's and locked there. His face didn't move, but there was an awareness in his eyes, an appreciation she hadn't noticed before. He swallowed several times in a row, his prominent Adam's apple bobbing.

She wanted to twirl her skirt around her knees and flutter her lashes at him and basically do all the things she did to flirt on a stage. Only, they weren't characters in a play, and they most certainly weren't onstage. So doing those things was bound to draw more attention than she needed at the moment. Instead, she offered him a small smile and looked toward Dusty.

"Hey," she croaked with a wave of her hand.

"Is that a real camera? Like a TV camera?" Dusty jumped from his platform, landed like a barn cat, and scurried forward. "Are you guys going to film in here? My mom saw your clip on the news with Miss Ahern and said little Victoria getting covered on the Charlottetown news was pretty exciting. Are you going to film me?"

Dusty immediately began primping, running the fingers of his too-big work gloves through his wild hair. The dirty gloves only left gray streaks throughout his sandy tresses already in dire need of a cut. And he didn't touch the smudge of dirt across his cheek.

Gunner chuckled. "I was hoping to get this guy on camera." He pointed his chin toward Levi. "What do you say?"

Kelsey's shoulders turned tense as she watched Levi try to measure out his response.

"I don't think so," he finally said.

"Come on." Gunner put an arm across Levi's shoulders. "Show me what you're doing here."

Levi looked at Gunner's button-up and tie like he'd wandered into the wrong building. Pointing to the pencil notch on the board, he said, "Cutting new floorboards."

Gunner's brown eyes darted back and forth from the boards to the cement floor. "For what?"

Levi grabbed his goggles and slipped them on before picking up a circular saw. He motioned for Gunner to step back before he lost his tie, and when the whirring split the air, Gunner did indeed jump out of the way.

In one precise swipe, Levi cut the board. He picked it up and held it out to Dusty, who scurried to carry it to the trailer. The flatbed had almost a whole new floor, save a few more rows.

"Are we going to be performing on those?" Gunner asked.

Kelsey grinned. "It's the easiest way to move a stage to the park."

"Vic." Gunner swatted the other guy's arm. "Get some footage of this." He paused for a split second. "Assuming Levi doesn't mind. No speaking part required."

Levi shrugged and turned back to his saw, its high-pitched squeal drowning out almost everything else. When

Gunner leaned in toward Kelsey, she had to read his lips as he said, "Smart idea."

She waited for Levi to stop. "It was his."

Gunner stood watch, hands on his hips and chest puffed out, as he waited for Vic to record what they needed. By the time Levi had finished cutting the boards and hopped up on the bed beside Dusty, Gunner had clearly formed a plan.

"Hey, can we get an interview with all three of you? Levi, I promise, you don't have to say a word. Just stand there and smile at the camera."

Levi looked ready to be bowled over by a feather. But they needed this coverage. They needed Gunner. Whatever the cost.

Sidling up beside Levi, Kelsey bumped her knuckles against the back of his leather gloves. "I'll do all the talking. Well, me and Dusty."

The teenager in question looked ready to vibrate right through the floor. And she couldn't let him go on air looking like that. He was a few centimeters taller than her, his feet too big, his limbs still gangly. He'd probably grow a head taller than her in the next year, but for now she could reach everything she needed to.

"Do you mind?" she asked, licking the pad of her thumb.

"No, ma'am."

She swiped the dirt off his cheek, and he held still like this wasn't the first time a woman had cleaned him up this way. When his face was in better shape, she ran her fingers through his hair, parting it to the side and combing it flat where she could. At least she'd gotten rid of the gray streaks.

"We better hurry before it comes back to life." Kelsey

chuckled as Gunner lined them up within the patch of natural light that came through the door. He placed her right next to him, Dusty half a step behind her shoulder, and Levi at the far end.

"Please say and spell your names for the visual team," Vic said.

Kelsey said hers, then passed the baton to Dusty. "Dusty Crowder," he said. Suddenly Levi shoved his shoulder, and Dusty glanced up into the face of his mentor, who didn't even look down. A smile plucked at the corner of his mouth as he tried again. "Dustin Crowder. D-u-s-t-i-n."

She couldn't put a name on what had just happened, but something passed between them, something that told her Levi had just encouraged Dusty—Dustin—to do something big. Something that mattered. At least to him.

Gunner pulled her attention back to himself as Vic counted down with his fingers then pointed to the newsman.

"You might wonder what an old tin barn has to do with saving a celebrated playhouse. Well, here in Victoria, it turns out, quite a lot. Today I'm here with Kelsey Ahern, the director and mastermind behind the benefit production bent on rescuing the old theatre that was damaged by Hurricane Adelle." He pressed the hand mic beneath her chin.

"We only have one theatre in town, so we had to get creative," she said. "My friend Levi Ross came up with the idea for a show in the park, which meant building a mobile stage." She stepped in front of Dustin and gracefully waved behind her. "We're extremely grateful for Mr. and Mrs. Herman, who have loaned us the use of these hay wagons that Levi and Dustin are restoring."

Gunner stepped past her, and she scooted out of the way as the mic landed in front of Dustin, whose eyes were wide and bright and full of joy. Not many students in Victoria made the island news. She prayed he'd be lauded for it by his friends.

"Mr. Crowder, how did you end up as part of this production?"

Dustin froze. Silence reigned. For a second, she thought Gunner was going to move on. But then, from her vantage point toward the back of their line, she saw Levi flick the kid's arm. It was like flipping a switch.

"I usually help Mr. Herman during the summers on his farm. But the hay isn't quite ready to come in because of the rain. So he sent me out here and said I should help Le— Mr. Ross. And he's been teaching me all sorts of things. We've fixed an axle and a couple of hitches, and now we're redoing the floors so they'll be stable for when the actors— when you—get up there to perform. Plus we're going to start building the frame to hold the curtain and the sound system. Mrs. Ross—not Mama Potts, but Mrs. Meg—she said she's going to help us on account of all of the electrical stuff she knows."

Gunner put on a face that was suitably impressed, and Kelsey had to bite her tongue to keep from asking why he hadn't emoted so much during the callbacks.

"It sounds like half the town is involved, between the cast and those chipping in behind the scenes," he said. "And the community here in Victoria has certainly welcomed this guy from Charlottetown to join them. But we need your support. Visit the website on the screen to get your tickets now. Only twenty dollars per ticket, plus your additional donation goes to reopening the Victoria Play-house. We'll see you next week with another interview to save the playhouse."

Vic motioned that it was a cut, and Gunner flipped back to not-TV mode.

Maybe that was part of his problem with stage act-ing. He had a TV personality, and he had a regular one. Maybe he hadn't put together that the TV one should be the actor. She filed that away for their first rehearsal later that week. Before then, she had to set something else straight.

"Um, Gunner, we don't have a website."

"Seriously?" His tone implied that he hadn't realized he'd signed up to be part of such an amateurish troupe.

"We'll have it done before this airs," Dustin said.

She caught Levi's gaze over Dustin's head. He looked as surprised as she felt.

"What? It's not like it's hard. I know somebody."

"Good. Send me the URL as soon as it's up." Gunner held out his hand toward Vic. "Now we just need a waiver from the minor. Parent's signature."

For the kid who would have no trouble setting up a web-site to sell tickets, a waiver seemed to be a different story. "Um . . . my mom's . . . You sure you need her to sign that?"

"Is it going to be a problem?"

Dustin dug the toe of his sneaker into the cement. "I haven't exactly told her . . . The thing is, she usually doesn't care what I'm up to, so long as I'm not in trouble. But if I bring her something to sign, she'll think it's either to get her money or to get me outta trouble."

Gunner's eyes narrowed, his lips pursing to the side.

"Fine. Come on, kid. I'll drive you home and explain to her that you're about to be a little bit famous."

Dustin nearly jumped out of his pants. "Really? That'd be so cool!" With a quick goodbye to Levi, he darted toward the van and clamored into the back.

To his credit, Gunner gave Kelsey a long look. "You okay to get home?"

"I'll drop her off." Levi hadn't asked if she needed a ride or if she wanted to walk the kilometer or so to her own front door, but she didn't argue.

"Thanks, Gunner," she said. "I'll see you at rehearsal on Wednesday."

He waved farewell, and the van flew down the lane, spitting red dirt behind it with every hiccup and hole.

With all the commotion gone, just the two of them left, the silence was oddly heavy. And while her sundress had seemed like a great idea earlier in the day, now she felt out of place. "Sorry I'm not really dressed to help you work today."

Levi shrugged and didn't complain. Not that he would have even if he wanted her help. "Do you want . . . I can give you a ride home."

"Or you can finish up what you're working on. I'll just . . . Oh, I should have brought my script with me. I could have made a few set notes. You know, while I'm inspired by the stage."

He held up a finger to indicate he'd be back in a second, then he darted outside. A moment later, his truck door slammed, and he bounded back inside, squinting from the outdoor brilliance and holding out a book. His fingers dwarfed the tiny paperback, and she realized that the books she usually saw him with were three, four, or five times larger.

Before she accepted it, she knew what it was—his own personal copy of the script. Some of the pages were dog-eared, and the spine was close to giving up. She cracked it open to the first page to find his name printed in all caps across the top.

"How long have you had this?"

Pulling back his hand, his fingers brushed hers. He moved slow, like he was afraid that if he went any faster, the friction between their skin would ignite. It was already threatening. Heat rushed up her arm, sparks shooting to the tips of her fingers.

Had it been like this the night of the storm? She couldn't remember much. Only that she'd been so cold and then suddenly there'd been warmth. His warmth. His protective arms had held her against his chest, which had risen and fallen with his breath against her temple.

The memories rushed over her, the flames licking at her neck. And the ridiculous square neckline of her sundress was not doing a thing to help.

Yanking the book to her chest, she spun and walked toward his work area. "Thank you."

The blue pencil that had been behind his ear earlier—the one that had had absolutely no business being so attractive tucked into the ebony waves of his hair—fluttered in front of her eyes. "Keep it as long as you need."

twelve

The next evening, Levi stepped into the noise and bustle of Carrie's Café. The dinner crowd was out en masse, nearly every seat full. Carrie sashayed between the tables to a perfectly choreographed dance, dropping off meals, picking up empty plates, accepting compliments along the way. Her black curls had begun to fall from where she'd clipped them up in the back, but she couldn't have looked more pleased.

"Levi," she called, the welcome in her voice drawing a dozen pairs of eyes to him. "You looking for Mama Potts?"

He hadn't been. But now he was.

His gaze washed over each table, into every nook and corner, until he found the familiar face. Her eyes were nearly glowing tonight.

And she wasn't alone.

Her slender fingers—always stained with the island's red clay after years of crafting her signature pottery—rested beside her empty plate on the table, just a breath from another hand that could have easily swallowed hers. Levi followed the thick forearm up to the man's shoulder, then to the clean-shaven, square jaw.

Patrick Macon.

Levi had been looking for Dustin, but that could wait. Patrick and Mama Potts could not.

He tried not to stomp across the floor, tried not to disturb anyone's meal or attract any more attention than need be. But they were nearly making a scene, so wrapped up in each other's gaze that they didn't notice him until he was literally bumping into their table for two. Way in the back corner.

"Levi?" Patrick looked surprised but didn't pull his hand away from Mama Potts's. "Good to see you."

"Honey? What are you doing here? I thought you were working on the show."

"I am." He waved toward wherever Dustin and his web guru friend might be sitting. "What are you doing? Are you . . . together?" The word tasted like beets, and he cringed at the mere suggestion.

Mama Potts's eyebrows dipped with a touch of sadness. "We're only having dinner."

He'd told his mom that he would be eating out. Because he still checked in with her and still lived in her home. Eli had insisted on taking the apartment above the garage when Oliver got married and moved in with Meg. Levi had stayed put in his room at the top of the stairs. The one he'd been in since he was sixteen. It was comfortable and familiar.

Exactly the opposite of whatever was happening before him.

"We can talk about this at home if you want," Mama Potts said.

He shook his head. Hard. He did not want to talk about this. And he sure didn't want to think about it.

"Oh, sweetie. Your dad's been gone a long time."

But his dad wasn't dead, and to the best of his knowledge, his parents had never divorced.

Which meant he didn't want to be a witness to whatever was happening, and he sure didn't want to draw any more attention than his beeline toward them already had.

"Levi, look. This is all completely innocent." Patrick didn't look embarrassed or concerned. He didn't even look like he was bothered by the interruption. "We've been friends since you were a kid. And I've always known your mom is a beautiful woman. But lately . . ."

Nope. He did not need the details, but he sure wanted to know how much his brothers knew. The problem was that texting them to ask was guaranteed to make sure they came charging down to Carrie's to investigate.

Holding up his hands to ward off any further details, he backed up, right into another two-top. Mumbling a quick apology, he made a straightaway for the entrance. But a hand reached out and grabbed his sleeve.

"Levi! You made it." Dustin tugged him down into the empty seat across from a teenage girl. She looked older than Dustin by a few years and vaguely familiar. Probably from the school.

She skipped the introductions and went straight to her line of questions. "You're Coach's brother, aren't you?"

His head was already spinning, unable to set aside the terrible vision of his mom. On a date. With his mentor. *Former* mentor. Whatever his connection to this girl, he couldn't make sense of it. "Um . . ."

"Coach Ross?" she said. "I was on the Stars."

Right. He'd seen them play a few times during the last spring season. But he couldn't have supplied her name.

"Audrey."

He nodded, one quick jerk of his chin.

Dustin looked almost as dumbfounded as Levi still felt. "Eli Ross is your brother?"

Levi couldn't move, but Audrey quickly confirmed. "Coach Ross is the oldest." With a nod, she motioned toward him. "He's the youngest."

Dustin's shoulders twitched with a chuckle. "You never said nothing." Then he let out a full-on laugh. With a hitch of his thumb, Dustin spoke to Audrey. "He doesn't talk much, but he can build just about anything. It's pretty wild, actually." Shifting his feet, he said, "Audrey is friends with my sister. She can make a website in a few minutes. Watch."

So that was what Levi did. Audrey flipped open a laptop not much bigger than his hand, connected to Carrie's ever-ready Wi-Fi, and went to work. Her fingers flew, the sound of them slapping against the keyboard carrying over the hum of voices and bursts of laughter.

Resting his elbow against the table, Levi squeezed the bridge of his nose between his thumb and forefinger and closed his eyes. The problem was as soon as he was in his own darkness, he could clearly see his mom's fingers reaching for Patrick's.

His eyes flew open. He couldn't keep from glancing over his shoulder where they still sat, leaning forward, whispering who knew what to each other.

"You want a menu?" Carrie's daughter had appeared

at their table, and she held a single sheet of paper out to him. Only then did he realize that Audrey and Dustin were chomping on fish and chips. He had a feeling he was going to be footing the bill.

The smell of grease and vinegar combined to make his already unsettled stomach roll, and he shook his head. "No, but thanks."

When he looked back at the screen, he did a double take.

Somehow Audrey's greasy fingers had made magic.

In a font that would have been right at home in Queen Victoria's castle itself, the page announced the show and date and a simple cast list. Clearly Gunner got top billing, as he was going to be the biggest draw. The background featured purple and teal and white stripes, almost a Victorian circus tent. And at the bottom of the single page, a picture of the playhouse and a simple request. *Help us rebuild*.

There was a button to buy tickets and an option to give a little extra right to the theatre's foundation. It was simpler to let the nonprofit collect donations and sell the tickets. After all, every penny was going to them anyway—except what it took to produce the show.

"Kelsey is going to—"

"I love it!"

He looked up as the voice in question cut him off.

Dustin jumped out of his chair, waving for her to sit down and pulling over an empty seat from the next table. Introductions were quick and efficient, and then Levi could just sit back as the women talked details, leaving him to ruminate and keep an eye on the table in the back.

"Are you walking home?" Kelsey jogged to catch up to Levi even as he paused on the shoulder of the dim road, right in the pool of a streetlamp.

He shrugged.

"But isn't that your truck?" She pointed to the one parked across the street that she knew full well belonged to him. He'd driven her home in it the day before.

"I just felt like a walk. Figured I could pick it up tomorrow."

"Oh."

Suddenly his neck jerked, and his eyes focused on her. "Do you need a ride home? I can . . ." He pointed at the truck as though giving up on finding the words.

"I was going to walk home too. Mind if I join you?"

They strolled in silence for several minutes, only the chirps of evening crickets to entertain them. The lights in Carrie's windows were still bright, casting their shadows long down the road, and the popular local spot would stay open until the last body went home.

Levi had been distracted the whole time they'd talked about the website. He hadn't added more than a grunt or two to the conversation, which was pretty normal. But for some reason his response had felt off, as though there was a weight on his shoulders that only he knew. Kelsey wasn't sure he'd even realized that Audrey had made the website live with the press of a single button. So as soon as he'd gotten up, thrown enough money on the table to cover three meals, and excused himself, she'd followed right behind.

"Are you all right? You've been kind of . . . quiet tonight."

He chuckled under his breath. "That unusual or something?"

She elbowed his arm. "Give me a break. I'm just checking on you. You've been so different lately—nearly chatty."

This time he snorted.

"Oh, shut it. I just mean, it seems like . . . well, ever since that night at the school, like we're friends now. Not co-workers. Not former classmates. Not just someone you nod at when you see them at the grocery, but like someone willing to be there. And I know I sound like an idiot. You probably have no idea what I'm talking about. But *I* know. I appreciate you. You've helped me out of more situations in the last three weeks than . . ."

She waved her hand and stopped walking, hoping he'd continue on and they could pretend like her incessant need to fill the silence hadn't led to a complete overshare. But he didn't keep walking. In fact, he came to a stop right beside her, then stepped even closer. She could just make out his profile against the big silvery moon before a cloud whispered across its face, hiding him in the darkness.

He seemed content to remain silent, but his presence made her shiver. It wasn't the breeze off the water or the cool summer night. It was him.

And he didn't have a clue.

He shrugged out of his flannel shirt and laid it on her shoulders. It was softer than goose down, still carried his body heat, and smelled like wood shavings and his spicy aftershave. She couldn't help but slide her arms into the sleeves, even if her hands didn't come close to reaching the cuffs. He took care of that too, rolling up each sleeve until her fingers were visible once again.

When he stepped away, she stumbled toward him, bumping into his chest and shivering all over again.

"Are you warm enough?" he asked as he pulled the collar of his shirt closed beneath her chin, his hands brushing her jaw ever so slightly.

Basically on fire. Thank you for asking.

"Uh-huh."

"Come on then." His hand on her back, he ushered her along the road, keeping his pace even and short enough that she didn't have to hurry to catch up. He seemed content to walk in silence under the stars. Then suddenly he said, "I am too."

"Huh?"

"Glad we're friends—better friends."

Twisting her neck to watch his face, she asked, "Were we friends before?"

Without looking in her direction, he chuckled. "I thought so. But if you weren't sure, then it was my fault."

"But you always called me Ms. Ahern."

"True," he said with a thoughtful nod. "But I thought of you as Kelsey."

Well, if that didn't make the fire inside her burn brighter, nothing ever would. The way he said her name . . . like he was shielding it from the rest of the world. Like he'd rather be dragged across gravel than let her know pain.

When they reached the dirt driveway to Mama Potts's white cottage near the shore, he paused to stare down the lane at the dark shape. None of the lights were on in the main house, though one window above the garage shone bright.

Levi kept walking, his feet picking up speed as she scrambled to catch up.

"You missed your turn there, buddy."

"I'm not interested in being home when my mom gets back tonight."

"Why not?"

He walked as though he had a mission—arms pumping, eyes focused. "I think my mom was on a date tonight."

"Mama Potts on a date?" Her voice nearly chirped with delight. "With who?"

"Patrick Macon." His pace picked up again, and she ran three steps to catch up with him, grabbing the sleeve of his white T-shirt to keep him from racing off without her.

"I don't understand. Why is this a bad thing?"

Stabbing his fingers through his hair left the front standing on end. But it was probably better than him pulling it out altogether, which looked to be his next step.

"I can't—" He jabbed a finger in the direction they'd come. "She's been through enough. What if he hurts her?"

"Patrick?" She felt like a six-year-old trying to put together a puzzle with the wrong pieces. "Slow down. Take a deep breath." Grabbing his arms, she tried to ground him, to make him look into her eyes. "Tell me what's going on inside your head. You've gotten pretty good at that lately, so don't tell me you can't."

His cheeks puffed as he let out a long breath between tight lips. "I must sound like an idiot."

"Not at all. You sound like a son who loves his mother very much. Now tell me why you're worried."

"As far as I know, my mom has never loved anyone but my dad."

When he paused, she gave his arm a little squeeze.

"And we both know how that turned out."

"Actually, I don't."

Levi let out a snort of derision. "Seriously? You grew up in this town, and no one told you about him?"

She shook her head.

"And I suppose you're going to tell me that you didn't know we got evicted right after he left."

"Oh, Levi. I didn't know." Her grandma had always said that there wasn't much that couldn't be fixed with a hug and duct tape. Kelsey didn't have the latter, but she threw her arms around his waist and pressed her ear to his heart. "I'm so sorry."

For a long second, he didn't seem sure what to do with his arms, but then they wrapped around her back, holding her so tight that she couldn't have escaped if she'd wanted to. Not that she did.

His chest rumbled. "Mama Potts did everything for us. She worked three jobs, made sure Oliver and I got to school, took in Violet like she was one of her own—all while trying to pursue her own dreams of owning the studio."

"I know you want her to be happy," she whispered into the impossibly soft cotton of his T-shirt. "Patrick is a good man. He's not your dad."

When he nodded, his five o'clock shadow caught the hair on top of her head with a soft tug. "She deserves the best. And maybe that's Patrick. I mean, I don't think he'd ever walk out on her or leave her with piles of gambling debts or something like that. He's one of the best men I know. I just . . ."

She squeezed him, hoping the words would pop right out.

"I don't see how Mama Potts can be happy with another man without somehow bringing my dad back into the picture."

"What do you mean?"

"I mean, they're still married. They'd have to sign some paperwork, officially end what he abandoned twelve years ago."

"And you don't want that?"

The growl low in his throat buzzed right over her head, sending tremors all the way down her spine. "I never want to see that man again."

She didn't know how to respond to that except to hold him tighter. It wasn't the time to push, so she simply stood in his arms and let him lean on her. And she leaned on him a little too. Because that's what friends did.

It was hard to know how much time passed. It could have been hours or maybe just fifteen minutes. Not a single car drove by and no light was switched on at Mama Potts's house. Their little corner of the world was untouched, save the gentle clapping of the waves beyond the grassy bluff.

When Levi finally pulled back, she held a sharp breath, ready to say good night. But he looked down the road and whispered like he had a secret, "Would you like to see my dream?"

"Very much." No two words had ever been so true. She skipped to keep up with him as they followed the road past a few more homes on the seaside and a field of lavender lupin bathed in moonlight.

He stopped her short, resting his hands on her shoulders and gazing from behind her. "That's going to be mine."

The green house sat up on a little rise in the road. At this time of night she couldn't see its color, but she'd driven past it a few hundred times in the midday sun. Its deep green both blended into the surrounding lawn and stood out against a cloudless blue sky. She could almost hear children playing behind the dormer windows upstairs and see the glass lanterns illuminating the wraparound porch.

Suddenly she couldn't wait, and she raced across the lawn, the lush grass squishing beneath her shoes. "Can we go in?"

He laughed. "It's not mine yet. But hopefully by the end of the summer I'll have the down payment."

"This is why you accepted the money for the show."

He nodded slowly. "And it's why I'm helping Mr. Herman harvest hay next week and next month too. Between that and my regular salary, it'll be enough."

But what if it wasn't? What if her dream somehow kept him from realizing his?

Tugging her hand, he plopped in the center of the lawn and began telling her his plans even before she landed beside him. They were grand, filled with family and nieces and nephews, alive with hope for the future and a part of him she hadn't seen before. A part she couldn't look away from.

He talked for more than ten minutes, his tone thick, his pitch rising with excitement. "And then I'm going to turn the attic into a playroom or a bedroom or both. Oliver and Meg's little guys can come stay with me, and I'll take them swimming and fishing and . . ."

"And you'll be the family you didn't get as a kid."

He hung his head, his lopsided grin still visible. "Something like that."

"I think that sounds pretty perfect."

"What about you? What's your dream?"

Her lip quivered, and she bit into it before Levi could notice. "The theatre. Restoring the playhouse."

"To save your job?" There was a question beneath his question, a worry that her dream wasn't big enough.

If he only knew. But she couldn't tell him the truth, tell him the price she owed. A half-truth would have to be enough. "For my grandma." The backs of her eyes began to burn, and she quickly swiped a thumb over each eyelid. "All of my best memories are on that stage with her."

thirteen

Kelsey chewed on her lower lip, crossing her arms as she walked back and forth across the makeshift stage taped out on the cafeteria floor.

Gunner stood opposite Fredrick, who was playing Algernon—the other character pretending to be named Ernest. Gunner, without moving his body, said in a complete deadpan, "When one is in town one amuses oneself. When one is in the country one amuses other people. It is excessively boring."

Fred, with a mischievous grin in his voice, replied, "And who are the people you amuse?"

Kelsey held her breath as she waited for Gunner's next line, which was to be light and airy. Instead, she got silence. Fred shot a quick look her way.

"Gunner, that's your line," she said.

"Are you sure?"

Striding over to his side, she held up her script, the margins filled with scribbles, and pointed to his line. "Oh, neighbors, neighbors." She said it exactly as she'd expect his character to, all flippancy and disregard for the unnamed characters.

He repeated it, tying a lead weight around the words, ready to chuck them into the harbor.

"Okay, everyone." She bit back the sigh that threatened. "Let's take ten." For Gunner's ears only, she whispered, "It's okay if you're not off the book yet. We've only been rehearsing for a week. And right now it's more about getting the timing and rhythm right, so you can use your book."

Guilt pinched his nose. "I forgot it in Charlottetown. I'm sorry."

Steam built inside her ears, and she swallowed to keep it from escaping. "No problem." The words slid out between gritted teeth. "You can use . . ." She almost offered up the copy that Levi had lent her, but it would never survive Gunner's care. "You can use mine today." She thrust it into his hands and then walked to the side door and straight outside.

She stopped by her car and gulped in the fresh air, lifting her face to the serenity. The sky was filled with fluffy white clouds, so it wasn't going to make good on any threat of rain. Levi, Dustin, and the rest of Mr. Herman's crew had at least another day to clear the rest of the fields. Honestly, they couldn't finish fast enough.

It felt like a month since she'd seen Levi. Okay, it had only been a week. But there had been no time for leisurely strolls and talk of dreams. He hadn't given her another glimpse into what was going on in his heart, what had bothered him so deeply about the idea of his father returning.

"Miss Ahern?" Willow called from the side entrance. "Are you coming back in?"

"Be right there." She ducked into her passenger seat, snagged Levi's weathered book, and jogged back inside. "Let's set the scene," she announced when she flung the door open. "Two dandies sharing tea and talking about how terrible their neighbors are. This is a comedy. Think light. Gunner, how would you cover a bright, sunny day, temperatures in the low twenties?"

"The forecast?"

"Yes. Let's say the forecast for next week is absolutely perfect. Not a cloud in the sky or a chance of heavy winds. Just that summer breeze that makes everyone want to go for a swim at the beach. How would you deliver that?"

Gunner glanced at the faces of the eight other cast members, for the first time appearing a little less than cool and collected. Then the light in his eyes flipped on, right along with his grin. "Hose off your chairs and take the cover off your pool—you're not going to want to waste a second of this weekend indoors. Get out your sandals and shake out that beach blanket. The shore is calling, and it has your number."

Everyone broke out in scattered applause, and Fredrick pressed his fingers to the corners of his mouth to give his costar a piercing whistle.

"Just like that!" Kelsey cheered. "Very good, Gunner. That's the exact emotion for this scene. Instructive. Joyful. A little bit playful. Now let's see you do it like that."

Pride oozed out of him as he raised his script and read his lines with Fred. They managed to make it all the way from Jack's arrival at Algernon's solo tea party to the arrival of Gwendolen and her mother, Lady Bracknell, without a pause.

Not perfect, but certainly watchable. At least when Gunner didn't have his script in his face. Which, if she was honest, he usually did. But they had almost seven weeks to go. It was going to be tight, but they could make it.

As the cast began to pick up their stuff and file out after rehearsal, Kelsey stopped Gunner. "Do you have someone to run lines with?"

"I'll be okay. I'll run them on the prompter at work."

"Or, you know, most actors practice with someone else." She blurted it out before she did something ridiculous like telling him just how stupid he sounded. "It helps you get a feeling for the timing and back-and-forth with another person. You can come practice with me while I'm working on sets."

"Just the two of us?" His over-the-top wink was either his attempt at flirting or his idea of a joke.

She decided to play it straight. "Well, Levi and Dustin will be there too."

His big brown eyes turned soft. "I'll be there if you think it'll help."

Before saying goodbye, she patted his arm. "You did good work today." And she meant it.

"Thanks, boss. See you later this week."

Levi felt every year of his age—twice that of Dustin and the other guys in the field. He was still young, but he was a little out of practice. Even though Mr. Herman's machines did a lot of the work, there was plenty of pushing and pulling and manhandling the round bales into shape, then hauling them onto the trailers to be carted off and sold.

He wiped his forehead against his elbow, sweat and dirt sticking to the short sleeve of his gray T-shirt. Well, it had started the day gray, but it was now mostly a hodgepodge of green pollen, black sweat stains, and a crimson stripe where he'd wiped his hand after cutting himself on some baling wire. Rookie mistake, and the crew of older teenagers had let him know it.

That was all right. Better they laugh at him than hassle each other—or Dustin.

Dustin had tried to stick up for him, but with a wave of his hand, Levi let him know it wasn't worth the effort. They had formed some sort of shorthand over the last couple weeks in the barn—Dustin asking questions and Levi providing silent answers. It wasn't entirely unlike his relationship with Patrick had been all those years ago, and it was nice to be on the teaching side of things.

He pulled his truck up to the yard in front of the new barn, and the boys in the bed hooted as they jumped down, calling out that they'd see him the next day. He waved a hand out the window and crawled out, then leaned heavily on the door. They'd worked four days in a row, and he prayed one more would do it as he looked around for Mr. Herman, who had met him out here at the end of every day just as the light was beginning to fade. But he wasn't there.

Kelsey was. She walked across the yard, her arms crossed, her bottom lip nearly invisible as she chewed on it.

"Is everything okay?" he called as his boots ate up the ground between them. "Is someone hurt?"

Her face relaxed, revealing a quick smile as she drew near, her gaze sweeping over him. Suddenly her eyes grew huge, unblinking. All of the color drained from her face, leaving her ashen and stony. "What happened to you? You're . . . you're . . . bleeding."

She swayed, and every second of that night in the school flashed before him. She hadn't taken the sight of even her own blood well. And while his hand had stopped dripping after a few minutes, his stained clothing probably told a different story.

"I'm fine. I'm not hurt."

She blinked at him three times in a row, and her throat worked convulsively, every swallow audible.

"Should I go get Mrs. Herman?" Dustin asked from a few meters away.

"Maybe get a glass of water for Miss Ahern too," Levi called back.

The kid set off for the house, looking like this was a race he was determined to win.

"Come on. Let's sit you down for a minute here." Tucking one hand under her elbow and his other around her wrist, Levi tried to shuttle her to the truck without coming into substantial contact with her pretty purple sweater.

Apparently she didn't mind because she leaned against his side, gulping staggering breaths all the way to where he'd left the driver-side door open. Wrapping his hands around her waist to boost her into the seat, he couldn't help but smell the lavender on her skin or take a minute to breathe in her very essence. She bounced a little on the bench seat but finally settled so they were eye to eye.

"You want some water? It's probably got hay on it, but it might help." He reached for the dirt-caked insulated thermos, looking for anything to wipe the spout. His clothes were a lost cause, and even her ripped jeans were too fancy to be used as a rag.

She took the thermos, guzzling it until her skin turned more pink and less gray, never looking away from his gaze. When she set it in her lap, she gave a big sigh.

"Better?"

She nodded. "I think so. I just get a little woozy around—"

"This isn't the first time you've tried to pass out on me. At least you didn't succeed this time."

She chuckled, but then fear filled her eyes. "But you're okay?"

"Perfectly fine. I got careless today, and some wire took a little bite out of my hand." He held up the outer ridge of his left hand and pressed his finger to the scab already forming there. "I'm not bleeding anymore."

"But you thought wiping it on your shirt—the one covered in hay and—" She sneezed hard, which conveyed everything she needed to.

"I would have wiped it on my handkerchief, but I haven't gotten it back from you yet."

Her mouth moved, but no words came out. Whatever color she'd gained back leaked from her face in a split second.

Taking her hands, he chuckled. "I'm teasing you, Kelsey. I had already used my handkerchief with all of this." He motioned to his hair and the mess surely on his face.

He generally wasn't overly concerned with his appearance. There wasn't much to him aside from a lanky build. He had hair and eyes that matched his brothers', but they got the interesting features. Eli was the classically handsome one. Oliver with a crooked nose and big ears had character for days.

And then there was Levi. Pretty ordinary every time he looked in the mirror.

But now, watching Kelsey react to him, he wished he had something to make himself stand out. At the very least, he wished he was clean.

The truth washed over him, carrying his own scent, and the sudden realization made him gag. He took half a step backward, stumbling on his boots, but stopped when she whispered his name.

"Levi?" Her voice was soft, but not as sweet as the feel of her gaze on his skin.

"I'm sorry. I need a shower."

Her fingers brushed his temple, her nails combing through his untamed waves. Then she dragged her fingers past his ear and along the bottom of his jaw, setting his whole world spinning.

"I missed you this week." Her hushed words sounded surprised.

"Me too," he confessed.

Her fingers had landed on his chin, her thumb on one side and the rest lazily drifting over his whiskers on the other. Suddenly she found his dimple, and he was inclined to smile even more as her finger rocked in the little groove.

"I always forget you have that. Maybe you should smile more."

He wasn't sure how to explain that up until a few weeks ago, he hadn't had much to smile about. Until she'd kicked down the walls he'd been using to isolate himself for years. Including one around his heart.

His hand jerked to his chest of its own volition, scratching at the spot where his heart slammed into his ribs. It hadn't done that before she'd walked back into his life. It hadn't ever had a reason. And now she sat in front of him like she'd just been waiting for him to notice all the heavy dismantling she'd done.

For maybe the first time in his life he desperately wanted to say something. He just didn't know what. Anything he said could break the magic spell that kept him locked in her gaze, and he couldn't risk losing that.

He reached for her wrist near his cheek, swiping his thumb over her pulse point. He was pretty sure he'd read somewhere that checking for a pulse with the thumb didn't work. But he could feel hers pounding a steady rhythm that matched the thunder in his ears.

Maybe that was his own pulse. Or maybe they were in sync.

When Kelsey finally blinked, his gaze fell toward her lips, the corners slightly turned up, full of color and life once again. Perfectly sweet. Perfectly kissable.

Heaven help him, he wanted to kiss Kelsey Ahern.

He knew she was smart and savvy and as beautiful as the evening sky overhead. But the desire that crashed through him wasn't a fleeting sunset. It was the everyday moments made special by the one he was with. It was fifty years down the road in a rocking chair, teasing and being teased by his wife. It was Oliver and Meg, Eli and Violet, and Mel and Faye Herman.

What he felt was Adirondack chairs on the porch of the green house, the attic playhouse filled not with nieces and nephews but with strawberry blonds who had their mama's blue eyes.

Levi had skipped about a hundred steps to get to that image, but one thing he knew for certain. Kelsey was leaning into him.

His tongue darted out to lick his lips. Placing a hand on her knee to keep himself steady, he closed his eyes.

"Mr. Ross! Mr. Ross! I got Mrs. Herman just like you said, and here's some water."

Levi jumped back just as Dustin tripped over his own feet and the cup of water in his hand went flying.

There was no time to move, no chance to react. All Levi could do was stand there as water splashed into his face and dripped down his shirt and Kelsey's smile lit up the cab of the truck.

He couldn't contain his own smile, giving her one more view of his dimple before Faye bustled up to check on the patient.

—————

"Dustin, will you read Gwendolen's part?"

Kelsey watched as the young man turned every shade of red she'd ever seen, finally landing on crimson from his neck to his hairline.

"I'll do it," Levi said before Dustin had even stammered out a whole word.

"I don't need a scene partner," Gunner said.

Kelsey shot him a look that told him not to argue with her.

"But how are you going to finish the stage if you're reading?" he asked Levi.

Levi popped a few nails into the corner of his mouth and raised his hammer. "Pray don't talk to me about the weather, Mr. Worthing." His voice had jumped a couple octaves, a false soprano that brought a smirk to every face in the barn. "Whenever people talk to me about the weather, I always feel quite certain that they mean something else. And that makes me so nervous."

Gunner's grin began to melt, first like ice in the midday sun, then like snow on the first day of June. "You mean you know this play?"

From his perch on a trailer where he was putting in the last of the new floorboards, Levi plucked one of the nails from between his lips, held it in place, and smashed its head with his hammer. Running a thumb over the top to make sure it was flush, he looked up to meet Gunner's gaze. "Yep."

"You've memorized it? The whole thing? All the parts?"

Another nail. Another nod.

"You're kidding, man." Gunner crossed his arms, a hint of a challenge in his stance. "No way you know all the parts. No one would memorize them all."

Kelsey chewed on her thumbnail, not sure how Levi was going to respond but certain he would take a stand.

Slowly he pulled the nails from his lips and stood tall on the makeshift stage. "I *do* mean something else." His voice had dropped to a pretty good impression of Gunner's. Well, a version of Gunner that did a better Jack.

Kelsey clapped a hand over her mouth to hide her smile.

A slight shift in his face indicated that Levi was changing characters back to Gwendolen. "I thought so. In fact, I am never wrong."

With a subtle change in his posture and a drop in his

tone, Levi slid back into Jack's role. "And I would like to be allowed to take advantage of Lady Bracknell's temporary absence . . ."

High-pitched Gwendolen rushed on. "I would certainly advise you to do so. Mamma has a way of coming back suddenly into a room that I have often had to speak to her about."

Dustin cracked up at that. Clamping both hands over his mouth wasn't enough to cover the snorts as Jack made another appearance, hesitant and cautious.

"Miss Fairfax, ever since I met you I have admired you more than any girl . . . I have ever met since . . . I met you."

Gunner lost it then too, dissolving into a fit of laughter. Dustin had to lean on his knees just to stay upright.

With some degree of difficulty, Kelsey kept her lips closed and managed not to ask Gunner to perform his lines *just* like that. Maybe Levi would serve as inspiration though.

Dustin whistled low. "Man, Mr. Ross. You're crazy. Where'd you learn all that?"

Levi arched an eyebrow, almost a question. "Where does anyone learn anything?"

Dustin looked confused, but Kelsey immediately pictured the worn-out copy of his book. Read. Reread. Loved.

What she wanted to know was how he'd learned to perform. The man had a knack for it. Why hadn't he shown up to auditions to do more than collect contact info and shuttle people into groups? Probably because that was all she'd asked of him.

She wanted desperately to ask him how he could slip so easily into the voice of another as though he hadn't struggled to talk to her at first. As though he didn't say more than a few words around Gunner. But that wasn't a conversation for this place in front of these people.

Levi knelt once again and slammed a few more nails into place. Long after she thought he had chosen not to answer Dustin's question, he simply said, "I like to read."

"I do too, but that's something else." Gunner chuckled. "I appreciate your help today."

Kelsey got him set up on a chair near where Levi continued to work. Dustin was silent for once as he shuttled fresh planks from the pile near the door to the trailer.

Gunner read from his script—hers, actually. The one he hadn't returned yet. Levi filled in with every other character. She'd thought she'd have to play most of the parts, but Levi did a commendable Algernon and a pretty hilarious Lady Bracknell too.

She should have been paying attention to Gunner, preparing notes, but all she could do was wonder where Levi had been hiding all of this talent. And why he hadn't let it out.

After about an hour, a soft voice at the sliding door called out to them, carried in on a gust of wind. "Well, there's more of you out here than I expected."

Kelsey spun in her chair to see Mrs. Herman standing there, a cup in each hand.

"Thought you boys might need some lemonade on a warm day like this. Didn't know we had visitors." Her smile was genuine for each of them. For once a woman didn't fall all over herself over Gunner.

Levi leaned back on his heels, wiping his forehead with the back of his forearm. He'd discarded his flannel at least half an hour ago, but she'd just noticed that his olive-green T-shirt was sticking to his arms and shoulders.

"You're a kind woman, Mrs. Herman," Levi said but waved for Dustin and Kelsey to receive the drinks in her hand.

Kelsey took a long sip, the tart lemonade quenching a thirst she'd barely known she had. "Thank you," she said.

"I'll be right back with more." Mrs. Herman disappeared into the bright sun, strolling back toward the farmhouse.

"I suppose this is a good spot for a break," Kelsey said. "How did that feel, Gunner?"

"Good, but I'm ready for that break." He stood and stretched his neck, which had been hunched over the script the whole time. "Mind if I take a few pictures for my social media accounts? The station is after me to push the series some more."

Dustin jumped up, sloshing a bit of his lemonade onto his hand then licking it off. "Sure."

"I'd love to get one of Levi too."

Levi's face pinched, but finally he nodded.

"Hop on up there." Gunner motioned to the trailer, and Dustin scrambled onto it.

Kelsey knew her skills in that department were lacking. Levi must have remembered too. Leaning down, he held out both hands. Holding on to her, Levi tugged sharply, and she popped up almost to his level and stepped onto the finished part of the floor.

"Thanks," she whispered, all of the butterflies she'd felt with him in the truck flooding back.

"Levi in the middle, Dusty over there, Kelsey on the other side. Good?" Gunner held up his phone as Levi draped his arm over her shoulders and nodded.

She plastered a smile into place, staring at the phone until there was a commotion at the door. She looked up, expecting to see Mrs. Herman back with more drinks. But the stocky silhouette in the frame wasn't hers.

"Well, this is something, isn't it?"

Levi froze against her side. Even his lungs stopped. A muscle in his jaw ticked, but he seemed unable to look away from the phone Gunner still held up—even though Gunner too was looking over his shoulder at their new visitor.

"Who's that?" Dustin whispered.

When Levi didn't say anything, their visitor filled in the blank. "Is that how you're going to greet your old man after all these years?"

fourteen

Levi couldn't move.

In one word that voice transported him back in time to their old home, the dark lawn, his pathetic plea. And Dean Ross, sneer firmly in place.

The trip stole his breath, and his knees buckled as he leaned on Kelsey under one arm and Dustin under the other. Simultaneously they wrapped him up, the only thing keeping him standing. Through the dense ringing in his ears, he just made out the sound of his name on repeat, each time more urgent, more worried.

Sucking a hard breath into lungs that didn't want to do their job, he straightened his legs and forced himself fully upright, dropping his arms from his supports. He wanted to say something. The trouble was, he had no words. Worse, he had no idea what he wanted them to be.

"Aren't you even going to say hello?" There was a taunt in Dean's voice, a challenge that Levi didn't care to accept. Dean sniffed, the sound filled with every bit of derision he'd ever poured on his youngest—the one who couldn't perform on the ice or work hard enough to help keep a roof over their heads.

It wasn't his fault that Mama Potts hadn't allowed him to work. He'd barely been fifteen. And she'd demanded her boys finish high school. No exceptions. He'd mowed lawns all summer, giving Mama Potts every single dollar that came in.

Which Dean then took to his bookie.

Levi's gut burned, fire shooting all the way to his throat, and a primal scream inside him demanded his dad hear everything he had coming to him. His fists shook at his sides, his nose flaring.

The whole time that Levi stared down the eyes so much like his own, no one spoke a word. Even Gunner kept his mouth closed, somehow seeming to understand this wasn't a man worth charming.

Levi jumped from the trailer, landed on both feet, and stalked silently out of the barn.

"Boy never did have much to say," his dad said behind him. "But he wasn't raised to be rude like that."

Someone in the barn snarled, and Levi didn't know if it was Dustin or Kelsey. If he were a gambler like his dad, he'd put his money on both of them.

In his truck, he slammed the door behind him and curled his hands around the steering wheel, white knuckles swimming before his traitorous eyes. He gulped in the warm air and shoved it out through his nose. Then he punched a button on his phone.

Oliver answered on the first ring. "Levi? What's wrong?"

He grunted.

"But you're . . . *calling* me."

"Meet me at Eli's—at the garage apartment. Now."

"Like, right now? I'm supposed to—"

"Now. Bring Meg."

He hung up before Oliver could argue. Then he turned on his truck and called Eli while he bounced down the lane.

The phone rang three times before a sweet voice picked up. "Are you all right?"

Maybe he needed to call his brothers more often. Or maybe it was better if they assumed that every call was an emergency.

He didn't bother answering Violet's question. "Are you and Eli at the apartment?"

"Yes, but we were going to go to the rink."

"Stay put. Both of you. I'm on my way."

"But—"

She wouldn't appreciate being hung up on, but he'd deal with her anger later. Right now he just had to get there, to look them in the eyes so none of them had to experience what he just had. So they could figure out how to tell Mama Potts too.

He skidded into the driveway just behind Oliver, who was already helping Meg out of his truck when Levi slammed his door.

"What's going on?" Oliver called.

Levi nodded up the faded wooden stairs on the outside of the garage, bounded up them two at a time, and pounded his fist against the plain door. The cut from his run-in with the baling wire still stung, but he didn't stop until Eli swung open the door. Eli looked ready to slam him into the boards—no skates required.

Levi charged in anyway, his hand flying through his hair,

probably making him look like a madman. If so, he looked just like he felt.

Violet rushed to his side but stopped just shy of touching his arm. "Levi, you're scaring me. What is going on? Is Mama Potts all right?"

"Mama Potts?" Levi asked. "What happened to her?"

Eli gave his shoulder a solid shove. "Violet is asking you."

"I think she's—I don't know. I haven't seen her. I haven't—"

A huffing and puffing Meg arrived at the open door, using a spiral notebook to fan her face. "This better be worth it. We were going to get some food."

Levi stared into four pairs of worried eyes, his mouth empty, his brain dry.

"Spill it," Oliver said. "Whatever it is, it can't be worse than Eli dragging his bad decisions home last year."

Eli punched his brother's shoulder but didn't deny it.

Levi heaved a big sigh, closed his eyes, and blurted it out. "Dad's back."

It felt like all of the air had been sucked out of the room. The smallest wave could have tipped them all over. When Levi opened his eyes, the others were statues, Eli holding on to Violet's hand, Oliver with an arm supporting Meg around the waist.

He had a sudden urge to go get Kelsey, to have someone to hang on to through this conversation.

It was Violet—the only one who hadn't lived in Victoria twelve years ago—who spoke first. "H-how do you know? Maybe it was just someone who looked like him."

Levi shook his head. "It was him. He found me at the Hermans' farm."

Oliver managed to stop gaping long enough to say, "He sought you out?"

A short nod.

"How did he know you were there?" Meg asked, her hand cupping her extended belly, protecting the first in the next generation of Rosses.

Levi began to lift his shoulder but stopped. "Gunner Raines. He's been covering the show for weeks. It's been all over the news and his social media."

The man Levi had unwittingly invited into their show had brought the very last man he wanted to see back to the island.

Eli grumbled something under his breath that made Violet visibly squeeze him tighter.

"What's he want?" Oliver asked.

Levi wrinkled his face until one eye fully closed. "I didn't stick around long enough to find out."

"Does Mama Potts know?" Violet asked.

Levi scrubbed his face with a flat palm. "I don't know. I don't think so. I figured she would have told one of us if she'd seen him."

All four of them shook their heads. Violet wrung her hands together before blurting out something that had clearly been bothering her. "I think she's been hiding something." Every eye snapped in her direction. "She's been leaving the studio a little earlier than usual, and when I asked if she wanted to have dinner with me and Eli last week, she said she had other plans. I think maybe she's seeing someone."

Levi's gut twisted. "She is. Patrick Macon."

"What?" Both of his brothers nearly blew their tops, lightning in their eyes.

"How long has this been going on?" Oliver demanded.

"I don't know." Levi sighed, regretting every chance he hadn't taken to tell his brothers the truth. "But I saw them at Carrie's a couple weeks ago."

"And you're just telling us now?" Eli roared, hair officially on fire.

In the pause between someone else exploding, Meg whispered, "I think I need to sit down."

Everyone scrambled to find her a seat and a place to put up her feet. Oliver squatted by her side, pressing his hand to her stomach. "Are you all right? Is the baby okay?"

She patted her husband's cheek. "You're cute. I just got tired."

Oliver wheezed out a sigh of relief as Meg presided over her court from the only armchair in the small living room.

"Mama Potts is a grown woman who makes her own decisions," she said. "And Levi was under no obligation to tell you anything."

Eli opened his mouth like he was going to interrupt, but Meg shot him her best teacher look. He quickly dipped his head in deference.

"Whether or not Mama Potts is seeing someone doesn't matter. What matters right now is, who's going to tell her about Dean. And what are you going to do about his return."

Levi looked at each of his brothers in turn, their expressions as uncertain as he felt. Violet and Meg both had a close relationship with Mama Potts, but there was no question that the news should come from one of her sons.

"Unless . . ." Eli began. "We could just send him packing and not tell Mama Potts."

"You're kidding, right?" Oliver said.

"What?" Even though it had been almost two years since he'd played in the NHL, Eli's frame was still in great shape from hours on the ice every day, and when he shrugged, he looked like an ox.

"Well, I tried that with you, and it didn't go so well." Oliver crossed his arms. "You came back even though I told you to stay away."

"You know you wanted me to come back." A smug grin crossed Eli's face. "As I recall, you promised to punch me in the face if I ever did return. Still waiting on that. Besides, Levi gave up his house for me to be able to stay."

"And now I'm regretting that decision," Levi said.

The women hooted with laughter, Violet slinging her arm around his waist. "I'm so glad. I'm just so glad that we're a family."

Levi rested an arm across her shoulders. "Okay, but . . ."

"I don't suppose anyone gave Dad a similar talking-to before he left." There was a note of hope in Eli's voice that twisted something in Levi—tearing at the part that never wanted to see his dad again and the part that wished he had never left.

Oliver gulped, pressing his hands against his knees to stand. Meg looked at him, snaking her fingers around his forearm. "I saw him that night. That last night."

Eli's eyes narrowed, but Levi felt like he'd been hit by a two-by-four.

"He was . . . He hit Mama Potts, and I couldn't . . . I stepped in between them and got a black eye for it."

"That was from Dad?" Levi asked at the same time as Eli.

Oliver shrugged. "Better me than her." He took a deep breath and dropped his eyes. "Again."

Everything inside Levi felt like it had imploded. He wanted to scream, to lay into his dad for hitting their mom, but his lungs refused to catch a breath.

"Listen, guys." Oliver stabbed his fingers through his shaggy black hair, regret pinching his mouth into a tight line. Meg's squeeze of his hand made him look up, and he spoke without hesitation. "Maybe I should have told you before, but I came home that afternoon. Eli, you were at hockey practice. Levi, you were probably at the library or something. Dad had just hit Mama Potts, knocked dinner across the kitchen. He was drunk, and I just saw red. I went after him, punched him until he was down. Then I dragged him outside and told him not to come back. In the morning, he was gone."

"I should have been the one to do that," Eli muttered as Violet pressed her face into his shoulder. "I should have been the last one to send him off."

The truth hit like a flash—what Levi knew that none of them did. Oliver hadn't been the last to see their dad that night. Levi had.

And he hadn't told his dad to leave.

The brothers had been able to agree on exactly one thing. Mama Potts needed to be told her husband was back in town before the rumor mill passed that information along. The how, where, and when were still very much undecided. No one wanted to do the deed, yet everyone agreed it had to be done as soon as possible.

Levi was holding too many secrets and couldn't seem to find the words to express any of them. Even Dustin had asked why he was so quiet.

Levi looked up from where he painted a freshly sanded flatbed. The matte black spread over the boards, his brush following the grain as the sharp odor surrounded him.

"So was that your dad yesterday, or what?"

Levi shook his head. He didn't care if the kid took it as a denial or what it was—an indication that he was not going to talk about Dean's arrival.

Dustin had a brush in his hand too, and when he raised it, flecks of black paint splattered across his hair. Levi didn't bother mentioning it. He just kept on painting. But always, he kept an eye on the spot in the doorway where his dad had stood the day before. He watched as though his dad was a specter, like he might appear out of nothing. But there was nothing except the morning light. And the seasick feeling in the pit of his stomach.

"You boys ready to talk lighting?"

Levi's head snapped up as Meg strolled in, then quickly covered her nose and mouth with her hand.

"I'm going to wait outside," she said, her teacher voice only partially muted between her fingers.

Levi shot a pointed glance at Dustin, who shrugged and hollered, "We'll be right out."

Good kid. At least when he wasn't asking about Levi's dad.

They scurried to close paint cans and clean up their brushes, and by the time they made it outside, Meg had found a patch of grass right in the sunshine. She leaned back on both hands, her long legs stretched out before her, as her skin seemed to glow, soaking in the vitamin D. Eyes closed and face lifted, she sighed. "Isn't this a perfect day?"

Dustin quickly agreed, plopping down beside her and crossing his legs beneath him. "Thought you were coming by later. We wouldn't have started painting."

She smiled and patted the top of her stomach, which was stretching her tank top about as far as it could. "This little guy decided to do some acrobatics at three o'clock this morning. And I couldn't get back to sleep, so I've had almost a full day already." Swishing her blond ponytail, she sighed. "I'm going to need him to hurry up and make his arrival."

Levi frowned as he lowered himself to the ground. She still had something like five weeks to go, so he waved a blank notebook in her direction and grabbed the pencil from behind his ear. Maybe if she stayed busy, the last month of pregnancy would go by quicker.

Opening one eye, she took both pieces from him. Using her belly as a table, she began to sketch out a plan. "Here's what I'm thinking. If we build this frame across the front, it can hold the curtain, and we can wire it up. Then we can run lights from the front of the frame to the back wall—I think those metal grids will work to hold the backdrops. Then, of course, we'll need wings, so we'll really only need about eight meters across."

Her pencil moved as fast as her tongue, her rendering to scale enough for him to work out the dimensions. The frame would require more lumber than he had on hand. And they'd have to build it in pieces that could be easily transferred and then locked together, not unlike the stage itself.

When she finally finished, she looked up. Dustin's eyebrows were knitted in pure confusion. But Levi nodded. They could do this.

"So, who wants to take me to get coffee"—she quickly held up a hand—"decaf, and a cinnamon roll?"

Dustin's eyes lit up, his whole posture charged with the excitement that only food could provide to a young man.

"I can't fit behind the wheel of my car, so Oliver dropped me off before going out on the *Pinch*, and I need a pick-me-up." She batted her eyelashes playfully, and Dustin was already on his feet.

"Can we, Levi—Mr. Ross? Please."

Levi narrowed his eyes at the kid. Dustin was a hard worker both on the stage and in Mr. Herman's fields. And if he was completely honest, Levi wouldn't mind a bit of silence. He'd trusted Dustin to drive his truck attached to a trailer several times in the field. He was an overly cautious driver—probably because he didn't want to risk not getting his license in a couple years—and caution was exactly what this excursion called for.

Levi pulled out his keys and held them out to a wide-eyed Dustin. "Carrie's is a kilometer away. Can you handle that?"

Those big green eyes blinked slowly. "Yes, sir."

"You're responsible for the most precious cargo on the island. Got it?"

"Yes, sir!"

Holding out a hand to Meg, Levi helped her to her feet and asked with his eyebrows if this was all right.

"You trust him. So do I." She pressed a kiss to his cheek, then leaned back and looked carefully at him. "How are you feeling?"

The best he could offer her was a shrug. How could he explain the emotions that came with his dad's return when he couldn't even name them himself?

"Come over for dinner anytime you want to talk."

He chuckled. He'd thought the running joke might not be viable much longer. After all, he'd become downright chatty with Kelsey of late. Even stranger, he *liked* talking with her.

But one glimpse of his dad and Levi had suddenly become the fifteen-year-old version of himself again—a boy without anything worth saying.

Meg smiled at his glimmer of humor and squeezed his hand. "I know this isn't easy . . . but you're not alone."

Except he was.

When his brothers had *known* his dad needed to leave, Levi had begged him to stay. When the whole town had seen Dean Ross for the crook and blight that he was, Levi had asked him to stick around.

Not that it mattered to his dad. But it mattered now to Levi.

He waved as Dustin pulled the truck in a loop around the yard and took the lane extra slow, barely rattling the tools in the bed. Then he strolled back into the barn. He could finish the painting before Dustin got back.

As he dropped the notebook where Meg had sketched her plan, he noticed another book on the ground, tucked nearly underneath the wheel he'd replaced on the front trailer. He stooped to pick it up and brushed off the layer of fine dust on the cover. The power sander had a habit of coating everything in the building, and even hiding under the trailer, the script couldn't escape.

Flipping it open, he noticed the pretty handwriting filling the margins. Notes from Kelsey to herself.

Make sure they don't cluster together on the stage.
Ask Willow to look a little more in love.
Help Gunner maintain his tone.
Give Gunner some choreography.
Make sure Gunner gets to his mark.

Levi chuckled to himself as he sank to the floor, his back to the wall. Setting his foot on the ground and resting the script on his knee, he read through every single note. Most of them were for Gunner—but even those were kind and thoughtful. No mention of him flopping around like a fish, which was really the only fitting description of the way Gunner moved in the rehearsal Levi had walked in on days before. She could have pointed it out and made him look foolish in front of the whole cast, but she hadn't. She'd coached and cajoled and turned him into something of an actor. Just like he'd known she could.

Smart. Creative. Kind. Kelsey was always kind.

Which was probably why she hadn't hauled off and smacked him when he'd nearly kissed her.

He scrubbed his hand across his whiskers before thumping it on his knee. Stupid move on his part. She had been on the verge of passing out, and he'd thought it was a romantic moment. Clearly not.

But in true Kelsey fashion, she hadn't brought it up again. She hadn't embarrassed him or pointed out why that was the worst possible time for his overture.

Even if she hadn't been sick from the blood, he had been

covered in hay and sweat and probably smelled as good as a pig barn. It was like he'd never tried to kiss a girl before.

He hadn't, actually. It was hard to get close enough to kiss one when he couldn't talk with them.

He'd thought Kelsey was different. Or at least that *he'd* been different with her. But since his dad's return, he hadn't said a single word to her.

It had only been twenty-four hours, and he missed her.

He pulled the pencil that Meg had given back to him from behind his ear and pressed the lead to a bare spot in the script.

You're the perfect person to lead this show. Victoria is so lucky to have you.

fifteen

Kelsey pulled up to the barn and squeezed the steering wheel of her sedan. Holding her breath, she prayed that Dustin wouldn't be inside. Or maybe that he would be.

Pressing her fists to her eyes, she sighed. This was stupid. Whether Dustin was there or not didn't matter. Levi was most certainly inside, though his truck wasn't parked out front like usual. The barn door stood wide open, a shadow moving within.

She was there to see Levi anyway.

Just about every time she closed her eyes since the other night at his truck, she saw his face and thought about what it would have been like to kiss him—if they hadn't been interrupted. She wondered if he thought about it too.

Probably not. He was far too busy with his work and his family and . . . well, she most likely didn't rank in his many thoughts lately.

Dustin or not, she needed to go inside to talk with Levi about sets. This was about the play, and she wasn't going to delay it just because she wasn't sure what Levi did or didn't think about what definitely didn't happen.

Extricating herself from her car, she walked stiffly toward the door. Even from a few meters away, she could hear someone puttering around inside.

The smell of paint washed over her as she stepped into the dimness, and it took a moment for the black spots to clear before her eyes. When they did, she didn't see Levi until something clanked in the far corner.

Hidden behind scraps of lumber and squatting low behind a trailer, he loaded tools into his arms. As he stood, his gaze darted toward her, then almost returned to his task before he completely computed that she was standing in front of him.

His eyes went wide. Something in her belly swished as she waited for his greeting.

But he said nothing. Only a dip of his chin in that move he so often made. The one he gave to other people.

The one she'd thought they were past.

"Hey." She lifted her hand in a tentative wave.

He moved toward her slowly, then faster. He stopped with several meters still between them, his eyes a little wary.

"I'm sorry about your dad. Is . . . have you talked with him?"

Levi shook his head hard.

All right. So that was a no on having talked with him *and* on wanting to talk with him.

"Do you know what he wants?"

Levi shrugged, leaving her once again facing a stone wall. Just like he'd been all those weeks before.

Her chest tightened, and for some reason her eyes burned. Stupid eyes. Must have been the paint fumes. She had no other reason to feel like sitting down and having a really good cry.

Sucking in a breath through clenched teeth, she tried for a smile. "Can we talk about sets?"

He nodded, dropped his tools near the sawhorses, and picked up a spiral notebook. He pulled a pencil from behind his ear, and she immediately flashed on a memory of him sliding it between his teeth.

It shouldn't have been attractive. There was nothing special about the movement. In fact, it just made him look more bookish, a little scholarly. Smart men kept writing tools handy, and Levi was as likely to wield a hammer as he was a pencil. Of course that combination made her heart flutter.

Stupid heart.

Levi pushed a script into her hands, and she realized it was hers, the one that Gunner had borrowed and probably forgotten here after Dean Ross's interruption. They had all stood around for a long, silent moment after Levi bolted.

Dustin had looked at her like she would know what to do or say, but she only saw red, wanted only to smack the smug look right off Dean's face. That was how he greeted his youngest son after twelve years?

Too soon after Levi's truck disappeared, Dean turned to Gunner. "You in charge here?"

"No. She is."

Dean looked less than pleased to have to address her. It was probably the scowl that she didn't even try to hide.

Or maybe the flames shooting out of her eyes. Because she was definitely trying to set him on fire.

"I heard about the show on the news." Dean hitched a thumb toward Gunner. "From this guy." Hiking up his pants beneath a belly that hung over them just a bit, he said, "I thought I could make myself useful."

"We don't need any help." Not from the likes of him, anyway. A few extra pairs of hands to paint sets would be nice. But Levi was in charge of that, and she wasn't about to invite his dad to pitch in.

"Well, I'll be around. I'd like to help get the theatre reopened."

She glared at him through narrow eyes. "Why does it matter to you?"

Dean shrugged in a motion that was altogether too familiar, too much like his youngest son's favorite move. "I was a member of this community for years. I took my boys to see a dozen shows at the playhouse. Lots of good memories there."

Kelsey didn't ease up on her scowl. The man was a terrible actor.

Gunner jumped in. "Could we interview you for a segment? We're looking for more people to talk about the history of the theatre and what it meant to them years ago."

Dean's barrel chest puffed up, his crooked grin filled with pride. "Well, sir, I'd sure like to do that for you, but there's a few people I need to talk to before I announce that I'm back in town."

Gunner shook his hand as though every part of Dean didn't make his skin crawl. And if that was true, then Gunner was the only one in the barn who hadn't needed a shower to scrub Dean off their skin.

But that was a day ago, and Levi still looked as stunned as he had at the first sound of his dad's voice. If it had been any other friend, Kelsey would have said something. There was no reason why Levi should be different.

"Levi?"

He held her gaze for a long moment, the blue depths there fighting back gray storm clouds.

"Do you want to talk about it? About your dad?"

He dropped his gaze and shook his head.

"He . . . he wants to help with the show."

Levi's eyes snapped back to her, no longer holding back the storm. Lightning flashed through him. He'd pushed up the sleeves of his Henley at some point—probably when he'd undone the three buttons at his collar. The dark hair on his forearms stood on end, and she couldn't look away as energy sizzled off him.

"He said he took you and your brothers to shows at the playhouse."

He snorted with such derision she wasn't sure he hadn't spoken the word. *Liar.*

She'd thought the same thing.

Pressing a hand to his arm, she expected a shock but found only warmth. "What happened with your dad?"

Levi didn't shrug her off, but he didn't answer her question either.

"Levi, is there a reason why your dad doesn't want to be interviewed on television?"

"Gunner." Levi seethed the solitary word.

It wasn't a question. Levi understood what had happened.

The problem was, it wasn't an answer either. And it made her chest ache. In the deepest part of her soul, she knew that Dean Ross was the reason Levi had put up the wall around his heart, brick by brick. That wall encompassed his voice too.

If Grandma Coletta had taught her anything, it was that a person's words were tied to their heart. What the mouth said came from the wellspring of the heart.

What didn't make sense was how Dean Ross could have so fully destroyed young Levi. No one deserved that—especially Levi. He had been quiet and a little bit shy as a boy. But he'd always been kind, helping teachers pick up after a busy science lab or offering to mow a neighbor's lawn.

"Oh, Levi. What can I . . ."

Waving her off, he turned his back to her.

Well, he'd have to do more than that to get her to give up.

Throwing her arms around his waist, she pressed herself against the back of his shirt, which was worn soft and smooth. The top of her head barely reached his shoulder, but when she pressed her cheek to the spot next to his spine, the rhythm of his jagged breathing filled her.

"I'm so sorry."

Maybe she shouldn't have pushed. The Lord knew she had a past she didn't want to share, mistakes she couldn't shake. And no one had asked about them—at least not directly. It was better that way.

But Levi's past couldn't be ignored. Not when it had literally walked back into his life and tried to insert itself into her show.

"I'm so—"

He pressed his hand to hers, holding it right over the pounding of his heart. Everything inside her hummed, her own heart quickening its cadence, bumping into her ribs.

"I. Can't." His voice was filled with splinters, each word aching as it passed his throat.

She'd give anything to take the pain from him. "What can I do?" Her breath left a warm, damp spot on his shirt, but he only squeezed her fingers a little tighter. She fisted her hand into the fabric at his chest and held on. When there was nothing else to do, she could just be there.

Levi wasn't sure how long they stood together, Kelsey's arms a brace that kept him standing as every regret from the night his father left slammed into him. As every worry about what his return would mean to their family tried to take him out at the knees. It rippled through him, catching in the back of his throat, halting his heart.

He wanted to tell Kelsey all about it. About that night. The truth about why Dean wasn't advertising his arrival in town.

Some may have forgotten, but Jeffrey Druthers certainly hadn't. He'd been more than clear during Oliver's first season as captain of the *Pinch* that he hadn't forgotten how much Dean had stolen from him. How Dean had almost sunk his lobster fishing business. And Druthers had plenty of friends who weren't eager to forgive either.

Dean knew that. So why had he returned? He couldn't possibly be trying to get in good with the family. Not after that initial greeting. Not after what he'd done to Eli in the last two years.

Levi heaved another sigh, and Kelsey's hand knotted even harder into his shirt.

For the first time in twenty-four hours, he grinned. He loosened her fingers from the fabric and slowly turned around in her arms until he was facing her so he could wrap his arms around her too.

He could sense the moment she saw his smile, her straight white teeth digging into her lower lip. "Good?" she whispered.

"No."

Her face began to fall.

"But better. Thanks."

"What are you going to do?"

He sighed, resting his ear on top of her sleek ponytail, all strawberry blond and softer than satin. She smelled of coconut. Coconut and sunlight.

He didn't know what he was going to do about his dad, but he knew what else he had to do. No matter how much he hated the prospect, Mama Potts deserved to know. If anyone would know how to handle Dean's return, it was the woman who had dealt with his gambling debts. Twice.

Eli had tried not to get her involved in his mess, and it had nearly cost him Violet. It had nearly cost him *all* of them. Levi had given every penny to his name to keep their family together. He wasn't going to let Dean Ross split them up again.

"I need to go see my mom."

Kelsey nodded, but she didn't drop her embrace. If anything, her grip around him tightened.

He chuckled. "Soon."

"Okay."

She still didn't make a move to let go. So he sank into her, into her sweetness and her strength. Inhaling her. Praying to borrow some of her confidence and maybe a few of her words.

"What are you going to say?"

He shrugged. "The truth, I guess."

Once he'd spoken the words, he had to act on them. Stepping back, he carefully extracted himself from Kelsey's arms, and her comfort fell away just as quickly. He gave her a quick smile but bolted before he was tempted to have her wrap his heart up again.

He walked out of the barn without a backward glance and strolled down the lane toward Mama Potts's Red Clay Shoppe. She was certain to be there at this time of day. She and Violet would probably be side by side at their wheels, chatting and creating beauty from the island's famous red clay.

When he walked around the back of the little blue shop, there were no cars parked in the dirt yard, but the rolling garage door was wide open, sunlight filling the shop and two forms hunched over their wheels, hands wet and red.

Maybe he could just turn around. Mama Potts didn't need to know that he'd come by. He could walk home, open the new Detective Alec Blodger, MD, book, and get lost in a mystery.

If he did that, he'd label himself a coward forevermore.

The alternative was admitting that he couldn't hide from this situation. It wasn't going to disappear even if he locked himself in his room. He'd done that a lot after his dad left. He'd gone to school, spoken to no one, and returned home only to tuck himself into the far corner of his room. As a kid, he'd liked to stretch out on the floor. As a fifteen-year-old still reeling from his father's abandonment, he'd curled into a ball, pulling a blanket over his head and making himself invisible.

But he'd never managed to disappear. And now his mom deserved to know the truth.

Mama Potts looked up, swiping at her graying curls with the back of her wrist. He could see his name on her lips even before he could hear her.

No escape now.

Violet looked up too, her hands stilling over the bowl-shaped piece of clay on the wheel. The light in her eyes flickered, and he knew she knew why he was there. With a small smile of encouragement, she waved at him, spraying clay over her apron.

"Hi, honey," Mama Potts called.

Levi was still a few meters away, but he lifted a shoulder in greeting.

"Hi, honey," Violet mimicked.

He scowled at her but couldn't hold it for long. Out of habit, his gaze dropped to her left hand and her naked ring finger. Then again, if Eli had proposed, she probably wouldn't be wearing a ring at the wheel.

"Not yet." She laughed, knowing right where his eyes had gone. "Trust me. I'll let you know."

Mama Potts chuckled too. "Why don't you just ask your brother when he's planning to ask her?"

Violet pressed her fingers to her lips—almost—leaving just enough room so that she didn't mess up her face. "Whatever do you mean? Is Eli going to ask me a question?"

Levi snorted. Good thing Violet hadn't tried out for the cast. She was a terrible actress.

"So what brings you here today?" Mama Potts asked. "I've barely seen you since you started working on the play. Seems like you're spending all your time with Kelsey."

His ears burned, but he refused to look at Violet, the weight of her knowing gaze too heavy. No need to tell his mom that he'd just come from seeing Kelsey. That he'd held her and let her hold him. That he'd wanted to kiss her, to brush stray hairs behind her ears and count every single one of those freckles on her nose.

Yeah, that was not a conversation to have with his mom. Or Violet. Or either of his brothers. That was one thought to hold close to his chest.

The smile that Kelsey brought to his lips began to fade as his mind swung back to why he had come. "Mom . . . I need to tell you something."

Mama Potts scooted up in her seat. "Well then. This sounds serious." But there was still a soft grin on her pink lips, a contentment that she always seemed to have. He didn't want to be responsible for wiping that away.

Chewing on the corner of his mouth, he closed his eyes and crossed his arms.

"Is there something wrong?" She didn't sound worried, but that didn't do much to relieve the knot in his stomach.

Just blurt it out.

Get the words out. That was all he had to do. They were simple—short.

Just.

Say.

Them.

With a stuttering gasp, he closed his eyes, pressed his fists to his sides, and forced the words out. "Dad's back."

The air rushed out of the building, every sound silenced. No cricket presumed to make its call. No bird risked singing. And Levi didn't dare to breathe.

After a long moment, he forced himself to open his eyes.

Slowly, soundlessly, Mama Potts stood, her fists dripping down her front, eyes wide, nostrils flaring. "Dean is back? How do you know?" Her words were surprisingly flat, as though if she infused them with any emotion, she'd have to give them all of her emotion.

"I saw him."

"Saw him? As in, from a distance?"

Levi shook his head. "He found me at the barn."

Mama Potts's eyes narrowed. "He sought you out." Then, under her breath, "Just like Eli."

"Listen, Mom. I'm sorry. I'm—"

She held up her hand. "That spineless jellyfish. If he had any integrity, if he was half a man ... oh ... " Her words seethed from between her teeth. "That man had better stay away from my boys. If he wants something, well ... he can come find me."

Levi looked at Violet, whose shocked face must have matched his own.

"Mama Potts?" Violet asked, her words like those for a feral dog.

Mama Potts swung her arm wide, almost slugging Violet, who ducked out of the way just in time. "That man has some nerve. *Some nerve.* How dare he waltz back into town?" She slammed her fist against her other palm, and the drying clay there hissed and squished, a sound that probably didn't punctuate her words as she'd hoped. But it didn't seem to deter her.

Her eyes had been unfocused, but suddenly they snapped on Levi. Sharp. Clear. "What did he want from you?"

I don't know. He tried to communicate it with a slow shake of his head.

Mama Potts understood. She always did. "Well then." She marched toward the sink beneath the stairs to Violet's apartment. With urgent, crisp movements, she scrubbed her hands before wiping them on the seat of her jeans. "You don't look very surprised, Violet."

Violet ducked her head, appropriately shamed.

"I suppose that means all of you kids know. And you're just now telling me."

Levi wanted to slink back toward the ever-present clapping of the waves beyond the grass and swim until he fully disappeared. Except there was nowhere that this mess wasn't going to follow him.

"I'm sorry, Mom. I'm sorry that I ever wrote to the TV station, that Gunner started covering the play. That I let him take pictures."

Mama Potts froze in the middle of pacing. "That's how Dean tracked you down?"

Hanging his head, Levi wrapped his arms around himself.

"Oh, honey." She rushed to him, clasped his cheeks between her cool hands, and forced him to meet her gaze. "This is not your fault. This is your dad's doing." She swallowed audibly. "I don't know why he's here, but I'm afraid it's probably not good. So keep your distance if you can. Don't—" Her voice cracked, and she took a stabilizing breath as she patted his shoulder. "Don't believe him. Whatever he says."

sixteen

How was that, boss?"

Kelsey cringed, schooling her face to keep the truth from full display. "Good," she lied to Gunner. Out of the corner of her eye, she saw Fred press his script to his face. Yeah, he'd been on the receiving end of Gunner's "good." Which had included at least three missed cues, relying heavily on his book, and a performance that made her wonder if he thought he was playing Pinocchio. Maybe she should remind him he wasn't a wooden boy.

Gunner's grin rivaled that of his on-air personality. So where was it when he was on their makeshift stage?

"We doing another scene today?" Gunner asked.

Someone groaned behind her but tried to quickly cover it with a cough.

"I think we're done for the day. Levi said the stage is just about ready. So we'll have our next rehearsal at the barn. See you all on Thursday."

A chorus of goodbyes echoed as the small cast picked up their things and trotted toward the side door. The metal clanged as it closed, and stillness surrounded her. It wasn't quite the serenity of a silent stage, but she could hear her own thoughts as she sat on one of the tables, her feet perched on the bench seat.

Maybe it wasn't such a good thing to be able to hear her own thoughts. Because every thought could be distilled down to the exact same question. Had she made a terrible mistake?

There were more than a few mistakes on the table. Thinking she could save the theatre. Thinking she was the right director for this show. Picking this script. Inviting Gunner to play the lead.

She hadn't even asked him to audition first. That was the rookiest of rookie mistakes.

She'd been swept away by his charm. And she knew better. Grandma Coletta had taught her better. Personality offstage did not always translate to personality onstage.

But she couldn't back out now. She wouldn't. There was too much at stake.

So how was she going to fix it?

Rubbing her palms up and down her jean-clad thighs, she prayed for an answer, even a hint that would lead her toward a solution. But if she'd hoped for a hand to write on the wall, she was disappointed.

It was just her and her script, the one she'd marked up from the beginning. With a thumb to the pages, she flipped through it. Notes in different colors, all in her own hand-writing, popped out. Then she passed a blocky note written in pencil, its gray lead blunt. She'd flipped too quickly and swiped the pages back to see the note more clearly.

The words had been written right below her own notes in a scene they hadn't worked on in a week or more. When she read them, they took her breath away.

You're the perfect person to lead this show. Victoria is so lucky to have you.

Her stomach rolled all the way over, her skin tingling in a way that it hadn't before. Maybe ever.

She glanced over her shoulder and searched the corners of the room, as though she wasn't supposed to be reading this. As though this was a message for someone else.

Only it wasn't.

Her pulse fluttered at her neck as she opened the book again, rereading the message. Lips twitching with a smile she couldn't contain, she flipped to another page only to find another message from the same pencil, in the same blocky writing.

Your grandma would have loved seeing you in this role.

She gasped, clutching the open pages to her chest and blinking against a sudden dampness in her eyes. Her lashes stuck together as she swiped a line of black mascara across the back of her knuckle.

She wanted to ask the writer if it was true. To ask how they could be so certain.

But she was alone. Alone with a book that spoke words she hadn't even known she needed to hear. Words that contradicted everything she'd thought about her work.

Who had written them?

Tracing the letters with her finger, she spelled out each word of the second message, hoping the shapes would give her a hint as to who had wanted her to see this. The writing was unfamiliar, its sentiment less so. She could almost hear the words somewhere deep in the recesses of her mind, and she closed her eyes, trying to see the face they belonged with. There was only darkness.

Squinting at the cover, at the title in proper calligraphy, she tried to remember the last time the script had been out of her possession. The last time she'd had to borrow Levi's book.

Gunner.

Her eyes flew open as the idea sifted and swirled like fog over the bay, never quite solid but too present to ignore.

She'd loaned her book to Gunner, and he'd had it for more than a few days. He'd taken it home with him. He'd had plenty of time to . . . what? To read her notes? To understand her insecurities? To read her mind and know exactly what she needed to hear?

It wasn't . . . completely outside the realm of possibility.

His face—his square jaw and television good looks—flickered across her mind. Warm brown eyes flashing as he combed his dark hair off his forehead.

He was a smart man. Kind. Charming. She hadn't pegged him as especially perceptive, but maybe she'd been too focused on critiquing his acting skills to notice the heart beneath. But how had he known about—

She'd mentioned her grandma during their first interview. He'd remembered.

A flutter in her chest caught her off guard, and she pressed her hand beneath her throat even as a smile tugged at the corners of her mouth.

Suddenly a big body slid onto the table beside her, bumping her shoulder and making her drop the script in question. Jerking her head around, she watched unblinking as Levi stooped to retrieve the booklet and handed it to her with a questioning eyebrow.

"Sorry. I was just thinking about Gunner."

His eyebrows pinched together, three lines forming right above his nose.

"Just . . ." She shrugged. She couldn't very well tell Levi that she had gotten a secret, unsigned message from the meteorologist. "I just don't want to fail him—or the show."

He leaned forward and rested his forearms on the blue coveralls stretched across his knees. He'd tied the long sleeves of his uniform around his waist, revealing a fresh white V-neck. Craning his neck, he stared at her, and she could practically hear the question he wasn't asking.

"I can't replace him. I can't." Squeezing her eyes closed, she rubbed her palms up and down over her face, probably leaving a trail of mascara in their wake.

Why not?

He hadn't asked. But he wanted to. It vibrated off him, out of the tense muscles of his shoulders.

"It's too late to add someone else. A replacement wouldn't have time to learn his lines and the direction. Besides, Gunner is our biggest draw, our best hope for a full house."

He snorted and nudged her knee.

"Okay, a full park. But it doesn't matter. Gunner has done more to spread the word about this show than anyone else. And if half the island shows up, they'll all be here to see him perform."

Levi gave a slow nod, his gaze still fixed on a spot on the far wall of the room. When he paused, she knew he had another argument. Whatever it was, it would be a good one.

She sighed. "My grandma wouldn't have."

His gaze flashed in her direction, settling heavy.

"She used to . . . she's the one who taught me . . . Well,

204

pretty much everything I know about theatre and acting I learned from her." She tried to smile, but her lower lip refused to cooperate, so she chomped into it. "She was so talented. And she had a way of making everyone else onstage with her better. She had a magic touch, a presence that drew every eye and stole the show but only made the rest of the cast shine brighter. I have to do what she would do."

Pressing the side of his knee to hers, he silently encouraged her to go on. For the first time in more than a year, she felt safe enough to do it.

"She got me onstage the first time when I was seven. I was terrified. I remember my hands were shaking so hard that I kept dropping the candle. It was *A Christmas Carol*, and I was playing Tiny Tim's sister. I didn't even have a speaking line."

She chuckled at the memory, and Levi's shoulders shook in shared humor.

"Grandma Coletta was the Ghost of Christmas Past, an absolute vision in white. She wasn't on rigging, but I'm telling you, she floated across that stage. The last spirit—the one of Christmas Future—scared me, and I remember my grandma made me meet the actor, so I could shake his hand and put a real face—not a dark cloak—to him."

A strange lump formed in her throat, threatening to strangle her, and she tried to cough it clear. It took several tries, and even when she spoke again, her words were raw.

"That was the first Christmas my parents decided to travel without me."

Levi snapped to attention, his wide eyes flashing first unbelief then compassion.

"It's all right. It's happened a lot since then."

"It's not all right." His words were low and certain.

Tears flooded her eyes, and she had to duck her head and look away to keep him from seeing them as she rubbed away whatever was left of her makeup. "I had Grandma Coletta. She was always . . . well, I think she wanted me to have something to look forward to." Her laugh was garbled by the knife twisting in her chest. "There's nothing like a new show to keep a kid distracted."

"I didn't . . ." Levi reached for her hand, then dropped his back to his lap. She could almost feel his calluses, the gentle pressure that hinted at the power of his embrace. Staring at his fingers balled into a fist, she prayed he'd reach for her again.

He didn't.

"I'm fine. Really. My parents didn't completely ruin me. I promise." She plastered a large if unimpressive smile into place.

It wasn't her parents who had let her down. She'd let down Grandma Coletta.

The next day, Levi ran his finger down the list of sets that Kelsey had given him, a vice twisting his stomach.

Interior Victorian flat.

Exterior garden of a manor house.

Inside room of the manor.

It was only three sets. All completely different. All needing unique touches that would make them come to life. A tea table for one. A picnic setting and trees for another. Chairs that could pass for a Victorian sitting room for the third.

In five weeks.

Apparently his worry was written across his face, as Kelsey rushed to amend the list. "We don't have to do all of them if it's too much."

Ruffling his hair, he sighed. There was no way he was going to let the town down. To let Kelsey down.

"The thing is that we have to bale hay again for Mr. Herman in a couple weeks," Dustin said. "The grass has already been cut, and with all this sun, it'll be dry and ready to go soon."

Dustin had been interpreting for him a lot lately. To Mel Herman. To Meg. To Kelsey. The kid was pretty good at translating, but he shouldn't have to.

Kelsey's shoulders deflated as she eyed her list again. "We can make do with something more simple. Maybe a solid backdrop?"

"You shouldn't have to," Levi gritted out.

Kelsey and Dustin both stared at him, mouths hanging open a little bit.

It wasn't a good sign when he surprised his friends with a spoken word. It meant he had gone silent for too long. He just hadn't had much to say since . . . well, since he'd talked with Mama Potts. Since his dad's return.

Sucking in some courage, he said, "Maybe Eli and Oliver can help."

Kelsey shook her head. "Meg asked Oliver, but he's busy with his fishing tours. And Eli said he's got a lot of work to do to get ready for the high school hockey season."

Levi let out a long sigh.

"We have the stage and the frame for the lights," Kelsey said, clearly trying to make him feel better. "That's the most important part."

Despite the buoyancy of her words, he felt the weight of their condemnation. The most important part wasn't the only necessary part. And he'd promised. In that first meeting in his office with Meg, he'd told Kelsey she could count on him.

All right, he didn't remember saying those words—or many words—exactly. But he wanted her to be able to count on him. He never wanted her to doubt that he would come through.

But he couldn't do both the baling and the set building. There weren't enough hours in a week. He had to sleep at some point. And after the previous round of baling, he knew he'd have to sleep more than a couple hours a night.

Kelsey's big blue eyes looked up at him as though he would have the answer. Her hair was swept back in a color-ful handkerchief, and the loose overalls that hung off her shoulders fit right into the barn.

"I'll figure something out," he grunted.

"Yeah, we'll figure it out," Dustin echoed.

Levi couldn't help but ruffle the kid's shaggy mop—even as Dustin ducked away—and Kelsey offered a tentative smile.

"We don't have rehearsal today," she said. "I can help out."

"You looking for some help?"

All three of them turned toward the door and surveyed the source of the voice.

Dean stood there, hands in his pockets, shoulders re-laxed, and a smug grin across his lips. He'd rolled up the sleeves of his white dress shirt, revealing a handful of faded tattoos across his forearms. His hair was combed and he was mostly clean-shaven, but there was something unsettling in his gaze. Something that made Levi want to move Dustin and Kelsey behind him.

"What are you doing here?" Levi ground out as he stepped forward.

Dean glanced over his shoulder then back with a questioning look. "I thought I made that clear. I'm here to help. I heard about the show, and it seems like you could use a hand. I'm pretty handy with a paintbrush."

Funny. Levi couldn't remember him ever doing projects around the house or deigning to paint anything. He crossed his arms. "Thanks. We're good."

"You didn't sound good. I heard you as I was walking up. Seems like you have a lot of work and not enough hands to do it." Dean's gaze dropped heavily on Dustin. "At least the right kind of hands."

Dustin's chin dipped, his mouth pinching as he reached across his middle to hold his other arm in a lopsided hug.

Fire lit in Levi's belly, a hundred memories sparking to life of his dad saying something similar to him.

"You're never going to be as good a hockey player as your brother. You're not worth the cost to sharpen your blades."

"Why can't you mow the lawn like Oliver? At least he doesn't miss a spot."

"Help your mom in the house. Maybe you won't mess that up too."

Dustin had started off the summer raw, but he was eager to help, eager to please. Just as Levi had been at that age.

Only there was no pleasing his dad. Ever.

His hands shook as he dropped his fists to his sides. His fingernails biting into his palms somehow kept him in the moment, kept him from sliding all the way back into the memories. They kept him present enough to find the words to fight back.

"Enough," Levi growled low in his chest. "Dustin belongs here—which is more than I can say for you."

Dean looked shocked for only a split second before a dismissive laugh erupted. He opened his mouth to speak, but Faye called from the yard.

"Dusty! Your mama just called. She needs you at home."

Levi looked down at Dustin, who didn't move—save for a turn of his head and a questioning raise of his eyebrows. With a low smile, Levi said, "It's okay. You can go on home. Get some rest. This is going to be a busy week."

"Yes, sir, Mr. R—" Dustin paused, shooting a quick glare at the other Mr. Ross in the barn.

Levi clapped him on the shoulder. "Good work today. I'll see you tomorrow."

Dustin nodded and took a step toward the open door. But he wasn't fast enough. Faye had already arrived.

"Dusty, did you—" Her fists went to her hips as she laid eyes on Levi's dad. "Dean Ross. Haven't seen you in a decade. Haven't missed you either."

Kelsey snorted, then clapped a hand over her nose and mouth to muffle her laugh. It didn't help much, but it made Levi smile. He should have figured Faye Herman wouldn't put up with a visit from Dean.

For his part, Dean didn't look fazed. Maybe he was used to that kind of greeting. Or maybe he just didn't care. Either way, he plastered an undeniably fake smile into place and reached out his hand to shake Faye's.

She didn't bite.

"Good to see you again, Mrs. Herman. It has been a while. How's Mel doing?"

"Well, right about now, he's probably calling his good friend Jeffrey Druthers."

The fluorescent lights in the barn gave nearly everything and everyone a yellow tinge. But at the mention of his former boss, Dean turned whiter than a bleached sheet. His smile vanished, and his shoulders began to twitch.

"Have you been to see *him* yet?" Faye asked. She clearly didn't expect an answer, nor did she rush to fill the painful silence that followed.

A hand slipped into Levi's, and he looked down to see Kelsey's slender fingers engulfed in his. There was a strength to her grip that flowed through him, making his breaths come a little easier and his thoughts a little clearer.

Faye crossed her arms over her chest, her gaze drilling into Dean. "Why are you here?"

His grin returned—at least a shadow of it. He tried to put on a breezy air, but he tugged on his ears and flared his nostrils like he wasn't as at ease as he wanted them all to believe. "Just wanted to offer to help."

"Well, you're not welcome to help here," Faye said. "We'll get the help we need from right here at home."

Dean's eyes shifted back to their small cluster, clearly taking in Levi and Kelsey holding hands.

Levi wasn't about to let go. And Kelsey only clung tighter to him.

Faye smacked her lips with distaste. "You'd be wise to get out of town and stay out."

But no one had ever accused Dean Ross of being wise.

seventeen

After Dean left—Faye close on his heels—and Dustin reluctantly loped off toward home to do his mother's bidding, Kelsey looked up into Levi's face. His eyes were focused somewhere past the big white farmhouse, past where Dean had disappeared down the lane with one look over his shoulder.

Her hand was still tucked into his, and he hung on like she was a lifeline. If she was honest with herself, she was hanging on to him just as hard. If he let go in that moment, they'd both go under.

Whatever Dean's motives, Kelsey was certain he could ruin her show. She didn't know how or why. She only knew she didn't trust him.

She and Levi stood in relative silence, only the crickets and herons singing to them as the afternoon sun slowly sank toward the horizon, outshining the barn's interior lights.

"What do you think he wants?" she whispered.

Levi lifted one shoulder. Silent again.

She wanted to personally see Dean to the ferry and be-yond to make sure he never returned to this town, never made Levi clam up again. She didn't know what had caused it, but she knew something for sure—Levi had barely said two words to her since his dad returned. There was no way that was a coincidence.

"What do you want to do?"

He looked down at her then. With a small squeeze of her hand, a tip of his head toward his truck, and a wink, he asked if she wanted to go with him.

That was an easy answer.

He helped her into his truck, finally letting go of her hand before closing the door and walking around to jump behind the wheel. They drove in silence for long minutes, the yellow canola fields flying by on their left as the blue of the bay glittered on their right. She'd thought he might turn to take the main road that ran the interior of the island, but instead, he stuck to the two-lane winding roads of the tourist department's recommended coastal drive.

She'd been in Toronto for only a few years, but the sight of the bright red cliffs topped by fortifying pine trees still stole her breath. Nowhere else in the world compared, and she let herself be lulled by the soft rumble of the truck and the gentle sway of the winding road.

Nearly asleep, she jerked herself alert when Levi's deep voice suddenly filled the cab. "I'm afraid to ask."

"Huh?"

Looking at her for a brief moment, he sighed. "What my dad wants. I'm afraid to ask him."

Her stomach did a full flip, tumbling out of the truck and down the embankment and landing somewhere in the bay. She was pretty sure she could hear the splash as they bounced along the road toward Charlottetown.

Levi had turned back to watch the yellow lines zip by, and she knew she needed to ask a follow-up question. A simple "Why?" seemed too banal. And she couldn't risk shutting him down again.

"I don't think I ever met your dad until earlier this week. What's he like?"

She was pretty sure the new sound in the cab was the grinding of his teeth, and she held her breath, hoping—praying—that he would say something. It didn't have to be much.

But with every passing second, she had to bite harder on her lips to keep from filling the space, to keep more questions from pouring out in a deluge.

Let him start talking.

If he knew it was safe to start, maybe he wouldn't stop. At least not right away.

She'd nearly drawn blood—and the Lord and Levi knew that could only lead to disaster—by the time he looked at her through squinted eyes and took a deep breath.

"I guess I don't know my dad very well. I haven't seen him since I was fifteen." He paused, his face twisting with something that looked like pain. "Well, I mean until he showed back up."

Levi's hand rested on the stick shift between them, trembling with the old truck. And forcing Kelsey to keep her distance. Instead of sliding across the bench seat, she shifted her whole body to face him, tucking her left leg under her so she could watch him. He gave her a quick perusal and a hint of a smile before clearing his throat.

"He walked out on us. Left Mama Potts with three teen-age boys—well, Eli left pretty quick after that. But she still

had to put up with Oliver and me. And my dad's debts."
He paused to swallow, his Adam's apple bobbing slowly.

"Debts?"

He almost smiled then, still facing the road but clearly interested in what she'd said. "You really don't know about him, do you?"

"No." Not when she'd been raised mostly by Grandma Coletta, who refused to be a stop on the gossip train. Not when her parents hadn't been in the area long enough to pick up the latest town news, let alone pass it along to their daughter. "But I assume he wasn't a great dad."

He snorted, the sound filling the cab. "You could say that. You could also say he was a thief and an addict."

"Addict?" Kelsey knew of a few men who had chosen liquor over their families—over their own health too. But drug addicts were rare on the island, at least in Victoria.

"Gambling. Drinking too."

"Oh."

Levi's knuckles turned white as he gripped the steering wheel, a muscle in his jaw jumping in quick succession as a bead of sweat trickled down his temple. After a deep breath, he released his words on a sigh. "My brothers and I didn't know how bad it was—or even that he was gambling. Maybe Mama Potts did, but she never talked about it. She was working so hard to keep our family together—afloat. I didn't notice." He stabbed his fingers through his hair. "Maybe I didn't want to."

The regret in his words clawed inside her chest. "But you were a kid."

Levi looked directly at her, his eyes flashing his argument. "I was fifteen."

"But how did your dad . . . I mean, why did he leave?"

All of him tightened, his body seeming to curl in on himself. "He was supposed to work Jeffrey Druthers's boat that season, but I guess Mama Potts confronted him about the gambling, and . . . well, he left."

He was leaving out part of the story. She could read it all over his face, and she wanted to push. But the timbre of his voice was so sweet that she couldn't risk silencing him again.

"He took pretty much everything that Druthers had— his truck and anything that wasn't nailed down on the boat. And he took off."

"To pay off his gambling debts?"

"Nope. He left those for Mama Potts to deal with."

Her voice turned soft. "I can't even imagine."

Levi shrugged. "We were homeless for a few months that year."

Her throat went cotton dry. "Homeless?"

"You didn't hear the rumors? I figured everyone knew."

She could only shake her head, could only try to shake free a memory of young Levi always in the shadows, never the spotlight. He'd been quiet before—even more so their tenth year and beyond. Maybe he hadn't had new clothes or a fresh haircut at the start of the year.

But homeless?

"What did you do?"

"You know how the ladies at the church are." He smiled fondly. "We lived in one of their basements. They brought us bags of groceries, fresh-baked bread, frozen meals. They helped my mom find work—a second job."

"All four of you in one basement."

Levi's shoulders twitched. "Eli was gone already. Just Oliver and Mama Potts and me."

Kelsey suddenly felt carsick. Of course. Way to remind him of his brother's ten-year absence. Eli had left for the NHL. Everyone knew that. That wasn't so much local gossip as it was local legend. Eli had put their tiny village on the map. Then he'd come back. She still didn't know what had prompted his return. But if the way he wrapped his arm around Violet's shoulders during Sunday morning services was any indication, he had no plans to leave. Maybe ever again.

Yet he had left. Right after their dad.

"Was that . . . I mean, that must have been terrible."

He raised an eyebrow.

Oh, no. They were not going back into silent mode.

Sitting up a little straighter, she squared her shoulders, her back resting against the rattling door as the beauty of the southern coast gave way to the city.

"What was it like when your brother left right after your dad?"

His smile said he knew exactly what she was up to, and for a minute she thought he might refuse to say another word. Finally he shrugged. "I imagine it was like being paralyzed and then losing your leg. We were numb, nearly destroyed. We hadn't even begun to figure out a way forward when Eli left. But it wasn't that he left that hurt so much—it was the silence."

She shot him a sardonic grin that she hoped told him he was one to broach that topic.

"He didn't reach out to us for eleven years. We didn't have his phone number, email, or mailing address."

Choking on her gasp, she coughed and sputtered, her face burning as she tried to catch her breath. "You can't be . . ." But he *was* serious. Completely.

Sadness. Pain. Regret. They all haunted his features as he turned onto the road that ran along the shoreline.

"I don't know what to say."

He shrugged, the corner of his mouth tilting up. "That's my shtick."

Pushing his shoulder playfully, she said, "I'm serious. I had no idea. You all seem so close now."

"We're getting there."

"But why did Eli come back?"

"You suggesting I'm not worth coming back for?"

"Oh, be quiet. You know I am."

He laughed loud and full at her joke, and it wrapped around her like a hug, making her want to wrap him up in an embrace of her own. "Eli was kicked out of the NHL."

She'd been grieving Grandma Coletta—she hadn't been buried beside her. Of course she'd heard about Eli. Everyone had heard about him being ousted from professional hockey. The why was a mystery—one that the church ladies still speculated about more than a year after his return. One that Levi probably knew the answer to.

"Why'd he get kicked out?"

Levi stared hard at her for a long moment. "Between you and me?"

She nodded, eagerly leaning forward.

"He had a run-in with my dad."

"But no one has seen your dad in years—well, until this week."

"Except Eli."

Her jaw dropped as the pieces tried to fit together in her mind. One dirtbag father. One hockey-playing son. One gambling addiction. "Did your dad dump his debts on Eli and take off?"

Levi said nothing. But his eyes confirmed everything.

Kelsey saw red. She barely knew Eli except as Meg's brother-in-law. They were shake-hands-at-church acquainted. Sure, she'd gone to a few of his local games as a kid, sat with her friends, and cheered for the home team. And more than once she'd wondered how the Ross brothers could look so similar—all with dark hair and blue eyes and dimples to swoon for—yet be so different.

So even though she didn't really know Eli, she was absolutely convinced in that second that he had been slighted. And she was ready to fight someone for him. She was ready to fight Dean Ross. Or at least see him kicked off the island for good.

There had to be a list of personae non gratae on Prince Edward Island. If there wasn't, she'd be delighted to start one.

"Is that why you stopped talking to me when your dad showed up?"

"I've been talking the whole drive."

She pushed his shoulder. "No, I mean before. Earlier this week. You suddenly went silent again. You let Dustin interpret for you."

"You noticed that, eh?"

She pursed her lips to the side. "I missed hearing your voice. I missed hearing what you had to say."

He snorted as he pulled his truck into the paved parking

lot before a few small storefronts. "That's a question for another time."

———

Levi swallowed, his throat oddly sore as he slammed the door of his truck and walked around the front. He hadn't felt much like speaking lately. But the words had been building up, bubbling up for too long.

As he offered Kelsey his hand to help her hop down, he was reminded again that she was safe. When everything else in his life felt off its axis, she was stable. She'd put the pieces of Eli's story together, but he was certain she wouldn't say a word.

She was safe for secrets. He just wasn't certain if she was safe for his shame.

"What is this place?" she asked, looking at the empty windows. There were no signs or banners on any of the three doors that opened from the sidewalk. The gray-shingled roof dipped in front, eaves so low that he'd almost have to duck to enter.

"I know a guy."

"That does not answer my question," she said, her steps slowing in the parking lot as he ambled toward the middle door.

Holding out a hand to her, he winked a *Trust me?*

She playfully rolled her eyes and shook her head but reached for his hand and let him tug her to the entrance. He pushed it open, and a bell right above them clanged an ominous greeting as they stepped into the near darkness.

Kelsey wrapped her other hand around his forearm and tugged. "Are you sure we're supposed to be here?"

Before he could assure her, a voice from the farthest corner of the room called out, "That you, Levi? Let me get the light."

Overhead bulbs popped like lightning, and he blinked hard against their force. Kelsey pressed a hand over her eyes but quickly dropped it to look around the room.

Enormous rolls of fabric lined the walls, stacked three and four patterns deep. There wasn't much organization. At least there hadn't been when Levi was here before, and it didn't look like much had changed. Florals leaned against checks, which were mingled with solids. Bright and soft colors lived side by side, unruled by any system.

"What is this place?" Kelsey whispered.

"Welcome to my gallery." Will stepped from behind a couple of spools and gave a little flourish of a bow. His hair was graying at the temples, and his face had a few more weather lines than when he and Levi had first met. "Will Sluiter. At your service, miss." He held out his hand, and when Kelsey slipped her fingers into it, he raised them to his lips.

Levi clapped a hand over his gut, which twisted in protest. He couldn't tell if it was from Will's kiss to her fingers or her titter of response.

"Kelsey Ahern." She ducked her head in a way that would have fit right into her play.

"It's a pleasure to meet you. How do you know this miscreant?"

Kelsey eyed him suspiciously. "Levi? A miscreant?"

Will winked at her. "Oh, he's still on his best behavior with you, I see."

Kelsey looked between them, clearly trying to figure out

if Will was to be trusted or if Levi had been putting on an act for the last twenty years.

When it was clear that Will wasn't going to give up his game, Levi sighed. "Will's a friend of Patrick's. He does upholstery."

"Oh, you did the new seats in the theatre a few years ago."

"Guilty as charged," Will said with another wink.

"They're lov—" The flame in her eyes flickered. "They were lovely."

Will's smile dimmed too. "I heard about the storm. I'm sorry to hear the old building took a hard hit."

When Kelsey didn't immediately dive in about the show, Levi leaned into her arm, shooting her a pointed look.

"We're putting on a benefit show," she said. "To restore the theatre. To keep it open."

"Seems I heard about that." Will scratched his chin. "Our local weatherman is sure excited about it."

"Oh, yes! Gunner. He's very . . . He's a big part of the show. And he's been very good at getting the word out."

If Will picked up on her hesitation, he didn't say anything. He pointed toward the far wall. "I heard you might be looking for some backdrop fabric."

"Yes, but how did . . ." She turned, and her smile lit Levi up.

He shrugged. So he'd made a call. Actually, he'd sent a text. Either way, it was the easiest thing he'd done since they started this journey. And Will had been more than happy to order cloth backdrops from his supplier.

Leading the way over to three large white rolls, Will said, "These should fit the measurements you gave me, Levi. The fabric is good for painting, and it shouldn't crack if you roll them up for storage."

Kelsey's mouth opened and closed several times, but no sound came out.

Levi couldn't help but point out the facts. "You're not usually the one at a loss for words."

When she blinked up at him, a teardrop was stuck to the end of her lashes, and there was a distinct quiver in her lower lip.

Over some fabric.

Will was looking at them like this was definitely a first in his gallery, and Levi had a sudden urge to get them out of there.

"Will this work?" he asked quietly.

Rubbing an edge between her thumb and forefinger, she nodded quickly. "It looks perfect."

"Great. We'll take it." Levi reached for the wallet in his back pocket. "How much do I owe you, Will?"

"No, I'll pay for it," Kelsey interrupted.

Of the two of them, Levi was the only one with a guaranteed job for the next school year, so he shook his head. "I've got it."

Will held up his hand, which stopped Kelsey from attempting to argue. "How about we call it my donation to the theatre? Maybe you put my logo on the website as a sponsor or something?"

When Kelsey finally agreed, the men loaded the bolts into the back of his truck. Levi didn't miss the way Kelsey hugged Will around the neck, that stupid knot in his stomach making an ugly show again.

He wasn't jealous. He wasn't. Not of Will anyway. Will was probably old enough to be her father. Maybe not quite. But some women liked a mature guy. Will was definitely charming, his quirky dramatics fitting for a lover of the arts.

But it wasn't like Kelsey was interested in the man. She'd just met him. And if she gave Gunner even a milliliter of encouragement, the meteorologist would probably fall at her feet. Any man in his right mind would.

No, he was jealous that the other men had the courage to flirt with her, to put themselves out there. Meanwhile, Levi was too cowardly to kiss her—to do more than dream about running his fingers through her hair. So he had no right to be jealous. No right to wish she was wrapping him up in her arms the way she was holding Will.

He could almost feel the coolness of her hands against the back of his neck, the smooth curve of her body against his. He could almost smell the coconut of her shampoo and the scent of coffee still clinging to her skin from that morning. He could almost hear the steady rhythm of her heart against his, setting a new tempo for them both—a little quicker, a little harder.

Because it was just the two of them. Together.

"We should get going," Levi blurted out while Kelsey was still in Will's embrace.

"Thank you again," Kelsey said as she waved to Will. "We'll save you a seat right up front!"

Levi slammed his door harder than necessary, which drew Kelsey's gaze as her door shut with a soft click.

"You okay?"

He nodded. But she had to know it was a lie. He could feel his ears burning and his throat closing, and all he wanted was to hold her. Instead, he'd rushed them out of

Will's gallery and toward home, effectively cutting their time together short.

"Are you ... hungry?" she asked.

As if on cue, his stomach growled. "Yeah." That was a good excuse for his strange behavior. He hoped.

"I know a great place for fish and chips."

Thirty minutes later, they were settled onto the tailgate of his truck, overlooking the harbor, each with a red and white checkered basket of fried fish. The grease pooled on the paper liner and seeped through the cardboard, and Levi licked his fingers before popping a salty fry into his mouth.

A few small fishing boats were out in the bay, but they were dwarfed by the enormous cruise ship that had docked the night before and would spend less than forty-eight hours in the harbor. Birds squawked, gliding and diving on the wind off the water.

It ruffled Kelsey's hair, and she set her dinner down long enough to tie her hair back in a low ponytail and shoot him a smile. "Better?"

Taking a bite of his crunchy, flaky fish, he nodded.

With a fork, she tore off a bite of her own golden fillet. Then with a wicked grin, she said, "So, this is another time. I believe you promised to answer my question."

eighteen

Levi choked on his fish, coughing as it caught at the back of his throat.

"You okay there?" Kelsey leaned over to him and thumped him on the back.

"You gotta give a guy"—he coughed again—"some warning before you start saying things like that." And preferably give him a chance to change the subject.

"It couldn't be helped," she said around another bite, a cheeky twinkle in her eye. "You promised."

Taking a deep breath, he wiped away the moisture in his eyes. "I don't recall putting a time frame on that promise."

"Well, now's as good a time as any, don't you think?" She looked around the parking lot, and his gaze followed hers to the empty spots surrounding theirs in the large lot across from the visitors' center. It had a good view of the bay and the strips of land on either side that reached toward each other, almost locking out the ocean beyond. Two tiny points of light flickered on the far side of the water, lighthouses on each side of the harbor entrance visible even in the early evening sun.

"You're one to be talking," he said. "You want to tell me why some backdrop fabric was making you emotional?"

She paused, a bite of fish almost to her mouth. "You noticed that?"

"Hard not to."

"It's just . . . this play. I don't know. Some days I'm not sure it's going to happen at all. Some days I regret even *thinking* I could pull it off."

"What do you mean? You're doing great."

"I'm doing . . . I'm surviving. I mean, we're getting there, but some of the actors still don't know their lines." She didn't have to say Gunner's name. "And we're only now getting the fabric for the backdrop—which, by the way, thank you for knowing a guy. Will is great! But it feels like something I should have been on top of weeks ago. And we need to start practicing on the stage, putting down our spikes for the set pieces. But we don't even have set pieces yet."

"I'm working on it."

She shook her head, finally setting her food next to her and swinging her feet from the pale blue, rusty tailgate. "You shouldn't have to. It shouldn't be all on you. You have a real job. Two of them, for that matter." Her voice rose in pitch and volume, her breaths coming out long and hard.

When his dad showed up, she'd put her hand in his, and he'd felt better. Not perfect, but somehow more calm, more secure.

Sliding his hand across the tailgate, he slipped his fingers across her palm. Her skin was smooth like cream, and her fingers spread to interlock with his. She held on tight but never quite looked at him. Still, he noticed her shoulders rising and falling a little slower, the clench of her jaw beginning to relax.

"I wish you didn't have to work two jobs on top of this one. I wish I could pay you more—pay you now instead of after the show."

He grunted. "There's lots of things to wish were different, but hard work isn't one of them."

Finally she turned toward him, her eyebrows tugged close together. "You like working for Mr. Herman, don't you?"

He hadn't really thought about working for Mr. Herman so directly before, and he paused to consider it, letting the low clap of the waves against the rocky shore fill the space. Kelsey didn't rush to end the silence. Her hand gently squeezed his, telling him she would wait.

"Truth is, I need to work for Mr. Herman a lot more than he needs me to work for him."

"For the green house?"

He nodded, the cottage flashing before his eyes. The dream sat somewhere in his gut, stirring a hope that he couldn't quite put a voice to.

"He's a good man, isn't he?" she asked.

"One of the best men I know." Aside from Patrick.

Except his regard for Patrick had become jumbled and sticky since that evening at Carrie's. Since he'd seen Patrick and Mama Potts together. Add in his dad's return, and Levi didn't know what to think or how to work through it all. Truthfully, he didn't want to. Not right now. Not when he was sitting beside the prettiest girl around.

The island hadn't been as bright when she'd left for those few years.

"What brought you back to Victoria?"

She blinked rapidly. "Where'd that come from?"

One of the hazards of staying silent was forgetting that others couldn't hear his thoughts. Levi tucked his chin into his chest with a rueful shake of his head. "Never mind."

"No, I mean, it's fine. I just wasn't expecting it," she said. "Things in Toronto were fine. But it wasn't like I was getting lead roles in big productions or anything."

"Their loss."

She laughed, bumping her shoulder into his arm. The sweet sensation zipped across his chest, settling right over his heart.

"I'll be sure to send the directors a message to let them know they missed out." She didn't sound like she was even trying to keep the giggle out of her voice. "I was still working a few hours a week at a coffee shop to make ends meet." She cocked her head, her lips pursing to the side. "But like you said, there's nothing wrong with working hard. It made me feel strong, empowered, I guess. Like I could make a life for myself doing what I loved, on my own. Even my grandma didn't make theatre her career, though she could have."

He squeezed her hand. "Your grandma was really talented."

Surprise flashed through her eyes. "You saw her perform?"

He nodded. He'd seen them perform together several times.

"I assumed when your dad said he'd taken you to the theatre as a kid that he was lying."

"He was."

"So you . . . came to see the shows."

"I came to see you."

Oh no. He had not meant for that to escape his brain. But there it was flapping in the wind, making her cheeks turn pink and her eyes shine like sapphires.

Nibbling on her bottom lip, she asked, "Me?"

His face was on fire, the flames licking from the collar of his shirt all the way to his hairline. Everything inside him wanted to jump down and make a run for the cab of the truck. But since he'd driven her into Charlottetown, he couldn't exactly leave her behind. Maybe he could give her the keys and let her drive back. He'd ride in the bed with the fabric. Or hitchhike.

Yes, that was a much better idea. Hitchhike and pray that someone heading over the Confederation Bridge would take pity on him. Eli had done it. Disappeared. It couldn't be that hard.

Except Levi could still remember Mama Potts's face when she'd realized that Eli wasn't coming back. There was no way he would be the reason she made a face like that again. He might not be the star of the family or the most talented or the most driven. But he knew Mama Potts loved him. She would miss him. And Meg and Violet would. His troublemaking brothers too. So a total escape was out of the question.

Which left one option. Telling Kelsey enough of the truth to explain why he'd just blurted out that he'd gone to see her shows at the playhouse. Back when he'd barely spoken a word to her in high school.

She was still looking at him, curiosity in the angle of her head and the line of her pink lips.

Gulping a deep breath, he forced what he hoped was a smile. "I had . . . um . . . I read *The Adventures of Tom Sawyer*, and then I saw that the playhouse was putting it on."

"The summer before we started high school. I remember. I played Becky Thatcher, and my grandma played Aunt Polly. You saw that?"

He nodded, pinching his lips together. "I snuck in."

A laugh bubbled out of her, sweet and joyful. "You did not."

"I did. I didn't have any money for a ticket, and there was no way I was going to ask my dad for it. He'd just say it was a waste. And my brothers would have mocked me for wanting to go. But I was curious to see how the show compared to the book. Was it like I'd imagined?" He shrugged. "So I snuck in with a big family and hid in the shadows until the curtain went up."

"And you kept coming back."

Dear Lord, let that be enough for her.

He didn't know if he could confess that he'd fallen in love with her the moment she stepped onto the stage, her two long braids hanging over her shoulders—hair and freckles more like Anne Shirley than Becky Thatcher. It didn't matter. She was Kelsey Ahern, and he'd spent the next school year wondering if it was possible to count every single one of those freckles peppering her nose and cheeks and arms and legs.

When he didn't say anything, she squeezed his hand. "Thank you. That's maybe the nicest compliment I've ever received."

Then she needed to hang out with different people. Because every day he found new things to admire about her, not the least of which was that she wanted to hear about his dad. Well, that wasn't quite right. She didn't care about Dean. She cared about how his actions had affected his sons.

Levi swallowed thickly. Even if she didn't care about him specifically, she cared about others. About her students, her community, and most of all her grandma.

And if he wasn't careful, all of that was going to come popping out of his mouth too.

Letting go of her hand, he hopped to the ground. When he turned to help her down, she was already standing at his side.

"We should get back," she said. "We have a lot of work to do."

It was a truth universally acknowledged that the less time there was, the faster it passed. Kelsey felt that acutely every day leading up to the show. They needed every minute to pull this off.

And she needed to stop thinking about how much she liked spending those minutes with Levi. Especially since this was his week to bale hay.

She chewed on her thumbnail as she eyed the stage that he and Dustin had pushed together in the barn. They'd even set up the frame so Meg could try out the lights.

"Is it going to work?" Kelsey asked.

At her side, Meg winced, pressing a hand to her back. "It looks good. We just need to start the generator to see for sure." With a dry laugh, she said, "But I can't bend over far enough to do tha-at." She wheezed on her last word.

Kelsey grabbed her by the elbow. "Are you all right?"

"I would be if this little guy didn't insist on taking up all of the room that my lungs would like to use." Meg grimaced as she stretched backward, her belly round. "And we'll get along a lot better when he quits giving me acid reflux."

Kelsey wasn't sure if she believed her friend, who had been groaning and twitching since she arrived at the barn three hours before. Meg had claimed that there was nothing comfortable about being thirty-seven weeks pregnant. But she'd checked the lights and breakers and wiring until she was satisfied.

"Can you start the generator?" Meg asked.

Kelsey had hoped that Levi would be here for this part. But he and Dustin and the rest of the boys were out in the field, bringing in the summer's second yield.

"I can try." But yanking on the cord of the old gas-powered generator felt like she was trying to dislocate her shoulder. She tugged and pulled, and the engine sputtered and chugged, teasing them as it got close but never quite caught. "Almost. Let me try again."

Meg grunted behind her.

Kelsey pulled again, her elbow slamming back, snapping her hand holding the cord to her shoulder. The generator coughed but sputtered out again.

Come on. Come on.

She mouthed a silent prayer for divine intervention. Just as she jerked the cord one more time, Meg let out a terrifying scream, and the motor choked to life. Its rumble drowned out everything else, and Kelsey hopped from foot to foot.

"Did you see that?"

Meg didn't respond, and Kelsey spun to look at her friend, whose eyes were wide, her hands cupped beneath her belly. Slowly Meg looked toward the ground and took a step back. There was a puddle where she had stood.

"I think my water broke."

Kelsey read her lips rather than heard the words, but still they clanged inside of her, turning her stomach, making her head spin.

Don't look at it. Don't look at it.

The chant echoed in her head as she tried to focus on Meg. Who was having her baby. Kelsey wasn't going to let that happen in this dirty old barn, no matter how much work Levi and Dustin had done to clean it up.

Flipping off the generator with one hand, she pulled out her phone with the other. "I'm calling Oliver."

Meg's breaths came in big gulps, her eyes pinching hard at what had to be a contraction.

Kelsey was a couple rings into the call when Meg finally let out a soft sigh. "He's on the *Pinch* today."

"What's he doing on the water?" Kelsey scolded the phone in her hand. "Doesn't he know there's a baby on the way?"

"We're supposed to have another three weeks." Meg breathed hard through tight lips. "He thought he'd take the boat for a test run for the season before there was a chance of the baby coming."

"Well, he thought wrong." Kelsey punched the red button on her phone to silence the incessant ringing. They didn't have time. Meg was about to have a baby. And Mr. and Mrs. Herman weren't at home. She'd thought it sweet when Mr. Herman said he was taking his bride out for a lobster dinner and some antiquing in New Glasgow.

That had been a couple of hours ago. Her opinion on the date was decidedly different now that she was alone with a woman in labor. A woman who needed to get to the hospital.

And Kelsey could not go into one. Especially not now. Not after what had happened. After what she'd done. Or rather, not done.

"I'm fi-ine," Meg said between clenched teeth. "If you can just drop me off at the ho-ospital."

Sweat broke out across Kelsey's forehead, and she swiped at it with the back of her hand. "I walked today. But I'll find you a ride. I promise."

Spinning in a quick circle, she looked for a chair or something for Meg to lean on, but there was nothing except the sawhorses stacked against the tin wall. And they were covered in dust and wood shavings. She didn't know where to go or what was needed. She was not good in an emergency.

Levi. Levi was good in an emergency.

Pressing her phone's voice activation, she said, "Call Levi." And then it was ringing.

Please let them be on a break.

But it rang again. Still nothing.

Meg groaned and bent over, then grunted something toward her shoes. It was probably meant to reassure her, but that was supposed to be Kelsey's job. Only, she could barely get enough air into her lungs to keep herself upright. She couldn't possibly keep Meg on her feet too.

Levi rarely answered his phone. Maybe she should text

him. But he might not get it right away. And if the way
Meg's face had gone paler than usual was any indication,
they needed help right away.

Lord, let Levi answer.

Out of the silence, his voice rang out. "Kelsey? You okay?"

"Levi!" She nearly shouted for joy, and even Meg gave a
little sigh of relief. "We're at the barn, and Meg's in labor.
Her water broke, and I don't have a car, and we can't get
ahold of Oliver, and—"

"I'll be right there. Stay put." Before he ended the call,
she heard him shouting at the boys to unhitch the trailer
and ordering someone to call Mama Potts.

She should have thought to call her. Or Violet. "Do you
want me to call your parents?"

"They're seeing a specialist out of town."

Meg's mom had a rare illness, and they had to take ap-
pointments whenever the doctors had availability. But
right about now, Kelsey wanted to have a word with the
scheduler at that office.

Suddenly Meg let out a piercing scream. Kelsey lunged
for her, holding her up by the elbow as the pool at her feet
began to turn pink.

"I don't know what's"—Meg panted a few breaths before continuing—"happening. I don't think this is right."

Kelsey blinked hard against her narrowing line of vision, spots dancing before her eyes as she tried to inhale
deeply. "It's okay. It's gonna be okay. Levi is on his way."
She didn't know if she said it to remind Meg or herself.
But for a second her knees didn't feel quite so weak, and
her stomach didn't threaten to overthrow her breakfast.
Still, her hands trembled and her arms had no strength left.

"I feel . . . I feel a little bit . . ." Meg sagged against her, and Kelsey let out a cry of defeat. She couldn't fight any longer. But maybe, when she fell, she could cushion Meg.

Protecting the first of the next generation of Rosses was the last thought on her mind before two gangly arms wrapped around her and Meg was whisked away. Words reached her as though through water. "I've got you."

nineteen

Kelsey didn't know how long she sat alone in the cab of Levi's truck in the parking lot of the Prince County Hospital in Summerside. She recalled Levi swooping in to pick Meg up and carrying her away. She somehow knew that Dustin had put her arm around his shoulders and trotted her toward the truck. Levi had pushed her in beside Meg and then wedged his long limbs behind the wheel.

They had driven mostly in silence—save Meg's groans—Kelsey holding her friend and trying to pray for her and the baby as the fog ebbed and flowed across her mind.

Levi was there. Sturdy and strong. Everything she knew him to be.

Then they arrived at the hospital. "Are you coming in?" he asked as he scooped Meg up.

For once Kelsey had nothing to say. No words could sneak past the lump in her throat. No thoughts could form amid the chaos in her mind.

So she sat there while Levi did his hero thing, and she tried not to remember the last time she'd sat in this very parking lot, hating herself for not going in but knowing she couldn't do it. Telling herself a story that everything would be all right.

It hadn't been. But that had been more than a year ago.

Now she waited and watched the entrance and whispered gibberish prayers, thankful that the Lord knew the deepest longings of her heart. Wrapping her arms around her legs, resting her chin on her bent knees, she chewed on her lip.

At some point during her wait, Mama Potts, Violet, and Eli had charged across the parking lot. Shortly after, Oliver had followed, his black hair wild and untamed like he'd been running his fingers through it nonstop.

She looked at her phone, hoping Levi might have texted an update, though she didn't deserve one. Information was for the ones brave enough to go inside, not the ones who got weak-kneed at the sight of a little blood.

Pressing her forehead to her knees, she closed her eyes and let out a long breath. She wasn't part of the family, and she shouldn't interrupt their time, whatever the result of this hospital visit.

She should—

The driver-side door swung open, and she turned her head so fast that her neck cracked. Levi stood there, one hand on the door and the other on the frame, his eyes wild and his grin brimming with joy.

"Is she . . . ?"

"Mom and baby are doing great!"

"Baby?" Tears rushed to her eyes, and she frantically wiped at them. "She had the baby?"

Levi hopped into the cab, closed the door behind him, and scooted along the seat past the steering wheel until his warmth began to chase away the shivers that had been racing up and down her spine.

He paused for a moment, his arm twitching. Then with a sudden, decisive movement, he reached around her and hauled her to his side. He was even warmer than she'd thought, and she sank into him, letting her softness mold into his strength.

"Walter Whitaker Ross. Tipped the scales at more than three kilos and so long he needed a bigger crib." Pride filled every syllable as he pulled out his phone and showed her a few pictures of a wrinkly little guy swaddled in a striped blanket. A blue hat was pulled low over his brows, and his eyes were pinched closed, his skin an uneven red. But it was the little fist tucked into his cheek that made her waterworks start again.

"And Meg?" she whispered into his shoulder.

"Probably glad that labor didn't last very long."

She snorted into him, crinkling her nose. "I'm serious."

"Me too. The doctor said it went faster than he's ever seen before. Oliver barely made it in time."

She leaned into his side a little harder.

"Her blood pressure was getting high. He said it was a good thing we got her here when we did. It could have been bad. But it wasn't yet."

"I felt so helpless." The words were out before she'd had a chance to unpack them, but Levi somehow knew exactly what she needed to hear to loosen the band around her lungs.

"You were great. You did everything right."

"But I couldn't reach Oliver. I didn't even think about calling your mom. Or maybe I should have called 911. Or—"

"Hey," he whispered, his arm tightening around her shoulders. "It's all right. Everyone's all right. Except maybe you."

She should have made a run for it while he was still inside. Maybe it wasn't too late. She made a half-hearted attempt to scoot across the bench, but he refused to let go.

"Talk to me. Tell me what's going on. Why wouldn't you leave the truck today?"

The depth of his voice settled in her stomach, warm and comforting, hot tea on a cool night. But she still didn't want to answer him. At the moment she was the only person who knew what she'd done—the only living person anyway.

And there it was, that twist of her insides that made her want to curl up and disappear. She held on to her knees even harder, trying to be smaller. But the weight of his gaze never diminished, the weight of his question never growing lighter.

"I can't go into hospitals."

His squeeze asked her to go on.

"I'm afraid—well, you've seen me. I nearly pass out every time I see blood."

"Nearly?" he asked with a teasing chuckle.

She pushed against his chest and rolled her eyes at him. "That was one time. And I had just been clobbered by a tree, as I recall. I was probably dehydrated too."

"Sure. From all the rain pouring in through the window."

She jerked her head up and looked at his lips, which twitched with the hint of a smile he was clearly fighting.

"Okay, so it wasn't my finest hour." She didn't exactly regret it either. Without that night, she doubted she'd be sitting in the cab of his truck now, breathing in the smell of hay and wood and Levi, enjoying his steady shoulder beneath her cheek. "I can't help it. I've always been this way, ever since I was a kid. Even when I scraped my knee, I'd get too weak to walk home, and I'd just sit by my bike on the sidewalk until my grandma came to rescue me." Smacking her hand over her face, she shook her head. "I can't believe I just admitted that."

"I think it's cute. I can picture little Kelsey with pigtails and a skinned knee."

He wouldn't think that of the rest of the story. Not if he really knew.

"I was afraid to go into the hospital, afraid that I'd see some blood. Afraid I'd pass out and embarrass myself."

"When? Today?"

She shook her head, her vision going blurry as she stared at his chin and the few days' worth of whiskers there. It wasn't terribly long, but the dark stubble stood out against his skin, and she tried to focus on just one hair, on a single point. Maybe then she wouldn't dwell on what she was about to reveal.

The truth sat low and painful in her stomach. Truth she hadn't ever spoken aloud. Truth she hadn't fully admitted to herself.

But denying it didn't make it any less true. Just like hiding from it didn't make it disappear.

Letting a stuttering breath out between tight lips, she curled into Levi's side and pressed her face against his shirt. He seemed to know that something heavy was coming because he reached his other arm around and held her with both.

"My grandma—Coletta—she died in there."

A sound from deep in his chest conveyed all things sympathy and comfort, and he somehow managed to hold her even closer.

Maybe she could stop there. Maybe that was enough of a reason for why she couldn't go into that hospital.

But that didn't explain why she'd moved back to Victoria. Why she'd thrown every minute into a benefit show that might not be enough to save her job. But it hadn't really been about her job. She could find work in another city. She could move again. There was nothing tying her to Victoria—except maybe the arms holding her at that moment.

There was no one else she wanted to tell. She could trust him. And she did.

"It was a little over a year ago. She called me." A sudden sob jerked her shoulders, but Levi's hold stayed firm. "She said she had a cough. It was getting worse, so I told her to go to the hospital. I told her to get checked out to make sure it wasn't serious. She called the next day. They'd admitted her. So I asked if she needed me." Kelsey pressed her hand over her mouth. "I think it was the first time she'd ever asked anything of me. I could tell she was scared. She asked me to come."

The truck cab felt like it was spinning, taking them back in time. Taking them to that horrible moment.

"I said I would. But I couldn't get past this parking lo-ot." Another sob surprised her as she pressed her fists to her eyes. "The doctors didn't seem that concerned about my grandma, and if I'd gone in there, I would have just been one more patient for them to take care of. She needed someone strong to hold her hand, and I couldn't do it." She gulped in a breath of air. "She didn't come out."

"Oh, Kels." His whisper ruffled her hair, wrapping another embrace around her.

"I . . . I wasn't there when she needed me."

"Your grandma loved you so much."

Head shaking, she refused to let him deny her pain. "But I let her down."

He nodded slowly, thoughtfully, biting his lips closed. She could almost see the battle inside him to let it go or to speak. Finally he sighed. "Maybe you did. But that doesn't change her love for you."

"But *I* didn't love her enough—"

"To what? To walk into a place filled with blood, knowing that you would probably pass out when the doctors told you she'd be released soon?"

"I was too scared, and I didn't do enough."

"But that still doesn't change—"

"She gave up everything to raise me when my parents took off. And I have to *do* something. I have to make it up to her."

Levi scooted back far enough to really look into her face, and the sudden loss of contact made her whole body shiver, so she curled in on herself again.

"That's why you came back to Victoria."

She nodded.

"Now that's why you're doing whatever it takes to save the theatre."

She nodded again.

"Kelsey, those are good things—things that honor your grandma and her legacy. But you never had to earn her love. You couldn't if you tried."

"How can you be so sure?"

Something bright and full of life flashed in his eyes for

a split second before his eyebrows pulled together. He looked deep in thought. Lifting his hand in fits and starts, he reached for her face. His thumb dragged over her cheek, brushing at the damp streaks there. "I guess because that's not how love works."

His touch was like fire, his words fanning the flame.

"Love isn't love because it's earned. Love is love because it's a choice. Your grandma chose to love you—no matter what."

She could barely hear his words as his finger looped toward her ear, making the hair on the back of her neck stand up in a most delightful way. Then it trailed along her jaw, finally stopping at the corner of her mouth. His nearly palpable gaze seemed to be locked there too, and she could do nothing but lick her suddenly dry lips.

Levi matched her movement, followed by a quick bob of his Adam's apple. Her stomach dipped in a similar motion, everything inside her mixed up yet hopeful.

She couldn't look away from the line of his mouth, from the unspoken promise. This was the moment. The one he'd hinted at and almost promised weeks ago in this very truck.

Right this minute, she knew with utter certainty that this was exactly where she was supposed to be. Where she wanted to be.

Levi's other hand slipped down her arm to her elbow, giving her a slight tug, an invitation to lean closer. He was all around her and deep in her heart. She could feel him egging on her pulse, encouraging the speed of her breathing and the thunder in her ears.

And she must look a mess. She didn't have a pretty cry

in her repertoire, at least offstage. Her eyes were almost certainly bloodshot and puffy, the tip of her nose assuredly stained red.

Yet he looked at her as though she was the definition of beauty.

For a moment, she thought maybe she could be. Maybe his opinion was the only one that mattered.

Closing her eyes, she leaned forward, took a little breath, and waited.

Suddenly the truck door flew open, and a familiar but unwelcome voice interrupted them. "What are you kids doing? Don't you know there's a baby to see inside?"

Her eyes flew open to find Levi turned all the way around, his hands gripping the steering wheel like he was going to tear it off the dashboard. And, of course, Eli—smug smile firmly in place—standing outside.

Just perfect.

Her cheeks flamed, and she pressed herself as far against the back of the seat as she could. But there was no disappearing beneath Eli's spotlight of a gaze.

"I was just going to take Kelsey home," Levi said. "She's had a long day."

Eli winked at her, then punched his brother in the shoulder. "They're going to keep Meg and little Walter overnight, and Mama Potts is going to stay with Oliver and them. Try to clean up a little bit before you stop by to see the little guy again."

Levi grunted as he shoved the key into the ignition and the motor rumbled to life.

"Where do you want me to stop?" Willow asked.

Kelsey pressed her fingers to her chin, pretending she was considering the question, when in fact her mind was far from where her four leads stood on the stage in the barn. It was still on the new message in her script.

She didn't know how long it had been there. A day, maybe two. Possibly more. It was the same blocky handwriting from her script before. The same kind tone.

This island needs more people like you. You're doing a good thing.

Now she couldn't help but watch Gunner's face, analyzing every feature and movement for some sign that he'd written the new message or wanted to tell her something more than that he thought he was ready to go off his book. He had been doing fairly well without it for the last twenty minutes.

Gunner and everyone else on the stage, however, were staring at her, probably seconds away from toe tapping and clock watching. Because she still hadn't answered Willow's question.

"Sorry, Willow. What was that?"

"When I come in here, where do you want me to stop? How close do you want me to get to Fredrick?"

"Oh, um . . . take a couple steps to your left, and turn toward the audience just a little bit . . . Perfect. Right there. And we'll have a tree in the background. It should line up right behind you."

Willow nodded and held herself perfectly still.

"Let's pick up from Fredrick's last line."

They easily fell back into character, even Gunner making his best effort yet. Maybe not quite believable, but he was certainly better. She couldn't take full credit, so when they reached the end of the scene, she said, "Well done, all. Have you been practicing without me?"

Most of the cast brushed off the compliment, knowing it was part of their role. Gunner nearly preened under the praise, and she gave him an extra grin.

The sound of an engine in the yard outside made her tingle all over. Levi was back from finishing up in the fields.

"Let's take a ten-minute break. Get some water, and then we'll go through the next garden scene."

The cast mumbled their thanks, all reaching for their bottles lined up against the side of the stage. Fredrick plopped down on the black surface, stretching his tennis shoes out in front of him as he leaned back on his elbows.

Kelsey turned to the open door just as two figures strolled in. They were little more than silhouettes, the bright sun behind them blocking everything else. She didn't need to see their faces to know that neither of them was Levi, and she took an involuntary step backward, bumping into the edge of the stage. Out of the corner of her eye, she saw Fredrick push himself up and Willow and Jade—the actress playing Gwendolen—both take a step closer together.

After a few more paces into the barn, the two visitors reached the glow of the fluorescent lights, which revealed faces she wasn't expecting or prepared to see.

With a quick step forward, Kelsey held out her hand to the taller of the men. "Mr. Trumball. Good to see you."

That wasn't even close to the truth. There could be no good reason why Mitch Trumball would stroll into the barn on a Monday afternoon. He should have other business. Like figuring out some way to help keep the playhouse foundation—the one he was the executive director of—running. He'd shown exactly zero interest in the show for the previous seven weeks, and whatever had caused him to cross town to show up at her rehearsal was probably not a good thing. Especially given the man standing beside him.

Dean Ross.

He was like a thistle in a flower garden. He kept popping up where he wasn't wanted.

"What brings you here today?" she asked, giving Dean a firm shake of her head when he reached out to grasp her hand.

"This is Dean Ross," Mitch said.

"We've met." If Grandma Coletta hadn't trained her with impeccable manners, Kelsey might have spit at his feet. She'd never had the urge to do that before, but it suddenly made perfect sense.

"Excellent." From the tone of his voice, Mitch was either blind or choosing to be oblivious. The tension between her and Dean was thicker than homemade stew, but it seemed Mitch couldn't care less.

She squeezed her hands into fists, pressing them to her hips and forcing her shoulders back. She'd been comfortable and confident before in her torn jeans and flannel shirt knotted at the waist. But Mitch's wrinkle-free button-up and tie screamed that she was out of place. Even in her own sanctuary.

What she wouldn't do to have Levi by her side. He'd had to take another day to finish the baling because he'd come to rescue Meg—and her. Because he'd dropped everything—including the job he needed—to take care of her.

She forced herself to face Mitch down. "What do you need?"

He crossed his lanky arms and narrowed his gaze, finally acknowledging her tone, even in silence. Tilting his head toward Dean, he said, "Dean had a pretty good idea that since the playhouse loaned all of our audio equipment to you for this show, we should make sure it's secure."

"You're worried that something is going to get stolen here?" Kelsey didn't know anyone who locked the door to their house, let alone secured their valuables.

"It is tourist season," Dean said. "You never know who might come through town."

His voice made her skin crawl and her stomach threaten to heave. Maybe it was his facade—so practiced, a complete performance. Actors recognized actors, and Dean was nothing if not rehearsed.

"I believe Levi and Mrs. Herman have asked you to leave this property," she said. "You're not welcome here."

Mitch straightened the knot of his tie and shot her a quick shake of his head. "Actually, he is. I hired him as special security for the show."

Several cast members behind her gasped as she spit out, "You what?"

"Security. For. The. Show."

Mitch spoke like he thought she was stupid, but he should have looked in a mirror. "Do you even know who this guy is? Do you know that he stole from his last employer here in town?"

"We talked about those rumors."

Rumors? Rumors! She wanted to stamp her foot and tell Mitch he'd fallen for an act, some con that was going to ruin her show. But it was her word against Dean's. Mitch hadn't been in town twelve years ago, and everything Kelsey knew was secondhand at best. But somehow Dean—his black hair slicked back, his jaw freshly shaved and his clothes clean if not new—had swindled his way into Mitch's confidences.

"But this is my show."

"And you're using my audio and lighting equipment. Equipment I want to be able to sell when the theatre closes."

He wanted to sell the equipment? He was that certain the playhouse was going to close?

Her stomach crashed to the floor, the whole building tumbling end over end. This was what it probably felt like in a hospital. Up was down. Right was wrong.

"But we're going to make enough to save . . ."

Mitch gave her a condescending pat on the shoulder and a superior smile that seemed to say "That's cute."

He didn't think the show was going to save the theatre, and he was already planning for its demise. She turned to look at her cast, and their faces were a mirror of her heart. Stunned silence.

Arguing now wasn't an option. Not in front of the cast. Not alone.

Mitch turned to Dean. "Go ahead and start your security sweep. Make sure all of my stuff is still here."

He could get started, but this wasn't over yet.

twenty

Levi dragged himself out of his truck just as the sun dipped beneath the horizon, shooting streaks of red and orange across the western sky as indigo rolled out its blanket of stars in the east. The lights were off in the Hermans' house, but he'd report to Mel the next day that they'd finished the last field, and all of the hay was in the new barn. Dustin had taken off a few hours earlier when his mom called, the rest of the crew shortly after that. Which had left Levi bone-tired and starving for more than the ham and cheese sandwich he'd inhaled at lunch.

At least his round of baling was done. Now he could rest. Or at least focus on only the school and the show. And soon—in a few weeks—there would be only the school. Well, the school and the green house. He prayed all of his work would be enough.

And he prayed the green house would fill the void he knew would come when he no longer had an excuse to see Kelsey every day.

The woman on his mind most days must have left the

lights on in the barn because the outline of the metal door glowed in the growing darkness. He shuffled over to it and slid the door open only far enough to step inside. Once there, he grinned. Kelsey hadn't forgotten to turn off the light. She'd forgotten to go home.

"Kelsey?"

She looked up from where she was perched on the front of the stage, her legs dangling, feet swinging back and forth. She'd been bent over a thick book that looked like one he'd left by the sawhorses a few days before.

"Levi." She said his name on a sigh, like he was going to rescue her.

"Whatcha reading?" he asked as he strolled in her general direction. Keenly aware of his hard day of labor and the dirt and grime still covering him, he kept his distance.

"Oh, just a book I found lying around. It's pretty good. This Dr. Alec Blodger seems to know his stuff. And so far he hasn't dealt with any blood."

Levi only had the energy for a low chuckle in response.

"How was your day?" she asked.

"Long. Yours?"

"Not great." She chewed on her lip, staring at the book now closed in her hands. Flipping it over and over, she didn't seem to see it.

"You want to tell me about it?"

She nodded. "Come sit next to me."

"I really don't think you want— You got up there all on your own."

"Well, you did add a ladder to the end."

He chuckled again but only moved to lean his arms against the chest-high stage.

"Come on." She patted the seat next to her. "I promise, I don't care how dirty you— You didn't cut yourself today, did you?"

He did a little spin to show her he was free of blood-stains, and when he had her nod of approval, he hopped up beside her. Not too close, but close enough that her sweet perfume fought its way through the dust and sweat and made the moment practically pleasant.

"So, what happened today?" he asked.

"Mitch Trumball—the playhouse's executive director— stopped by."

She swallowed thickly, and he wished he had a drink of water to share with her. And maybe one for himself. Wherever this was going, it wouldn't be good. Trumball hadn't deigned to visit even once. In fact, he didn't seem to care that much that Kelsey was even trying to save the playhouse.

"He wasn't alone. He . . . um, he hired your dad to be security for the show."

Levi let out a snort of pure disbelief. "So we really are hiring foxes to guard the henhouse now?"

"I'm sorry. I tried to talk him out of it. I told him not to trust your dad, but . . ."

Levi sighed as he leaned back and stretched out. The stage was hard, but he could probably fall asleep if he closed his eyes. Instead, he stared up into the rafters above the light frame and tried to wrap his head around this new discovery. "What exactly is he trying to secure?"

Kelsey leaned back too, speaking toward the ceiling. "The audio and lighting equipment. Mitch said he wants to sell them."

His chin jerked, and he turned to face her. "He doesn't think you're going to succeed, does he?"

"I guess not." Her voice was smaller than he'd ever heard it before. He'd heard her project from a stage, reach the back of a room with her perfect pitch, spread her emotion to every corner. But it was clear now what she feared most.

"You're going to make your grandma proud. You already are."

"But how? If this show flops, if the donations don't come in . . ." She paused, three little lines appearing between her eyebrows. "He knows how many donations have already come in from the website. And how many tickets have been sold."

Right. Dustin's friend had set up the site to connect directly to the nonprofit's accounts. Mitch had to know how they were doing.

"Gunner is still featuring the show every week on the news, and he told me a few weeks ago that his social media posts were getting his best engagement ever." Levi shrugged. "Whatever that means. But it sounds good. It has to be good."

"Unless Mitch wants to be done with the theatre. Unless *he* doesn't want to stick around."

By nature Levi wasn't a violent guy. When his brothers had been wrestling and fighting as kids, he'd found a quiet place to read. And when his teammates on the junior hockey team had been sent to the penalty box for brawling, he'd remained squarely out of the way.

But at this moment, as the truth of what Kelsey said sank in, he wanted to punch Mitch in the mouth. If that man was somehow hindering Kelsey from doing what she needed to, Levi would gladly take a few bruised knuckles.

"And where is he getting the money to hire your dad?" Her voice rose in volume with each word, her fire stoked with each realization. "I mean, given what I know about your dad, he's probably not working for free."

"Definitely not. Mama Potts knows he's here, but I don't think he's come out of hiding long enough to see her. Or anyone else I know either. I don't know what he's up to, but I can promise you, it's not good. He's not here to help anyone but himself."

"I'm just sorry he's going to be around more. I'm sorry I couldn't keep him away from this show."

Levi sighed. He was too. But his dad had always been able to talk anyone into anything, to make others believe he was the facade he put on. It was how he'd kept Mama Potts from leaving him. It was how he'd gotten Druthers to trust him with everything. It was how he'd talked Eli into taking on half a million dollars in debt.

It was how he'd gotten Levi to beg him to stay.

Dean Ross had a silver tongue, a way with words. He gave big promises that sounded sweet but never quite ripened.

Draping one arm over his eyes, Levi tried to drive away that memory. But it was there, right in front of his eyes and on the tip of his tongue. He licked away the salty sweat and dirt that still caked his lips, but it wasn't enough to pull him into the present. To pull him back from that terrible night.

"I was fifteen when my dad left, and I only just found out that Oliver told him to go, that my dad had hit him and Mama Potts that night."

Cool, gentle fingers tiptoed down his forearm before finding his hand and snuggling inside it. He squeezed her fingers because he didn't know how else to ask her not to take them away. He'd started something he didn't know how to finish, but it was something he needed to get out.

"I remember my brother's black eye. Man, I remember that. I also remember him never giving a straight answer about where it came from. Eli grilled him. I think he was ready to throw down with anyone messing with one of us. Classic big brother. But Oliver never admitted it. Not until about three weeks ago. I think maybe I had an inkling about what happened, but if I'd admitted it to myself, I'd have had to admit what an idiot I was."

"But you're not. You're the smartest man I know. Who would think to create all of this out of four old trailers?"

He squeezed her hand again, and this time she squeezed back, a gentle nudge to keep going, a reminder that she was still listening.

"I heard my dad packing up the night he left. He didn't try to be quiet. Closet doors slammed and boxes crashed together. I honestly don't know what he was packing because the house somehow felt just the same the next morning. But that night, I chased him out the door. Mama Potts and my brothers weren't around. Probably in their rooms. And Dad was stomping around like a bull. I could smell the liquor on him even from a few meters away. It permeated the air. Even worse, I realized I'd been ignoring that smell for years. More like running from it. Every time my dad came home angry and loud, I'd run for my room. My favorite reading spot was in the corner behind the door, under a blanket. He never seemed to see me there."

When Levi paused, the silence was filled only with Kelsey's scrabbling and scraping as she scooted toward him. Pressing into his side, she rested her head on his shoulder and her free hand right over his heart, which thundered at her closeness. If she could hear it, his racing pulse didn't scare her away. She was steady. Warm. Reassuring. A silent encouragement to keep going, that she wanted to hear what he had to say.

And if that was indeed true, oh, the irony of the story he was about to tell.

"I caught up to him in the front yard. There was a bright moon that night, enough for me to see the twist of his lips, the fury in the slant of his eyes. When I called out to him, he spun on me, throwing a box at my head. I dodged it, but it grazed off my shoulder. I should have turned around and gone back inside. I should have . . ." He rolled toward her just enough to see her face, the tight lines surrounding her mouth, and the glassy sheen to her eyes. "You ever realize a dozen years later what a fool you were?"

"Tell me what it's like."

"Everyone else in that house knew what my father was—they knew he was only going to destroy our family. But not me. I was the idiot out there asking him to stay. Begging him not to leave."

Levi could still feel the burning in his throat as he screamed that his dad had to stay. They needed him.

"What did he say?" she whispered.

Those words had been tattooed across his mind every day since. "He sneered at me and said, 'You think you're so smart? You think you have something worth saying? You think anyone wants to hear a word that comes out of your mouth? You're never going to say anything that anyone wants to hear.' Then he turned and stalked away. He didn't even bother picking up the box he'd thrown at me."

Kelsey gasped, and he held her hand even tighter. He tried to tell her it was all right, that he'd worked through it. That it didn't bother him anymore. But that couldn't be true. Not when his dad still had the power to silence him, to make him second-guess every word he wanted to speak.

"How could your own father say that?" She removed her hand from his chest and pressed her palm to his cheek, her soft thumb brushing away the dirt beneath his eye.

Levi shrugged. "I don't know. Sometimes I think he might have been right."

"Well, you stop thinking that right now, Levi Ross." Her words carried all the power of her teacher voice, which was pretty similar to her director voice, and he smiled at it. "Yes, you're smart. You're also kind and thoughtful. Do you even know what an impact you've had on Dustin?"

"He's a good kid."

"Yes, he is." She pressed harder on his cheek until he met her gaze. "But he needed someone to care about him. His dad is a thousand kilometers away and barely shows an interest in him. His mom is so overwhelmed that she barely has time to keep track of him. And then you came along and showed him respect and encouraged him to respect his mom. You trusted him with your tools and taught him how to not settle for good enough. You showed him what it means to be a friend, to care for your family."

"But that's just—"

"Look at me." Her perfect pink lips pressed together as one corner began to turn up. "There's no 'just' about it. What you did for him—what you've done for me—it's no small thing."

"Yeah, well, you're paying me."

She gave a delicate but firm snort. "You and I both know that you could be making a lot more money elsewhere. If I was paying you what you're worth, you could have bought the green house weeks ago." She plucked a piece of straw out of his hair. "And you wouldn't have to work a third job this summer."

"I would have helped you for free."

Her eyes flashed with joy, her grin growing. Pride swelled deep in his chest. It was a sweet victory to make her smile like that, and he wanted to do it every single day.

"Your dad only knows how to speak wickedness," she said. "His words are meant to wound. But you, Levi, you speak life. Always."

He ducked his head, already feeling the telltale signs of his pink cheeks. "Not always."

"Yes, always. Even when you asked him to stay, you did it to keep your family together, to keep it alive. There's no shame in that." She shook her head hard. "None."

But just because he wanted to believe her words didn't make them true.

Nearly a week later, Kelsey closed her hymnal as the church piano's last notes drifted away, ending the service. Behind her, Mable Jean Huxley hummed the refrain of "The Old Rugged Cross" one more time as the church filled with chatter and the squeals of children being swung into the air by proud fathers.

Her gaze immediately jumped to the Ross family pew. Oliver and Meg were conspicuously absent, certainly at home with little Walter. But Eli and Violet, Mama Potts, and Levi shuffled into the aisle.

As though he could feel her gaze on him, Levi looked up, his smile gentle and his eyes knowing. She'd already talked to him that morning, risking the hem of her maxi dress to stop by the old barn, where Levi had been checking the new industrial padlock on the sliding door.

"Anything?" she had asked as she climbed out of her car.

Levi shook his head. "Nope. Locked up tight. Everything is still inside."

Whatever Dean was up to, he hadn't stolen any of the equipment. At least not yet. Then again, maybe he didn't want to risk stealing from the location he was supposed to be protecting. He strolled the perimeter of the building during their rehearsals and tried to start conversations. Kelsey put those to a stop as soon as they started. After all, they were two weeks from the show. They didn't have time to goof off.

But Kelsey did have time to do a little investigating now, so after smiling at Levi, she turned to the couple behind her. "Mr. and Mrs. Huxley," she said, hoping her bright expression looked pleased instead of practiced. "Lovely to see you this morning."

"We sit in these seats every Sunday morning. Where else were you going to see us?" Mr. Huxley grumbled as he shuffled toward the exit.

Mable Jean pushed him along with a roll of her eyes.

"Ignore him this morning. Gerald stubbed his toe getting out of bed and couldn't even be appeased with a cherry Danish."

Kelsey bit back a laugh but didn't quite keep the humor from her voice. "I'm terribly sorry to hear that. But I am glad to see you. Do you have a moment to talk, Mrs. Huxley? Alone."

Her eyebrows rose. "It's Mable Jean, my dear. And certainly. Whatever can be so important that we should discuss it alone? Could it have something to do with the show?"

With a Cheshire smile, Kelsey ushered her into the flow between the rows of wooden pews and through the front doors. The summer sky wasn't as friendly as usual, puffy gray clouds slipping past the sun, creating patches of shade and hinting at afternoon showers. At least that was what Gunner had said on the news that morning.

The lush green lawn was filled with laughter as young children barely able to walk tottered around the base of a big tree in the middle of the yard while older kids played tag in the far corner. A few adults from the congregation streamed toward the gravel parking lot, but most had formed pockets of interest. The men discussed the coming fishing season, Sunday school teachers chattered about the new curriculum, and the town biddies gossiped about the latest news. Kelsey couldn't risk getting pulled into any of those groups, so she led the way toward a smaller tree near the corner of the church building.

Mable Jean apparently couldn't wait to hear more. "What on earth is going on, young lady? Has something happened with your show?"

Kelsey turned with what she hoped was a reassuring smile, but Mable Jean frowned.

"What happened? The show must go on. Gunner Raines has been talking about it on air for ages, and even my friends from out of town are planning their trip to come see it. You can't be canceling." Her high-pitched voice rang out across the lawn.

"No, no. We're not canceling." Kelsey looked around to make sure that they hadn't caught the attention of anyone else. When it seemed no one cared what they were talking about, she spoke in a low voice. "I just wondered if you know Mitch Trumball."

Mable Jean frowned, her gaze sweeping across the lawn. "Mitch Trumball? The playhouse's executive director? But I thought you and the youngest Ross boy—"

"It's nothing like that," she interrupted. Let Mable Jean think of that what she wanted. Kelsey had absolutely no interest in Mitch. And Levi *still* hadn't said anything official. He hadn't admitted to feeling anything more than friendship. But, oh, the feelings he stirred up in her, that made her stomach mad with butterflies, her skin feel both chilled and warmed in the same moment.

While she generally accepted any excuse to think about Levi, that was not why she'd pulled Mable Jean into this conversation. Clearing her throat, Kelsey said, "I'm worried. I . . . um . . . Mitch hired Dean Ross to oversee security for the show."

Mable Jean tsked loudly. "Well, that was a ridiculous idea. He certainly didn't ask anyone in town before doing so. Maybe that's what the board gets for hiring someone from away."

"I know Mitch hasn't been here for very long, but I wondered if you know him . . . or know what he's planning to do."

Crossing her arms, Mable Jean looked down her long nose, pursing her lips until her red lipstick seeped into the surrounding wrinkles. "Go on."

Kelsey quickly waved her hands in front of her. "I don't know anything. I mean, not much anyway. It was just . . . I got a bad feeling when Mitch brought Dean by to look at the sound and lighting equipment that we borrowed from the playhouse. He said something about selling them after the theatre closes, and—"

Mable Jean snapped to attention. Whatever had been casual before turned to granite. "He told you he was going to sell them?"

With a quick nod, Kelsey said, "He seemed sure that the theatre was closing, and, well, I wondered if there weren't enough donations coming in. Do you know anyone on the playhouse board?"

Mable Jean was generally prim and poised and every bit an island lady. But Kelsey had clearly said something that riled her up, because the older woman looked ready to gnaw on hay and spit it out on Mitch Trumball.

"Not enough donations?" She snorted. "I know for a fact that the other theatres on the island got together and donated more than five thousand dollars. And a real estate developer in Charlottetown pledged another ten. The money is there, and if *Mr.* Trumball is claiming otherwise, then someone needs to look into that."

"Would you?" Kelsey grabbed her hand, only then realizing that her own were trembling, hope and fear and gratitude all rolled together.

Mable Jean patted her hand and nodded. "Oh, I will. It will be my pleasure. And if I find out that anything unscrupulous is afoot, you can believe I'll do more than alert the media. I'll call the Royal Canadian Mounted Police myself."

"Thank you," Kelsey whispered. She locked her hands before her and dropped her gaze. She shouldn't ask. She'd promised herself she'd wait until after the show, but the closer it drew, the more she remembered that she didn't have a job after it. "Um . . . I was wondering too, has the school board . . ."

Mable Jean frowned. "I'm sorry, honey. Not yet." Then she added under her breath, "If that Henry Deering would quit dragging his feet . . ." Pushing a smile into place, she said, "Now, you just focus on that show. Make sure it's everything the town deserves."

twenty-one

The week of the show arrived bright and clear—the perfect forecast for a Friday night in the park, and Kelsey took a deep breath for the first time in weeks. The backdrops were almost complete with some extra help from Dustin, the generator had proven it could power the show, and all of her actors were off script.

Even Gunner was ready. He wasn't going to win a Tony—or ever be nominated—but at least he wasn't going to embarrass himself. Or her. He'd put in a lot of hard work, and she planned to give him his due when the cast arrived for their first dress rehearsal.

She strolled into the barn to find Levi squatting on the stage, his head bent over one of the brackets that connected the four parts. The back of his Henley stretched across his shoulders, his jeans pulling snug at his thighs, and she couldn't help but stare.

Just for a minute. Or two.

Everything about him reminded her of his steadiness, of the pillar of kindness that inspired everything else about him. Maybe it was true that good guys finished last. Levi certainly wasn't flashy or bright. He didn't have the easy charm of Gunner or the confidence of Eli. But his integrity, his genuine care for her—and the Hermans and Dustin and his family—spoke volumes. If she ever saw him holding his nephew, she knew she'd be a hundred percent smitten.

And if she found his long legs, sapphire eyes, and dimples gorgeous too, well . . . it couldn't be helped.

If only he'd get around to finally kissing her.

Her throat went dry, and when she tried to swallow, it turned into a cough instead. A loud one.

Off to her right, Dustin was high on a ladder, adding bushy leaves to the tree on a backdrop. "Hey, Miss Ahern. Is it time for rehearsal already?"

"Pretty soon."

Levi stood and stretched his back, shooting her a silent smile that spoke a thousand words—loudest of all, *I'm glad you're here.*

She winked at him as she strolled toward Dustin. "That's coming along really nicely." The garden scene was inviting and beautiful, at its center an expansive green lawn that disappeared into low, rolling hills. A garden of pink and purple flowers filled the lower right corner, the tree occupied the far edge, and above it all a bright blue sky housed whispering clouds. An unusual forecast in England, but perfect for the play's second act.

"I told him he should take art classes next year," Levi said.

"Hush, you!" She picked up a rag and playfully threw it at him. "He'll be in the drama class next year. Won't you, Dustin?"

Dustin's ears turned red, but his chest puffed out. "If you think I'd be any good at it."

"Good at it? You could lead the whole crew!"

Levi flashed her another grin, this one filled with gratitude. But she'd only spoken the truth. Dustin had picked up more from Levi in the past ten weeks than she could teach him in four years of productions. And with that, the confidence to lead.

"Come see me when school starts?" she asked.

He nodded fiercely as car doors outside the barn slammed closed. Jade and Willow strolled in arm in arm, character shoes hung over the shoulders of their costumes. The colorful floor-length skirts were on loan from the playhouse, and the white blouses had been purchased from Walmart. Puffed sleeves had come back in style just in time.

Dustin's blush spread from his ears, across his cheeks, and down his neck, and Kelsey caught Levi's eye, nodding almost imperceptibly at Willow. She was probably only four years older than Dustin and prettier than the peonies in his painting, her blond hair pulled back into a loose bun, her green eyes dancing.

Levi jumped down from the stage and strolled up to her. Lowering his head, he spoke right into her ear. "Don't even think about it."

"What?" she mouthed back at him, feigning innocence. But she was pretty sure he could read her mind at this point.

Then again, she'd take just about any excuse to have him this close, close enough to feel the warmth of his body and smell the oak on his clothes. Her insides did a little jig, and she let herself lean back against him. Just for a second.

"Give him some time to grow up."

Perhaps that was what Levi had needed too. Time to grow up. Time to finally take notice of her.

Only, she was pretty sure he *had* noticed her. There was no pretending that his heart didn't hammer at an unhealthy pace when she pressed her hand to his chest. And the man was twenty-seven, for heaven's sake. Not that she was impatient or anything.

He did have three jobs. She didn't even have one—not a paying one anyway.

Unfortunately—or perhaps fortunately—she didn't have the opportunity to dwell on her situation with Levi. Jade and Willow sauntered up, asking some questions about their parasol props and how to open them without letting them steal the scene. She chatted with them as the rest of the cast arrived in twos and threes. But when she looked up to begin, they were one actor short. One very conspicuous actor short.

"Maybe there's a traffic jam on the way from Charlottetown?" Fredrick suggested.

Jade sniffed. "More likely there's a tractor blocking the road."

Fredrick chuckled. "Same thing."

"Or maybe there was a weather emergency," Dustin said from his seat at the top of the ladder.

Everyone chuckled at that, but ten minutes later Gunner still hadn't arrived. Kelsey asked Willow to begin their scene before excusing herself to call Gunner. Stepping out into the sunshine, she lifted her face to the sky, inhaling the wind that carried the scent of salt and life.

By the third ring, her stomach began to twist, threatening a full flip. "Come on, Gunner. Where are you?"

The phone rang again.

Come on.

When the fifth ring began, she held her breath and sent a silent prayer heavenward.

Just before his voicemail picked up, Gunner's voice burst through her phone. "Kelsey. I'm so sorry. I forgot to call you."

On a sigh of relief, she asked, "Are you all right? Is everything okay?"

"Yes. It's great!" But his pause was filled with something that suggested it might not be quite so fantastic. "I mean, I'm fine."

"Okay . . . so, you're on your way to rehearsal?"

Gunner groaned. "Um . . . no."

Whatever flip her stomach had threatened before came to fruition, with an extra loop for good measure. "Gunner? What's going on?"

"Listen, Kelsey. I'm sorry. It's all happening so fast."

The guy sounded like they'd gone out on a few whirlwind dates instead of spending the whole summer working on this production. He sounded like he was breaking up with her.

Or with her *show*.

The air vanished, and her lungs ceased to remember their only function. "Gunner, tell me now," she wheezed as the earth tilted beneath her feet. Black spots danced at the corners of her eyes, and she tumbled to her knees.

He wouldn't. She was misunderstanding. He had too much invested in this show to give up on it now.

"I didn't know when I took the part how popular the segments were going to become. I mean, my Instagram followers tripled basically overnight after I posted the first video. And they weren't just locals either. Then the station out of Calgary called. They loved what I was doing, and they wanted to see more. More behind the scenes. More community involvement. And I couldn't say no. I mean, it's Calgary." He sighed loudly. "I didn't know they were going to offer me a job so soon. But I can't pass it up."

Her ears started ringing, and she pressed her hand to her forehead.

As though he were speaking through a tunnel, he said, "I'm moving there this week."

She knew every one of his words, but none of them made sense. "I don't . . . What do you mean?"

"I can't make the show on Friday. I'll be halfway to Calgary by then, and I start on air on Monday. The station lost their lead meteorologist, and their backup is out on maternity leave. They can't wait to fill the position."

"Can you wait just one day?" She sounded like she was pleading. Lord help her, she was pleading. "I mean, you can take off right after the show, and you'll only be set back a day or two."

"Kelsey . . ." He wrapped her name up in an apology that made it worse.

"No. Seriously. I'll buy you an airplane ticket." Perfect. Making promises her bank account could not back up.

"Listen, I know this isn't great news, but this is too big of an offer to pass on."

"But we don't have a show without you." Her words trembled. "And your fans are expecting you."

"I know. And I hate letting them down, but you'll smooth it over, I'm sure. Besides, I'll have new fans soon. More fans."

"You can't—" A sob surprised her, and suddenly there were tears in her eyes.

"I know this puts you in a tight spot, but you'll figure something out. You're a great director." He hung up.

And just like that, her dreams died. There would be no saving the theatre. No saving her job. No saving the memories of her grandma that lived on that old stage.

"Miss—Miss Ahern?"

She pinched her eyes closed at the sound of Willow's voice. She wasn't quite ready to stand and face her yet.

"What happened?" That was Fredrick, which meant that the whole cast was probably staring at her, waiting for her to get up and lead the rehearsal.

And all she could do was imagine how sad this would have made her grandma.

Wrapping her arms around her stomach, she curled in on herself, letting the truth wash over her. She'd failed. This town, the students, her grandma—she'd failed them all.

Another familiar voice broke through the silence. Deep and a little gravelly, sometimes out of use, always tender. "I think you all should head home now. We'll pick back up tomorrow."

A collective mumbled argument kept them in place for a few moments, but slowly they dispersed, the women squeezing her arm and the older men patting her head. All of them unaware that their work had been for nothing.

Then there was silence. It lasted for hours. Or maybe it just felt like hours.

Finally a shadow fell across the grass, and long legs squatted before her. Big hands rubbed up and down her bare arms, and Levi whispered words she couldn't make out through the thunder in her ears.

When she looked up, slowly unfurling, pain seared through her stomach. But Levi was there to pull her in tight. Then suddenly she was weightless, cradled in his arms like she had been the night this all began. He carried her to the barn and set her on the stage as though she were one of the porcelain Anne dolls sold at any one of a hundred shops on the island.

Standing before her, he cupped her face, a hand on each side. Then he pushed her hair behind her ears and smoothed his rough thumbs under her eyes and across her cheeks.

Nothing had ever felt better.

"What happened?" he finally asked.

"Gunner is moving to Calgary. He quit the show."

"But—but—it's four days away." His stilted words mirrored the uneven pace of her heart.

"I know." She flung a hand toward the yard where he'd picked her up, as though to indicate she'd put the pieces together already.

Levi's expression tumbled from disbelief to misery, his eyes turning nearly as gray as a thunderstorm. "He wouldn't."

"He did." Tears welled up again, and she swiped at them angrily. "Levi, I don't know what I'm going to do. I let my grandma down. Every memory that I have with her on that stage will be plowed to the ground. Not to mention the whole town will lose its heartbeat. Everybody's put so much work in—you've put so much work in—and I failed."

"This isn't your fault." He wrapped his fingers around her arms, holding her firmly upright.

"But it is. I'm the one who gave him the role. I invited him to be part of a community production. If I'd just stuck with locals . . ."

"You'd have had slim pickings. And not nearly the publicity."

She scowled at his logic. "But at least I'd still have a full cast."

"Maybe." He shrugged. "But people get sick or injured. There was never a guarantee. Even if you'd had an understudy."

She slumped down, calling herself all kinds of fool for not looking for an understudy. A bad actor—even one worse than Gunner—would have been better than nothing. Better than a canceled show. She huffed a breath toward her eyes, her bangs flopping out of the way.

"Before you cancel it, what are your other options?"

"It's not like there's just someone wandering around Victoria who knows the . . ." Her eyes went wide, her breath catching in her throat.

It took Levi several seconds to catch up with her unspoken train of thought, and she watched the realization wash over him, his face going one shade of white after another. He began shaking his head, taking a stumbling step back, before he was completely ashen.

"But it's perfect! You know all the lines. You've been at nearly every practice. You know the blocking and the spikes."

"But I can't get up in front of a crowd."

She launched herself off the stage and landed right in front of him. Grabbing his hands, she squeezed with every bit of strength in her. "You can. I know you can. It's not that hard."

He tilted his head like she was crazy. "Easy for you to say. You've been doing this pretty much your whole life."

"True." She dragged the word out on a long breath. "But you have natural talent. Remember that day you were running lines with Gunner? You played every other part. In character."

He shrugged and turned away, his shoulder blocking her view of his face.

"I'm serious, Levi. You could do this. You *can* do this."

"You don't understand. This isn't about knowing the words—this is about standing up in front of hundreds of people. I. Don't. Do. That."

She huffed out a sigh and pressed her hand to his arm. "Why not? You're amazing."

"Maybe I was okay in front of you and Gunner and Dustin. But . . ." Levi stabbed his fingers through his hair, leaving it standing on end.

"Is this about what your dad said?"

He shrugged again, choosing silence over explanation, and she wanted to tug on his arm until he opened his mouth. Until he told her exactly what was going through his mind.

So that she could persuade him to fill in for Gunner.

It was all right if he was a little nervous. Or even if he had full-on stage fright. She'd teach him the same things her grandma had taught her for how to deal with them. In four days. No problem.

"You know you don't have to come up with any of the words you're going to say."

He spun on her, his eyebrows meeting over his nose and his eyes narrowing into slits. "You don't understand. You can't understand."

"Then help me. We can work through this together."

With a hard shake of his head, he dismissed her, leaving her only one option. Begging.

Grasping one of his hands in both of hers, she pressed it to her chin. Her lip was trembling, but maybe that could speak the words beyond the ones she could find. "You know what this show means to me and to this town. What it would have meant to my grandma." She chewed on her lower lip for a long moment before adding, "I need your help."

He stared right into her eyes, his gaze filled with sadness and regret and so much pain.

"Please. If you care about me even a little . . ."

Extricating his hand gently from her grasp, he said, "If you knew me at all, you wouldn't ask." Then he turned and walked through the barn door without looking over his shoulder.

Wrapping her arms around her middle, she sank to the floor and let the tears come. The show was over. She'd failed in every possible way.

And she'd just confirmed the worst of it. Levi didn't care for her at all.

twenty-two

Levi started the page in his book for the fourth time. The words couldn't seem to hold still, blurring together, their meanings vanishing. Pressing his forefinger and thumb to his eyes and resting his elbows on the kitchen table, he tried not to see the look of desolation that he'd put on Kelsey's face the day before.

It didn't work.

It had been there every time he closed his eyes the night before, stealing his sleep. Which explained why he couldn't manage to read even a paragraph today.

Well, that or the rock in his stomach that just kept falling into a bottomless pit.

What had he done? He tried to pray for answers, but there were none, only recrimination from the voice in his head and a constant refrain. *She doesn't understand.*

The side door closed softly, and he jerked his head up, expecting to see either Mama Potts or Violet. There was no way Eli would be so gentle. And Oliver was pretty much glued to home since little Walter's arrival, except for the somewhat frequent diaper runs.

Sure enough, Mama Potts strolled into the kitchen, her arms wrapped around a box heavy with finished mugs. When she spotted him, her eyebrows nearly reached her graying hairline. "What are you doing here? I thought you'd be at the barn tonight, with the show only a few days away."

"I'm not sure there's going to be a show."

Mouth dropping open, she set the box on the table with all the tenderness of someone who had poured hours into each piece. She plopped into the chair across from him with much less care. "All right. Talk."

His mouth clamped closed out of habit, but Mama Potts shook her head in determination. "You don't get a pass today, Son. Not after dropping that bomb. You've worked way too hard to give up now."

Levi licked his lips, trying to find a way out of this. As he closed his book and tried to hug it to his chest like a shield, she grabbed his hand and squeezed it hard.

"Gunner backed out of the show."

"Excuse me?"

He hadn't mumbled, so he expanded. "He got a job in Calgary. Apparently the whole series on the news was basically an audition for him to get a job in a bigger market. And he's moving there this week."

Mama Potts leaned back, crossing her arms and sucking on her front tooth. The corner of her eye twitched, probably to hold in exactly what she thought of the meteorologist.

Levi hadn't ever trusted them—as far as the weather

was concerned anyway. Now he didn't trust them offscreen either.

After a few deep breaths, Mama Potts asked, "What is Kelsey going to do?"

"What *can* she do?"

"Isn't there someone who could step in?"

His gut twisted violently. He knew right where his mom was heading. She'd probably heard rumors already from Meg or Violet. "No."

Leaning forward, her voice all innocence, she asked, "No, what?"

"I'm not going to play the part."

That didn't seem to surprise her at all. Which meant she knew he *could* play the part. Which meant someone had been talking.

"Well, I think you'd be the perfect Jack."

"Mom, you don't understand. I can't do this."

Mama Potts raised her eyebrows, pulling her driving glasses to the tip of her nose. "Oh, so you *don't* know the part?"

Levi scrubbed his palms over his face. She didn't want to understand what this meant, what it would take. That it was a feat he couldn't manage.

Even if he tried, there was no way he'd get through it with his dad's voice ringing in his ears. *"You're never going to say anything that anyone wants to hear."* It didn't matter that he hadn't thought up the words. They would still have to come out of his mouth. And there would be a whole lot of ears not wanting to hear them.

Including his dad's.

"Honey, listen to me." Mama Potts caught his forearm

across the table and tugged at it until he met her eyes. Her gaze was firm but kind. "You're my baby boy—" She waved him off when he tried to argue that he was only a few years shy of thirty. "Age doesn't matter to a mom. You're always going to be my boy, and I love you. But I worry that I did you a disservice."

"You're amazing. What you did to keep our family together, to get this roof over our head—we wouldn't have made it without you."

Squeezing his arm, she smiled. "And I'd do again and again and again. As many times as it took to protect you boys. But did I make our home too safe for you?"

"Too safe?" He shook his head.

"I let you be quiet. I didn't make you speak up. After your dad left, I wasn't sure you were ever going to speak again. Some of the church ladies said I needed to take you to a child psychologist in Charlottetown, but you seemed content enough to stay by yourself. You didn't seem particularly sad, just . . . introverted. Should I have pushed you to get out of your shell?"

Levi's heart sank straight to his toes. He'd never considered that his own predilections would cause his amazing mother to doubt if she'd done a good job. "It wasn't you," he rushed to assure her. "It was—"

He nearly bit his tongue off. Apparently telling Kelsey the truth had opened a floodgate he hadn't even known he had. And teasing the story wasn't going to be enough for Mama Potts. Not with the way her eyebrows snapped together.

"Who?"

Levi let out a low groan. "I didn't know he'd hit you."

Her eyes flew open, and her lower lip quivered. "What did that man say to you?"

He zeroed in on one of the pieces of blue pottery still in the box. He was pretty sure he'd lose his nerve if he had to look her in the eye. "I begged him to stay. The night he left, I asked him to stay. And he . . ." Levi swallowed thickly, his mouth suddenly a desert. "He told me I wasn't ever going to say anything that anyone would want to hear."

Letting go of his arm, Mama Potts slapped the tabletop so hard that it rattled the box of dishes. "Sometimes I just want to shove that man into the harbor. And sometimes I plain feel sorry for him. He gave up everything good, turned his back on all that was right in his life." She took a deep breath and shook the fire out of her hands before looking right into his eyes. "You hear me, Levi Michael Ross, and you hear me good. *I* want to hear what you have to say. Every single day. And not because you're my son. Because you're smart. And you're kind. And you're the most compassionate person I know."

His ears burned, and he ducked his head away from her.

"Look at me."

He couldn't ignore her command.

"My sweet boy, God has given you a kind heart, a tender heart. And it's a gift." When he started to argue, she cut him off again. "Who was the one willing to give up his dream to save his brother? What you did for Eli—for this whole family—was no small thing."

He folded his hands on the table and stared at his knuckles. He hadn't even thought about that decision. Not for more than a split second anyway. There really hadn't been a choice. He could give Eli the money he'd needed to be able to stay—or he could watch his family's hearts break. And Violet wouldn't have come in to rescue them again. She would have been just as broken as them.

Violet's arrival had started their family on a path to healing after his dad left. After Eli left. Levi had not been about to stand idly by when he could be part of keeping Eli in town. And keeping Violet happier than he'd ever seen her.

"What else was I going to do?" he mumbled.

Mama Potts smiled. "Said like someone with true empathy. Your kind heart helps you understand others' pain. But it also leaves you vulnerable to their vile words. Your father has had a hard heart for years." She shook her head, her eyes focusing on a distant memory. "He wasn't always like that. He loved you boys—and me too—for a while."

"What happened to him? Why is he like this?"

"When his twin brother—your uncle—died, he didn't know how to deal with it."

His gut clenched. "Uncle?"

Mama Potts tilted her head with a sad smile. "You would have liked your uncle Dennis. He loved to read too. But most of all, he loved to fish. He and your dad worked Jeffrey Druthers's boat together for a long time. One day your dad went out even though there was clearly a storm brewing. When the rain started and your dad didn't come back in, Dennis went out in a dinghy looking for him. Your—your dad made it back, but Dennis never did. After that, your dad refused to let us talk about Dennis. He was so angry. He blamed God. He blamed Druthers. He even blamed me. But mostly, I think he blamed himself for being the one to survive."

"That's when he started drinking?"

She nodded. "And gambling. Anything to take his mind off his ghosts."

Levi knew they hadn't helped. And they weren't ever going to.

"Why did you stay with him? All those years. And please don't say it was because of us."

Mama Potts flashed a smile that must have been part of the reason his dad had fallen for her in the first place. "Because we do hard things for the people we love."

That landed like a punch to his kidney, and he wheezed out a breath.

"You know, you can do hard things for someone you love too."

He tried to shake off her not-so-subtle implication. He wasn't in love with Kelsey. Much.

Okay, maybe a little bit. But she certainly—probably—didn't reciprocate. And whatever she might have possibly felt for him had been thwarted by his declaration that he wasn't ever going to get up on a stage for her.

Except, if there was ever anyone worth making a complete fool of himself for, it was Kelsey Ahern. And if there was ever anyone who wouldn't let him look like a fool, it was also her. And not just because she cared about making her show a success.

Reaching for his hand once again, Mama Potts said, "I always figured you'd open up when you were ready—when you met someone special. And I've seen you blossom this summer beyond what I ever even hoped."

She was going to make him go up in a flame of embarrassment if she didn't stop. Yet he craved the words—affirmation he hadn't let himself admit he needed.

"Kelsey is good for you, my dear. She's going to stretch you and help you see life beyond the pages of a book. But more than that, you're good for her. You're the first person she's let get close enough to speak life over her since her grandma died last year."

He sat with that for a silent moment. Kelsey had used that same phrase—speak life—not too long ago. He was pretty sure it came from a verse in Proverbs. Each person had the power to speak life or death, and he'd spoken death over Kelsey's entire production—and her entire future in Victoria—with just one word. *No.*

It would take only one other word to speak life.

If he could just find the courage to say it.

———

Kelsey knocked softly on the door of the quaint home just a few blocks from the playhouse in one direction and the shore in the other. It was white with gray shutters and trim and had a bright turquoise front door. A small card had been taped over the doorbell to alert visitors: *We hope the baby is sleeping!* She smiled at that as shuffling steps on the other side of the door preceded the gentle snick of it opening.

"Kelsey, what a wonderful surprise," Meg said. "Come in, come in."

She stepped into the living room, its carpet littered with baby rockers and changing blankets and diaper bags. Just three weeks old and little Walter had begun taking over the house.

"Please ignore my mess," Meg said. "I'm just—"

"You just had a baby."

Meg sighed in relief. "Exactly. I assume you're here to see the star of the show." She chuckled, scooping up the little guy from the rocker where he was mostly asleep. He grunted, gurgled, and snuggled into his mom's shoulder.

"I brought a little something," Kelsey said, holding out a gift bag stuffed with white tissue paper.

Meg's eyes lit up. "I know they're for little Walter, but I love opening presents. Here." She deftly passed Kelsey the baby and took the bag in one movement.

Kelsey snuggled his feather-soft thatch of black hair, so much like his dad's and uncles'. She couldn't help but wonder if he'd end up with blue eyes just like theirs too. If he'd be tall and handsome with dimples that would steal a girl's breath.

The Ross genes ran strong, and when she blinked, she saw Levi's face, heard his words from the day before, felt the crash of disappointment yet again.

Distracting herself, she breathed in all the sweet smells of a baby, pressing her nose against little Walter's cheek as he grunted and wiggled and burrowed right into her heart.

True to her word, Meg didn't waste any time ripping into the gift bag and pulling out the little onesie in blue and white stripes, an anchor stitched over the heart. She held it out at arm's length, her face immediately melting at its cuteness. Then she turned it around and squealed at the little lobster sewn right onto the seat, in prime pinching position.

Little Walter must have recognized his mom's voice as he cooed and gurgled but couldn't quite be bothered to wake up.

"Where did you get this? Oliver is going to insist little

Walt wear this every day, at least during fishing season. I'm going to have to get him one in every size when he outgrows this."

Kelsey chuckled, delighted that she'd found the perfect gift. "One of the shops in Summerside. I saw it a few months back before he made his early arrival, and I thought you might get a kick out of it."

Meg hugged it to her chest and wrapped an arm around Kelsey. "It's perfect. Thank you." She sighed. "Now, if you don't mind, let's sit because I'm tired pretty much all the time." She lowered herself tenderly to the fluffy sofa behind her, patting the cushion beside her. "I'm delighted to see you, but I can't help but think seeing this handsome guy isn't the only reason you stopped by."

Kelsey carefully made her way to the sofa and perched on the edge of the couch, still soaking in all of the baby snuggles and trying not to think about how precious this little Ross family was. How once or twice she'd allowed herself to imagine a life in the green house by the shore. A life with Levi. Not a fairy tale but an imperfect life built on love and trust and . . .

Well, none of it mattered now. She didn't have a job, a life, or anything keeping her in Victoria. She was going to have to move.

An unexpected sob caught in her chest as she bounced poor little Walter, who grunted his displeasure and whimpered before she rubbed his back, soothing him back to sleep.

"Kelsey?" Meg reached for her knee, squeezing it gently. "What's going on?"

"It's . . . it's been a hard couple of days." Then it all tumbled out. Gunner dropping out of the show. Her begging Levi to play the part. Him walking away. "I don't have a benefit show at all. We'll have to give back all of the ticket sales. And the playhouse is going to close. *For sure.*" She pressed a kiss to the top of Walter's head, but not even his snuggles could ease the pain in her chest. "And I let my grandma down. Again."

Meg offered a sad smile, but her voice was firm when she spoke. "First of all, no. You've let no one down. Least of all Coletta."

Kelsey tried to interrupt, but Meg held up her hand, basically in teacher mode now. Her look said she was not to be questioned.

"Your grandma was incredibly proud of you. Always. And not because of something you did or didn't do, but because she loved you. Period. If she was still here, she'd have loved that you tried, regardless of the outcome." Meg's eyes turned sad. "You know that my mom is sick."

Kelsey nodded. She'd seen Sandra Whitaker at church only a handful of times in the last year, and each time her gaze seemed unable to focus, her steps uneven. She clung to Meg's dad like he was her lifeline. Maybe he was.

Meg swallowed hard. "The thing is, watching my parents these last few years has taught me a lot about love, about what it takes to love someone well. I've watched my dad sacrifice everything to care for my mom, and I know he'd do it over and over again. Your grandma loved you the same way."

"But I can't ever repay her. I wasn't even there when she needed me the most—when she died alone in the hospital." Kelsey blinked rapidly against the fire singeing her eyes.

"Oh, honey." Meg morphed into mom mode. "Love isn't about keeping score, and it's too big to earn. And love that is contingent on what another person gives is a cheap imitation of the real thing. My dad loves my mom, even though some days she doesn't even know who he is."

"I'm so-orry." Kelsey hiccuped on a sob, patting little Walter's back to keep him asleep. "That must be so hard."

"It is." Meg nodded slowly. "But it's a choice he made a long time ago. It's the same choice your grandma made, to care for you through the good and the hard."

Kelsey's eyes leaked, tears slipping down her cheeks.

Meg reached for a nearby burp cloth and handed it over. "It's clean," she said in a conspiratorial whisper.

Wiping her eyes and her runny nose and knowing she must look all kinds of ridiculous, Kelsey sighed the sigh of the heart weary. "I'm sorry. It's just . . . I didn't have anything to give my parents. So they left. Again and again and again. And I just can't understand why my grandma took me in when I didn't have something to give her. When I couldn't show her how much I loved her."

Meg's lips quivered, her eyes suddenly turning glassy. Waving her hand at her face, she shrugged. "Sorry. Hormones." Swallowing thickly, she said, "I'm sorry that your parents didn't show you what love looks like. I'm sorry they were too focused on themselves to love you well. Maybe God knew you needed your grandma Coletta. I think because she knew how much God loved her, she knew how to love you. And nothing you did or could have done would have changed that. Saving the playhouse is a beautiful idea, but she would have loved you just the same if they bulldoze it to the ground."

Kelsey's tears began in earnest, her shoulders shaking so hard that Meg reached for her fussing baby. "I'm such a mess."

"Not even a little bit." Meg chuckled. "Now tell me what's really hurting your heart."

Kelsey didn't want to say the words, but they flew out of her mouth anyway. "I blew it with Levi. I basically told him that if he wouldn't do the show, he doesn't care about me."

With a conspiratorial smile, Meg asked, "But he does, doesn't he?"

"I don't know." Kelsey shot to her feet, wringing her hands and pacing the small room. "I mean, I thought he did. There have been all these signs, but he's so quiet, and he's never . . . But I want him to. Care about me, I mean."

"Uh-huh. Care about you. Right."

That, among other things. Which all pointed to a life and family in the green house. With him.

She plopped back down on the couch, flopping her arm across her face in the most stereotypical theatrics ever. Heaving a sigh, she adjusted her arm until she could see Meg's face with one eye. "Do you think I have any chance of . . ."

"Winning him back?"

"I'm not sure I ever had him."

Meg snorted, and little Walter echoed it perfectly. "If I know one thing about the Ross brothers, they don't hide their affections very well. And Levi's have been on full display for the last ten weeks."

Kelsey wanted to believe that Meg was telling the truth, but there was only one way to know for sure. And it would mean giving up everything she'd worked for.

twenty-three

Kelsey didn't recognize the number that flashed on her phone that evening, and she wanted to ignore it, to shut out the rest of the world and hide under a blanket with a good book. But she didn't want to miss a miracle. She'd been praying for a solution for two days. She'd been praying she wouldn't have to tell the cast that she didn't have a solution to Gunner's departure and the show was canceled. Because when she did that, she knew it really would be.

"Hello?" she answered, hope and hesitancy matched in her voice.

"Miss Ahern? It's Dustin. Dustin Crowder."

She knew who he was, but she couldn't figure out what reason he'd have to call her. Unless he'd been able to . . .

No. A fifteen-year-old boy hadn't figured out how to save the show.

She forced a smile into her voice. "Hi, Dustin. What can I do for you?"

"Um . . . it's Levi—I mean, Mr. Ross. He, um, I got your number from his phone."

A brick landed in the bottom of her stomach as she squeezed the phone tighter to her ear, her fingers shaking. "What do you mean, 'from his phone'?"

"He dropped it. When they took him to the hospital."

"Who took him to the hospital?"

"Some of the other guys. I just figured you'd want to know. His leg got cut out in the field. We were going back over a field that hadn't dried before. A wire snapped, and he . . . he was bleeding pretty bad."

Her mouth felt like it was filled with cotton, and she couldn't breathe. She waited for the all-too-familiar sensation of seasickness, the one that always accompanied the sight—and usually the thought—of blood. But it didn't come. There wasn't room for it among the twisted knots already filling her stomach.

"How bad was it?" she managed to force out between uneven breaths. That was a stupid question. If he'd needed to be rushed to the hospital, it was bad. Very bad.

"It was—" Dustin swallowed audibly. "It was my fault. I didn't secure the wire before I cut it, and . . ."

She could hear his pain through the phone, and she wanted to reach out and hug him. "Dustin, it's going to be okay." She couldn't believe anything else. She couldn't stand for anything else. If something happened to Levi and he thought she didn't care, she wouldn't be able to live with that.

She couldn't let it happen again.

She took a shallow breath and let it out between trembling lips. "Where is he?"

"At the hospital in Summerside. He dropped his phone in the field and I picked it up, but they were already gone. They took his truck."

"Levi's?"

"Yeah. His and another one. I guess so the other guys wouldn't be stuck there."

They were going to leave him alone at the hospital? Her heart skipped a beat, then echoed in her chest.

"Miss Ahern, are you going to see him?"

Every bell in her mind clanged that she couldn't. But her mouth didn't get the message. "I'm on my way."

"Could you . . . could you take me with you?"

She sighed, imagining the scene at the hospital. Levi in surgery, blood transfusions, and her passed out in the waiting room. Bile rose in the back of her throat, and she swallowed it down as quickly as she could. She didn't want Dustin to see her like that. But more than that, she needed a moment alone with Levi, a chance to tell him how she really felt.

"Not this time."

"Okay." He sounded like his puppy had run off.

"But I'll tell him how sorry you are. And that it was an accident."

"Yeah?"

"Yes." She ended the call and tossed her phone into her purse, scrambling for anything else she might need. Why were there never any smelling salts around when she needed them?

Oh well. She'd make do without them. Because this was Levi. And she loved him a little bit.

Throwing her bag into the passenger seat of her car,

she dropped behind the steering wheel and flew out of the driveway of her bungalow.

Please, Lord, don't let Kevin be on patrol.

She didn't know if God answered the prayers of speeding drivers, but she hoped so. Because she wasn't going to slow down. She spent the whole thirty-minute drive to the Prince County Hospital with her foot pressed to the floor, asking God to let Levi be okay.

As she flew into the parking lot, she scanned each row for Levi's old blue truck.

There. It was parked next to a light pole, and she swung her car into the open spot beside it. Slamming her door, she raced for the emergency room entrance. Her gaze narrowed until she could see only what was right in front of her. Only what she was looking for.

At the sliding glass doors, she stopped, her feet refusing to take another step.

"Come on," she whispered to herself. "Just do this."

Not only for Grandma Coletta. Not just for Levi. She had to do this for herself. She had to know that she wasn't paralyzed by this phobia that had way too much power over her life.

One step. Then another. That was all she had to do.

So she did.

The smell of disinfectant assaulted her the moment she stepped inside, and she pressed her hand to her nose. *Ignore the needles. Ignore any sign of blood.* She could do this.

At the info desk, she pulled her hand down just far enough to ask, "Where can I find Levi Ross?"

The nurse at the station opened her mouth, but it was a deep voice from her right that filled the space.

"Kelsey?"

She spun to see Levi charging toward her, whole in body if not in his jeans, which had been sheared just above his left knee. She risked a glance down to find a pristine white bandage below his knee, covering a patch of skin about the size of his hand. If there was blood, she didn't see it.

She threw herself at him, wrapping her arms around his neck and pressing her nose into his shoulder. He smelled of hay and earth and that infernal disinfectant. The scent was sweeter than cinnamon rolls fresh out of the oven.

"What are you doing here?" he asked as he slipped one arm around her waist.

She couldn't answer him. This wasn't the place to confess all of her feelings. Instead, she asked, "Are you all right?"

"I'm fine. The doctor sewed me up with twelve stitches. But . . ." He pulled away far enough to look into her face, confusion written all over his. "I don't understand."

"I . . . um . . . Dustin called me. He said it was bad."

Levi's chuckle made his chest shake where her hand rested over his heart. "It looked terrible. Poor guy probably thinks it's his fault."

She cringed. "A little bit."

"I'll call him a little later from the house, since he has my phone."

Part of her wanted Levi to let Dustin off the hook quickly so he didn't beat himself up over an accident. The other part of her wanted Levi to keep on holding her like this until everything in the world felt right again. And it was starting to.

He wasn't badly injured. He was holding her like he did care. Like it wasn't too late for them.

"Come on." He tugged her hand toward the door. "You look like you'd rather be anywhere but here."

She didn't care as long as she was with him. But that was too cheesy to say out loud in front of the nurses, whose gazes were fixed on them as they ate up the scene. So Kelsey followed silently behind him, gulping in the fresh air when they reached the sun-drenched parking lot.

Levi didn't say anything as he strolled toward his truck and finally stopped by its side. She stopped behind him, close enough to hear his breathing, to reassure herself that he hadn't been significantly injured. That he was still with her.

When he turned to face her, he wore a sad smile, his dimples deep but not filled with joy. Scraping his hands down his face, he sighed. "I never expected to see you here. I was coming to find you."

Her heart slammed against her ribs, hope daring to fill up her lungs. "You were?"

"Yeah. I . . . What are you doing at the hospital?"

"I told you. Dustin called."

"But you were *inside* the hospital."

She sighed and shrugged. "It's where you were."

His smile lost its sadness, genuine joy trickling out of him on a chuckle that made her tingle all over the same way the sun on her skin made her feel alive.

"Levi." She sighed, pressing her hands to his chest because she needed to touch him, to know he was solid and stable and so many other things she loved about him. "I never should have asked you to do the show. I know why you can't, and I shouldn't have pressured you. I'm sorry."

He licked his lips, and her gaze couldn't seem to make it

any farther north. She was stuck there, mesmerized by his perfect smile, waiting for his response, praying an apology was enough.

"You came into that hospital for *me*?"

She looked down and would have dropped her hands, but he clasped them right where they were. "I didn't know how serious it was, and I couldn't let . . . I couldn't let those words the other day be the last thing I said to you. I just needed you to know—" She swallowed thickly before glancing up for just a moment. "It doesn't matter how you feel about me, but I wanted you to know that I care about you. I'm—that is—it's just that—"

Blerg.

When had words become so hard? Maybe when she had to come up with them on her own. She should have practiced on the drive over, but she'd been too busy praying that Levi hadn't been seriously injured. Too busy praying she'd have a chance for this moment.

Now she did, and she didn't have a clue what to say.

Levi released her hands and cupped her cheeks, tilting her head up. "I know," he whispered.

Maybe he could explain it to her then. "What?"

A muscle in his jaw jumped. "I know how much strength and courage it took for you to walk into that hospital. And I'm guessing you walked in there for the same reason I was coming to find you."

"You were coming to find me?" Oh dear. She needed to stop sounding like a broken record. "Why?"

"Because I don't want to hurt you. Because if it's in my power, I'll do anything for you. Because you had every right to ask me for my help, and I was scared to offer it."

"No—no—no," she stuttered. "I'm not asking you to be in the show. I didn't apologize so you'd change your mind."

"I know. I changed my mind before you apologized. It's what I should have done in the first place."

"No. You never had to prove yourself. Not to me."

Levi's thumb swept over her cheek and around the rim of her ear, sparks following its path, shivers racing down her neck and all the way to her fingers and toes. Her knees began to tremble, but not like when she had fainted in the past. This wasn't because of fear or pain. It was the sweetest feeling to be overwhelmed by him.

Not that it kept her legs from buckling.

He caught her just in time, swinging her against the side of his truck so she could lean on it as he cradled her cheeks. He leaned in so close that his breath fanned her face. "Okay there?"

She nodded, and he grinned. A little shy. A little fierce.

"Here's the thing. I'm going to do your show."

"But why, when you'll be miserable?"

"Mama Potts said something to me that stuck. She said we do hard things for the people we love. And I've been more than a little bit in love with you since about grade nine."

His words echoed inside her from the top of her head to the tips of her toes. They circulated to all the wounded parts of her, binding them up, speaking life. "That's a long time," she finally said, giggling.

"You're telling me." He rolled his eyes. "But when I saw you in the hospital, I thought maybe you'd done a hard thing for someone you love too?"

She started to bite into her lower lip, but Levi's thumb

was already there, tracing the line of it, teasing her with what could be. She could barely breathe for the fluttering in her chest. And if she pressed onto her tiptoes to get a little closer to him, well, that couldn't be helped.

Lord, please let him finally kiss me.

She'd been waiting for what felt like ages. And if she'd had any kind of brain, *she* would have kissed *him* long before.

But this was better. This moment in his arms. Just the two of them. Finding a completely private moment in a public parking lot.

Gazing up into his eyes, she watched him watch her. He seemed to inspect every angle of her face, his fingers tracing the curve of her forehead and the bridge of her nose. He studied her like an art historian studied the masters. As though she were a precious artifact.

"You're prettier every time I see you."

Her finger automatically flew to the mole that hid in her smile line, but he caught her wrist and gently pressed her hand back to his chest.

"All of you. Especially your freckles."

She wrinkled her nose. "I tried to get rid of them with lemon juice when I was a kid. But they wouldn't budge."

"I'm glad," he said as he pressed the pad of his finger to the dots spreading from her nose to her cheeks. He seemed to get lost in them, almost as though he were counting every single mark, each touch as gentle as a butterfly kiss.

Each touch not enough.

"Levi?"

He glanced up from her nose. "Hmm?"

"Are you going to kiss me or what?"

He laughed, the sound deep and rich and joyful. Then,

with a quick nod, he leaned in, pressing his lips against hers.

Finally.

His lips were hesitant at first, asking permission with sweet, soft movements. When she combed a hand into his hair and held him close, he sighed and leaned all the way in, the distance between them vanishing. His arms tightened around her, and his body pressed hers more firmly against the unforgiving side of the truck. She completely melted into him, clinging to the front of his shirt as her legs gave way.

Something akin to joy bubbled deep in her chest when one of his hands swept up her back until he cradled her head, protective and ever so solid. His hair felt like silk beneath her hands, and he shivered as she ran her fingers over the fine hair on the back of his neck. Then he let out a low growl that made her giggle. She'd remember that he liked that.

He liked it so much, in fact, that he kissed her harder, shifting his head for a better angle that sent tingles clear to her toes.

She hung on to his shoulders, the muscles there bunching as he pulled her harder against him. It didn't seem possible, but somehow he made it work as he breathed her in.

She wanted to inhale him too. To have him this close forever. And she wanted to kick herself for missing out on weeks—maybe years—of being in his arms, of leaning on his strength. But there was no time for regret as he pressed his nose into her neck, settling a kiss on the spot right behind her ear.

Pure delight washed over her even as she gasped for breath in preparation for another kiss. And if she was lucky, more after that.

Before she could kiss him again, Levi laughed. It wasn't a chuckle of embarrassment or even a chortle of uncertainty. It was a full-on laugh of humor.

She shoved his shoulders, though it probably hurt her more than it did him. "What's that supposed to mean?"

His dimples went into full effect. "I'm just really glad that my first kiss was with you—not on the stage."

"First? That was your first kiss?"

His ears turned that endearing shade of pink that they seemed to whenever he ducked his chin in embarrassment, and she grabbed his face between her hands.

"How is that possible? How did none of the other girls . . . ? But you're so handsome."

His ears turned a few more shades of pink. "No, Eli's always been the handsome one."

"Uh-uh. The girls have just been blind."

He shrugged. "Maybe I've just been head over heels for this one girl ever since I noticed that girls don't have cooties. And . . ." He lifted his shoulder again.

And he'd been too shy to say anything to her. Until now.

And he was going to be in the show and share a kiss with Jade as Gwendolen.

Her stomach trickled toward her knees, the air seeping out of her chest like a tired balloon.

She knew it was going to be a stage kiss, but now that she'd had Levi's first kiss, she wanted all of them. Pretty much for the rest of forever.

twenty-four

Levi pulled his truck into the park near the lighthouse, the string of trailers behind him toting all of the equipment needed to put on the show. The one he had agreed to star in.

When he looked across the cab at the smile on Kelsey's face, he knew it couldn't have ended any other way. He was always going to do hard things for her. He wasn't his dad, who ran when things got difficult.

"Are you excited?" he asked.

"I can't believe we're actually here. That the show is going to happen. If Mable Jean's source on the board is right, we've sold nearly a thousand tickets already."

He frowned as he put on the emergency brake. "Will a thousand people fit in the park?"

"I guess we'll find out." She laughed as she let go of his hand and hopped out of the cab.

Dustin jumped from the truck bed, his hands on his hips like a foreman overseeing his first job.

Levi clapped him on the shoulder. "Where are we going to start?"

Green eyes bright, the kid ran his hand through his shaggy mop. "Guess we better unhook the trailers and get them into place."

Their small crew got to work separating then reassembling the stage, setting up the backdrop rack, and connecting the lights to the generator. The overhead sun began to drop toward the point where the sea met the horizon, but the breeze carried more than birdsong. Cool air off the water blew by them, teasing Kelsey's hair and keeping the sweat at bay.

They worked for hours tightening every bolt and screw until the structure was stable and ready for the full cast.

Just about the time Dustin's stomach growled loudly, Meg arrived, little Walter in a carrier on her front and a white sack from Carrie's in her hand. "I thought you might want something to eat."

Dustin jumped from the stage and ran to take the food from her. He was halfway back to the flatbeds before he turned and said, "Thanks, Mrs. Ross." And that was the last thing he said for the next five minutes as he shoved fried fish tacos into his mouth.

Levi winked at him but was less interested in the food than his new nephew. He wrapped Meg in a hug and pressed a kiss to the top of the baby's head. "Thanks for coming over."

"Well, someone has to make sure that your lights and sound work."

He chuckled. "Where's Oliver?"

"Sleeping." The roll of her eyes couldn't diminish the

warmth of her smile at the mention of her husband's name. "He's been taking the night shifts with this little guy. He says he has to get in all the time he can with him before setting day."

Once the lobster fishing season started, Oliver would be up before four and on the water for most of the day every day for two months. No one could blame him for wanting to get as much time as possible with his son before that. Levi suspected Oliver was doing his best to care for his wife while he was available too. Which was probably one of the reasons Meg looked just as smitten with his brother as she had on their wedding day a year and a half before.

Levi risked a glance at Kelsey, who was testing the backdrops to make sure they rolled up and down as they were supposed to. Now he understood what his brothers felt, why they had fallen so hard. The right woman was a gift, and they'd do anything to make her happy.

"Would you like a demonstration?" he asked Meg, waving at Dustin, whose cheeks were full of taco.

Meg nodded once before freezing, her gaze locked somewhere over his shoulder.

Turning slowly, Levi already knew who she'd seen.

Dean strolled across the grass, stumbling a little bit as though his shoes were a size too big. As he drew closer, Levi could see that his eyes were unfocused, his nose red. And the kicker was the stench of liquor hanging all over him.

Levi cringed at the odor violating everything good and pure about the shore. He stepped forward anyway, putting Meg and little Walter behind him. Meg was plenty tall enough to see over his shoulder, but he was going to keep Dean as far away from the youngest Ross as possible.

"Who ya got there?" Dean slurred. "What happened to the redhead?"

Levi glanced up at Kelsey and saw a flicker of fear cross her face. He took a breath to steady his pulse and stared directly at his dad. "Go home."

"Aw, come on. S'posed to take care of the lights 'n' stuff."

Something about the way Dean said it didn't sound like he was there to protect the equipment. And if his job wasn't security, then he had another understanding with Mitch.

It made Levi's stomach twist until he blurted out more. "I'll be here all night."

Dean scowled, then tried to look around him at Meg and the baby. "That your kid? 'M I a grandpa?"

Meg gasped softly, and Levi stepped closer to his dad. His words were stuck on his tongue, so he did the only other thing he could. He stared him down until Dean stumbled backward, staggering toward the street.

"Be back tomorrow," he mumbled as he left.

Suddenly an arm looped through each of his, Meg on his right and Kelsey on his left.

"Thank you," Meg whispered, her gaze never leaving the disappearing figure as she cradled her free arm protectively around her son. "I don't think Oliver is ready for your dad to meet little Walter. I'm not either."

He nodded, wishing he'd had the strength to say what he really wanted to, to tell his dad the truth. But once again, he'd let his tongue get tied.

On his other side, Kelsey rested her head against his shoulder. "Are you really going to stay here all night?"

He grunted. "Guess I don't have much of a choice now. Whatever he wants, he's not man enough to go after it in front of an audience."

"Then I'm staying too," she said.

"Me too," Dustin said. At least, that was what it sounded like he said around a mouthful of taco.

"You guys don't—"

Dustin gulped down his food to interrupt Levi. "We're a team, right? We've been working on this together all summer. Let us finish it out."

"Smart guy," Kelsey said, cocking her head to the side.

There would be no arguing with them, so Levi pulled his truck keys out of his pocket and tossed them to Dustin. "You got some sleeping bags?"

"Yes, Mr. Ross."

"Good. Go get three of them and bring them back."

Dustin's eyes lit up, and he raced for the truck. He carefully maneuvered it around the stage and to the road, where it bounced along until it turned the corner and disappeared.

Patting his arm, Meg chuckled. "You're going to make such a good dad."

He prayed the evening light was enough to hide the pink on his ears. He fought the urge to glance at Kelsey, but he failed. She wore a thoughtful smile as her hand wrapped into his, and he couldn't help but imagine a string of red-headed kids running around the yard of the green house.

He'd never wanted to own that property more.

By the time Dustin returned with sleeping bags, they had

triple-checked all of the equipment, set the stage for the next day, and packed Meg and her little guy into the car and sent them home. The sun was already low, its glow reaching across the water with shimmering fingers. Dustin yawned loudly, then clapped a hand over his mouth as though he wasn't supposed to reveal that he was tired. But it had been a long day. A long week. In the fields and on the stage.

Levi couldn't blame him when he was feeling it too. "Why don't you get some sleep? I'll take first watch."

Dustin shot him a look of gratitude and unrolled his bag on the far side of the stage. Without a word, he slipped between the layers, the zipper hissing as he sealed himself inside. Levi and Kelsey had barely unrolled another bag when Dustin's breathing turned heavy, low snores mingling with the evening crickets.

"Guess it's just the two of us," Kelsey whispered as she sat down and patted the spot beside her.

Levi frowned as he lowered himself to her side. "You can rest if you're tired. I don't mind staying up."

Her gaze darted toward the sky, where the inky blue was just beginning to reveal the breadth of the stars. "And miss this time with you?" She snuggled into his side as he draped his arm over her shoulders. He held her tight and let the night fall over them.

After what could have been hours or merely minutes, she sighed. "Do you think your dad's going to come back tonight?"

The back of his throat turned sour. "I think it's more likely he's passed out in a ditch somewhere. And that Trumball is going to discover that he's working with a less-than-reliable partner."

"What do you think they're up to?"

Levi shook his head. "I honestly don't know. But I don't trust my dad—or anyone foolish enough to hire him."

"Do you think Trumball is really trying to close the theatre for good?" Worry etched itself into every word.

Combing her hair behind her ear, he smiled. "I think he can try. But he doesn't know who he's messing with. You won't go down without a fight. And you're not alone. Besides, you're the right woman for this job—the only one who could have made this happen."

She tilted her head and stared at him for a long, silent second.

"What?"

"You." She shook her head. "I should have known. I can't believe I didn't see it immediately. You wrote those notes in my script."

He ducked his chin and looked away. He hadn't meant to get caught or take credit. He'd just known she'd needed a bit of encouragement. And she was the one who had left her script lying around.

Either she didn't notice him squirming or she didn't care, because she plowed on before he could confirm. "I'm such a dolt. But . . . why didn't you sign them?"

"I don't know. I figured you needed the words and it didn't matter who they were from."

"Of course it mattered." She pursed her lips. "You always matter." She reached up to kiss his cheek before leaning more snugly into his side. "Thank you."

With her this close, he could barely feel the chill blowing in off the water.

"Do you want to run your lines?" she whispered.

He shook his head and combed her hair off her forehead before pressing his lips there. "Nah. I don't want to get too far into my head over it. I know the words, but if I overthink it . . . I just need to be in the moment."

She smiled into his shoulder, then craned her neck to look at Dustin, soft snoring still coming from the outline of his sleeping bag. "Are you nervous?"

He paused for a moment, letting the question roll around his head as he considered the true answer. "I'm not particularly looking forward to getting up in front of my dad, but now that I know why he is the way he is, I mostly just feel sorry for him. He blames himself for a tragedy that he couldn't have prevented."

"What tragedy?"

With a sigh, he told her about his uncle's death and all that Mama Potts had shared. "Instead of getting help in his grief, he made every other self-destructive choice. He sank so low that he's apparently afraid to speak to his own wife, let alone two of his sons. It's hard to fear the opinion of a man like that."

"He still hasn't spoken to your brothers? So he really didn't know who Meg was?"

"Nope. I figure he knows that Eli is none too happy with him. And the last time he saw Oliver, he got decked. Maybe he singled me out because he thought I'd be quick to forgive."

"Have you—forgiven him, I mean?"

Levi chewed on that thought, on the torment his father's words had caused for more than a decade. On the years he'd spent believing a lie. On the trepidation he felt every time he dared to open his mouth. "I think it's going to take some time."

Kelsey's arms snaked around his waist, her breath soft at his neck. "Sometimes forgiveness takes time. More often than not it's a repeated choice. And the trying is the choice."

"Know-it-all."

She giggled as he squeezed her, until Dustin grunted from the other side of the stage. Clapping a hand over her mouth, she gave his side a guilty jab as he pressed a finger to his lips.

When he was sure that Dustin was still asleep, he sighed. "When did you get so smart?" The silk of her hair caught on his whiskers as he rubbed his cheek across her temple.

"What can I say? This town basically gave me the keys to run my own show because they recognized my brilliance."

He snorted. "And humility."

She shot him a wide grin, her face glowing in the moonlight, her round pink lips shining like the stars. By degrees, her smile faded to curiosity, the corner of her mouth disappearing as she chewed on it. "Are you mad that I talked you into this?"

"You talked me into this? I've been blaming Mama Potts all week."

She playfully slapped his chest, and he snatched her hand to his heart before she could remove it. Warm and soothing, her nearness removed any fear that might have been left.

"Am I going to have some jitters tomorrow? Probably. A bit of stage fright?" He shrugged. "Maybe. But it's that good kind of anticipation. It's like . . ." His mind immediately jumped to the hospital parking lot, to that kiss. His heart thundered deep in his chest, echoing through every bit of him.

"Like what?"

"Like when I kissed you."

"You mean when you *finally* kissed me." She muttered something under her breath that sounded a lot like "Took you long enough."

"Yes, when I *finally* kissed you." He overemphasized the same word, hooking his finger under her chin until she faced him. "It's that feeling you get when you're a little bit nervous but you know it's going to be okay."

"Okay? You thought that kiss was *okay*?"

He shrugged off her question, which was apparently the wrong thing to do. She dove for him, tickling his sides with no mercy. Pleasure and pain mingled tirelessly as he writhed to get away from her devious fingers without waking their fellow watchman or alerting the locals.

"Okay?" she asked again, but he was breathless from silent laughter. That only made her tickle him more.

When he could stay quiet no longer, he encircled her in his arms, holding her still. They lay on their sides, their faces only a breath apart.

"Okay?" she grumbled.

"Amazing. Is that better?"

She gave a fake pout that lasted only a moment. "Fine."

"I knew it was going to be incredible. Because it was with you." He leaned in until his lips brushed hers, and her whole body relaxed with a sigh.

This—all of it, all of her—was incredible. Her skin was softer than silk, but she didn't seem to fear that he'd snag it with his work-worn hands as he dragged his fingers down her bare arms. Instead, she sighed into him, the sound in the back of her throat making his heart overflow.

When she finally pulled back, she said with a lazy but satisfied smile, "I'll accept incredible."

He would too.

Holding her so close, breathing in the sweet scent of her mingled with the salty air, was more than he could have asked for. She was the answer to a teenage boy's prayer. Shoot, she was the answer to a grown man's prayer.

Levi was pretty sure he was running on pure adrenaline. He'd gotten only a few hours of sleep the night before. Not that he'd minded staying up and talking with Kelsey until the sun began to turn the eastern sky pink and orange. He hadn't even minded Dustin's snoring.

But now, only fifteen minutes before the show, his hands shook and his head spun. Maybe it was those nerves he'd bragged wouldn't be too bad. Or maybe it was the sound of all those voices in the park. They wafted past the stage and through the opening to the makeshift dressing room that he shared with Fredrick and the older men in the cast.

"Whew! It's packed out there!" Fredrick said as he flipped open the tent's entrance. "Poor Kevin is out there trying to herd people into the pasture. And they're about as agreeable as hungry heifers."

"Did you see the news van?" one of the other men said.

Fredrick grinned. "Yep. Gunner's station is getting scooped! I saw the anchor from the other Charlottetown station interviewing Kelsey earlier."

All four of the other men laughed, but Levi could only

manage a forced chuckle. He felt the weight of this reality like a stone on his back.

He had chosen this path knowing it would be hard. Because he cared more about Kelsey's smile than he did about the butterflies assaulting his insides.

Squeezing his eyes closed, he forced himself to remember his why.

The audio system crackled, and Kelsey's voice split the air. She was probably making her announcement from a spot behind the stage. "Welcome to tonight's benefit show for the Victoria Playhouse. Please squeeze in so everyone can get a seat on the grass." She paused as a general murmur of excitement spread through the audience. "Tonight the role of Jack will be played by Levi Ross."

A hush fell over the crowd.

Levi held his breath, waiting for the grumbles to begin from those disappointed that Gunner wasn't going to show. Instead, a cheer went up from someone who sounded an awful lot like Mel Herman. It rippled through the crowd.

Fredrick pounded him on the back. "Guess we know who the star of the show is. Break a leg, man."

Before Levi could respond, Kelsey's voice quieted the crowd once again. "And playing the role of Gwendolen will be Kelsey Ahern."

The crowd exploded in cheers, and Levi ran from the tent, right into the woman of the hour. The woman of his dreams. "Gwendolen, eh?" he said as he caught her about the waist and swung her around.

She was already in costume, her pretty blue Victorian dress making her eyes glow even brighter than usual. Or maybe that was the joy shining from deep inside her.

"How did you—"

"When I told Jade that Gunner was out and you were in, she was worried she might not have the right chemistry with you—you know, without practice." With a wink, she added, "I didn't think we'd have any trouble."

He leaned in to kiss her, but she pressed her hands to his chest to stop him. "After. We can't mess up our makeup."

With that, she led him to the ladder and gave him a little shove into the spotlight as the curtain opened and the crowd roared.

twenty-five

Kelsey had never felt a rush so high as performing opposite the man she loved. Levi seemed to enjoy it too. At least he acted like he did. And the man could act. Every line, every movement—it was like he'd memorized every single piece of direction she'd given to Gunner and pulled them out one by one.

Grandma Coletta would have been proud.

Kelsey certainly was.

Regardless of the outcome, she'd done the best she could for her community, for her job, for her grandma's memory. As she stood hand in hand with Levi and took the final curtain call to the wild cheers of the audience, she prayed it had all been enough.

Levi squeezed her fingers, and she glanced at him. His dimples had never been deeper, nor the light in his eyes brighter.

"Thank you," she mouthed to him.

"I love you," he mouthed back.

That was all she needed to hear.

She floated off the stage and down the ladder, greeted by more hugs than she could recognize faces. All the joy and excitement swirled around her. Always Levi was by her side, never out of sight. Always with his unconditional love.

A high-pitched squeal broke through the chaos, and Levi disappeared into a cloud of family members. Violet practically jumped into his arms as his brothers grunted and thumped him on the back.

"I didn't know you could talk that much." Violet laughed. "You were amazing!"

"You too," Mama Potts said to Kelsey as she pulled her into a mother's embrace.

Kelsey had nearly forgotten how good that could feel as she leaned into the warmth and acceptance. "Thank you," she whispered around the lump that jumped to her throat at being surrounded by family. Levi's family.

And maybe—someday—her family.

Violet finally released Levi, cupping his face and pressing a smacking kiss on his cheek. The moonlight caught on her hand, and Kelsey stared at the shiny loop on her finger for a long second before it finally came into focus.

Meg, too, must have seen it because she squeaked with joy. "You did it," she said with a shove at Eli's shoulder.

He shrugged and pulled Violet to his side, and Kelsey couldn't tell if Levi was more thankful to be rescued from Violet's congratulations or pleased that his brother was finally going to make Violet a full and true Ross. Then everyone was talking at once again, congratulating the happy couple on their engagement, begging for the details.

"At the ice rink," Violet said. "Just the two of us. And he even asked Carson to play our song."

"Did he get down on one knee?" Meg asked.

"Of course," Eli said. "Like I'd do anything less."

Oliver smirked. "I'm surprised he didn't have the team spell out the question on the ice."

Eli rolled his eyes before Levi added, "Took you long enough to get around to it."

Kelsey laughed along with the others and elbowed him gently in the side. He was one to be talking. But as he looked down into her eyes, she knew he'd been worth the wait.

"Well, well." Mable Jean arrived like she was holding court and it was her show that would be the talk of the island for weeks to come. "It would appear congratulations are in order, my dears. All around." She turned to Eli first. "I fear you've broken the hearts of many a woman on the south shore, but we do adore Violet, and I wish you both my best."

"Thank you, MJ," Eli said—undoubtedly the only person on the island who could get away with calling her that.

Mable Jean turned to Kelsey, her face even brighter than the stage lights could manage. Reaching out both hands, she said, "Kelsey, you've done even more than I could have imagined! What a success!"

Kelsey squeezed the older woman's silky-soft hands. "Thank you."

"And you, Levi. You're a star in the making if you want it."

He quickly shook his head and ducked his chin, but his smile was filled with life.

Mable Jean looked at each of them, white eyebrows sagging low over her eyes. "And now for the bad news."

Kelsey's stomach twisted, and she grabbed for Levi. His arm was already around her waist.

"I've discovered a great many things about Mr. Mitch Trumball, most concerning that he has been petitioning the board to close the playhouse for quite some time."

Kelsey gasped. "But he's the executive director. How could he?"

"It would seem he's been offered another job, but he's been unable to get out of his contract to accept it."

"So he didn't want us to succeed."

"Indeed."

Sucking in a sharp breath, Kelsey jerked her head around, wondering if the man had dared to make an appearance. Surely his absence would be noted by the community. But maybe he didn't even care.

Instead of Mitch, she spotted Dean Ross strolling around the end of the park, his hands in his pockets, looking like he was whistling a tune.

"And Mr. Ross?"

"Ah, yes. As far as I can tell, he was supposed to steal the portable equipment yesterday to ensure that the show would flop and the community would agree there was no need for the theatre."

That was why he'd been loitering the day before. Kelsey wanted to push him into the bay.

"Apparently someone got in his way," Mable Jean said with a wink just for Levi. "He was also supposed to make sure that the large equipment—the pieces he couldn't move on his own—weren't damaged and could be sold for profit. They planned to say you had stolen it after you'd had to cancel the show. That way they could get the insurance payout too. Mitch was planning to take it all and disappear just as Dean Ross did all those years ago."

Levi saw red. He'd never understood that expression until this moment, when his vision literally took on a crimson tint.

"That man is—" Mama Potts looked like she was ready to spit nails, too mad to finish her thought.

Eli and Oliver both stepped forward, fists at their sides. They were physically intimidating for sure, all broad shoulders and fiery eyes. But a black eye or another bruise wasn't going to solve this problem.

Holding up his hands, Levi stopped them. "Let me."

Both of them looked uncertain, but Levi didn't wait for their permission. He marched across the lawn through the thinning crowd, straight toward his dad. For the first time since he was fifteen, he spoke the words that he wanted to.

"You've ruined a lot of lives, Dad. But that ends right now."

Dean's gaze swept up and down as he sneered. "Says who?"

"Says me." Levi licked his lips as he straightened the hem of his costume vest. "I won't let you hurt this family or anyone I care about any longer. You should have left town and never come back."

"That's not what you said the last time."

"You're right. I didn't know who you were then. I didn't know what you'd been through or what you'd done. But I know now. And I know the local RCMP."

Dean's face went wan, revealing a purple tint across his cheekbone.

"I also know that you and Trumball had some kind of deal."

"You can't prove that," Dean spit out, wincing at the movement.

Levi stared at him hard, but Dean angled the left side of his face out of the light.

"What happened? Were you too drunk last night to put a stop to the show? I bet Trumball wasn't very happy to find that out."

Fear flashed in Dean's eyes, then so much anger that Levi could hardly recognize them. Gone were the eyes that he saw in his brothers, that he saw every morning in the mirror. They'd been overtaken by fury and terror. Whatever shame and regret his dad felt, he masked them behind the other emotions.

But Levi knew they were there. Even if fear ruled in his dad's heart.

"Why did you come back here?" he asked.

Dean said nothing, and his gaze remained fixed on the ground.

"You thought there might be some con to be had, some money to be swindled?"

"It's none of your business."

"You're wrong about that." He swung his finger toward the small crowd a dozen meters away. "Every time you show up in our lives, you end up hurting at least one of us, and it's not going to happen again."

Dean squinted at the small group. "Did your brothers get married? Guess they're plenty old enough now."

Levi squared his shoulders. "That's no longer your concern. You've proved time and again that you don't want to be part of our family, so we're going to honor that. And you need to let Mom go—sign the papers, do whatever needs to be done."

His eyes flashed. "You don't have a say in that."

"Maybe not, but I think Jeffrey Druthers does."

Dean's face went redder than a beet, his mouth pumping but no words coming out.

"And the RCMP."

His voice trembled. "You wouldn't call the police on your old man."

Levi tried to find pity or regret, but neither was there. Only sadness that it had come to this, and certainty that this was what he had to do to protect his family. And the courage to speak the words that needed to be spoken.

"I already did."

As if on cue, the lights of Kevin's patrol car flashed, and he stepped out from behind the wheel. A man with a barrel chest and bushy beard exited the passenger seat.

Dean physically recoiled, his eyes larger than saucers. "No. No. It's been too long. There has to be a statute of limitations or something."

"Maybe, but they certainly have enough to bring you in for questioning. And I have a feeling they'll find enough to link you to Trumball and his schemes too."

"No. No. No." Dean shook his head wildly, his feet back-pedaling so fast that he tripped and landed in the grass. Even scrambling to right himself, he greeted Jeffrey Druthers and the police on all fours, sunk low. "I'll tell you everything," he said as Kevin hoisted him to his feet, already clicking handcuffs on him. "Trumball was going to take all the profits from the show. He was going to take everything and said he'd split it with me. But it wasn't my idea. None of it was my idea."

"I've been waiting a long time for this," Druthers seethed. "You almost sunk me, and now I'm going to see you behind bars."

Levi watched Kevin march his dad away. With a sad sigh, he shoved his hands into his pockets and strolled back to his family. Eli stood behind Violet, his arms wrapped around her. Oliver held Meg against his side with one arm and the baby in the other. Even Mama Potts was leaning into the comfort of Patrick.

For the first time in his memory, Levi had someone to hold too. Someone for comfort and support. He reached for Kelsey, and she stepped into his embrace and pressed her face against his shoulder. Warm and sweet, she somehow brought a smile to his lips despite all the somber faces staring at him.

"That was . . ." Eli trailed off, clearly not sure how to finish.

"Did you plan that? You called Kevin?" Oliver asked, a dose of admiration in his voice.

Levi shrugged. "When Dad showed up last night, I knew he'd be back. Kevin's been keeping an eye on him all night, making sure he didn't slip away."

Mama Potts pressed her hand to his cheek. "I'm so proud of you." Somehow her words covered all of it. Performing in the show. Having his dad arrested. Speaking up for himself—for them all.

For the first time since that night so many years before, he knew for certain that he had things worth saying.

The crowd lingered well into the night, the stage lights illuminating the children running around the lawn and the families enjoying the midnight sky. After Oliver and Meg took little Walter home, Eli and Violet disappeared and Patrick offered to walk Mama Potts home.

Not long before midnight, Kelsey took Levi's hand and led him behind the stage, finally having a moment for just the two of them. Pulling him in close, she snuggled against his scratchy costume vest and starchy white shirt—and she didn't even mind because beneath them was the truest, kindest heart she knew. One with the strength to do hard things for his family.

For her.

Even though he hadn't said it yet, she knew that she was his family. He was hers too.

"Thank you," she whispered into his chest.

"Hmm?"

"Thank you."

"What was that?"

She looked up into his eyes, which held a glint of humor. Even in the soft glow from the lights on the other side of the stage, she could make out his mischievous dimples. Pushing up on her tiptoes, she pressed her lips against his. "Thank you," she breathed.

"Hmm." His sigh might have meant "You're welcome." Or maybe it meant "Anytime." Or—she hoped—"I love you." It didn't matter too much because the way he wrapped her up in his arms promised all of that and so much more.

Someone behind her cleared their throat. Kelsey jumped and tried to put some space between her and Levi. But he didn't let her go all the way, keeping one arm around her waist.

Mable Jean stood behind her, hands folded primly, head cocked to the side, and eyebrows lifted. "I bring news from the playhouse board."

Kelsey's chest tightened, and she swayed against Levi.

"They're overjoyed that the show has brought in more than fifty thousand dollars in donations and requests from several businesses to sponsor next summer's theatre in the park."

"You're kidding me," Kelsey said breathlessly. "Fifty thousand? For one show?"

"It's more than enough to fix the playhouse. And since I suggested the board of directors revoke Mitch Trumball's access to the playhouse's accounts—shortly after you asked me about him—the money is safe and sound."

Levi squeezed her, pressing a kiss to her temple.

"I—that's—I'm so—I don't have any words. That's new for me."

All three of them laughed, but Mable Jean quickly turned serious. "It's good news for the playhouse, indeed. However, I don't have good news from the school board."

Kelsey's stomach hit the ground and burrowed right into the red dirt as unexpected tears sprang to her eyes.

"They decided this morning not to reopen the drama department. I'm very sorry."

Somehow they'd honored Grandma Coletta's memory and saved the theatre—but it hadn't been enough. Without a job, Kelsey had no way to stay in Victoria.

Levi immediately recognized the same. She could feel it

in the tension of his chest and the trembling of his hands. Then his arms turned to steel.

Kelsey tried to force an understanding smile into place, but it wouldn't stick for the quivering of her lower lip.

Mable Jean chuckled. "But I do happen to know that the playhouse will be looking for a new executive director. Would you like me to put in a good word for you?"

Levi let out a deep breath, easing his hold on her enough to let her breathe too. Or maybe that was the lifted weight from her shoulders.

"Yes. Please," she said. "Yes. I'd like that."

"Good, because I already did, and you have an interview on Monday." Mable Jean, clearly satisfied with herself, clapped her hands and nodded firmly. "Now, get back to whatever you were doing." With a wink and a knowing grin, she slipped away, leaving Kelsey to sag in relief against Levi.

Pressing his lips to her ear, he whispered, "I wasn't going to let you go, you know."

Shivers raced down her spine. "Oh yeah? And how were you going to get me to stay?"

"I'd have thought of something to say." He kissed her ear. Then her cheek. Then her jaw. He turned her slowly until their lips touched, sweet and tender and better than she had ever hoped to deserve.

Closing her eyes as joy washed over her, she wrapped her arms around his neck. "Go on, then. I'm listening."

Epilogue

The thing about dreams is that they aren't supposed to come true. At least in Levi's experience.

But here he sat in an Adirondack chair on the wrap-around porch of his very own green house, a bouncing baby Ross on his knee. Little Walter squealed and giggled as Levi tickled him, his chubby fists waving back and forth as he blew bubbles from his mouth. It wouldn't be long before he was tottering all over the house and yard.

"Levi! Get over here!"

He looked up at Oliver. "I'm taking care of your kid," he hollered. "Besides, why do we need a rehearsal anyway? We all know where we're going to stand."

"Such a guy thing to say," Meg mumbled as she stepped outside and scooped her ten-month-old from his leg.

"Well? I'm serious. If Eli and Violet can't manage to find each other at the end of the aisle, then . . ."

"What?" Long fingers jabbed him in the side, and Levi laughed as Violet swooped around him. "It's my wedding. And I want a rehearsal. I have no doubt Eli and I will find each other. It's you and Oliver I'm worried about."

He snorted but held out his arm anyway to escort her

down the porch steps and across the green lawn of his front yard. Rows of white chairs had already been set up facing the ocean, and a wooden arch—a Levi Ross original—marked the spot where Violet and Eli would say their vows the following evening as the sun cast its big orange glow across the water.

Violet's parents stood near the chairs, talking with Mama Potts and Patrick, who—Levi had been forced to admit—made his mom happier than he had ever seen her.

Violet hugged her mom, then looked around quickly. "Where's Kelsey?"

"On her way," he said just as her old Ford skidded into the driveway.

"Sorry I'm late," she hollered as she hopped from her car. She did a little dance as she straightened her sundress and raced across the lawn. "Sorry," she panted again as she gave Violet a quick hug and then pressed her lips against Levi's in a brief kiss. Too brief for his liking. But probably appropriate for their audience.

He'd circle back to that after the rehearsal.

"The show is coming along great," Kelsey said, "and I can't believe we're opening next week."

It had been a long year of hard work and late nights. If Levi hadn't spent the majority of them at the Victoria Playhouse, he wasn't sure he'd have seen Kelsey at all. But it was all worth it to see the light in her eyes when she talked about the first show of the year—sold-out performances the entire month.

Pastor Dell called them all to order, and Levi gave her another quick kiss before trotting around the chairs to meet his brothers at the front. Eli, who had never suffered stage fright, didn't look like he was about to begin, even when Oliver elbowed him and Levi asked, "Are you sure about this?"

"Pipe down, you two," he hissed with a smile as Kelsey and then Meg—carrying little Walter—stepped down the aisle. Then came Violet on her dad's arm, radiant in her white sundress and makeshift bouquet of wildflowers.

As the pastor read Scripture over Eli and Violet and asked them to repeat their vows, Levi leaned around them and caught Kelsey's eye. She smiled a secret smile, one filled with hope and promise, one that made him pat his pocket to triple-check that the ring was right where he'd left it.

He'd have to wait to finish the attic until he could save up more money. But some things couldn't wait—like making sure Kelsey knew the green house didn't mean anything unless she lived in it with him.

Long after the rehearsal dinner, after everyone had gone to their own homes, Levi lay in the grass beside Kelsey, staring up at the sky and listening to the waves ebb and flow.

"What are you going to dream about now?" she asked, linking their hands. "You have the house you always wanted, just one job, and the best girl in the world."

He snorted his laughter. "A humble one at that."

"What can I say?" Rolling to her side, she propped her chin on his chest. "It couldn't be helped."

Leaning forward, he pressed his lips to hers. She tasted like strawberry cake and sparkling cider and all of his favorite things.

After a lingering kiss to the music of the night, she smiled languidly. "So? What more could you want?"

For the first time in almost a year, he felt tongue-tied. Maybe he should have memorized a sonnet or written something to read. Or perhaps he should just put this on hold. The ring could wait, even though he had asked Violet if he could propose on her wedding weekend. While she hadn't technically said yes, her squeal of delight and thorough hug had made him think he had her blessing.

After a long silence, he uttered just one simple word. "You."

"Hmm?"

"You. You're all I want."

Kelsey chuckled softly. "You already have me."

He slipped his hand into his pocket and pulled out the platinum ring with the modest diamond. As he held it out beneath the moonlight, it glittered like a star. "Forever?"

Somehow he'd managed to leave Kelsey speechless. But her body trembled against his, her eyes shining like glass. She'd stopped breathing, and he brushed her hair back, cupping her ear.

"You're not going to pass out on me again, are you?"

She shook her head, finally reaching for the ring and sliding it onto her finger, then holding it up into the light, her eyes transfixed.

"So, is that a yes?"

She nodded into his shoulder but didn't make a sound.

"Forever?"

She nodded again, and he tickled her until she laughed. The melody wrapped around his heart, which was free from fear, free to love her.

Then, finally, "Yes. For always."

Acknowledgments

With much appreciation for the real Victoria Playhouse and the people of Victoria by the Sea, Prince Edward Island.

The hall—completed in 1915—has endured a number of storms, including the remnants of Hurricane Dorian in 2019. But as far as I know, it has never been threatened with closure due to damage since it became a playhouse in 1981. In 2007, the building was designated a historic place on the Canadian Register of Historic Places and remains the heart of the community, presenting over seventy performances a year. I hope you'll make it part of your next trip to the island.

The fact that this book has made it into your hands is a testament to God's goodness and the many people who have spoken life over me and my writing time and again. If it was up to me alone, I'm afraid I might have given up. But God knew I needed this community.

Rachel Kent and Books & Such Literary Management, thank you for cheering me on and believing in my stories.

I'm so thankful that we sat at the same table the first night of the 2009 ACFW conference. What a ride this has been. I'm privileged to call you not only my agent but my friend.

The amazing team at Revell, you are incredible. Thank you for making this book better than I could have made it on my own. Kelsey, Jessica, Michele, Karen, and the rest of the team, thank you! And Vicki—somehow nine books together seem to have gone by in a flash. I'll be forever grateful to you for seeing what the Red Door could be.

The Panera ladies, my fellow writers, confidantes, and friends—what a gift you've been to me. This year we celebrate five years of meeting for dinner, writing (sometimes), and doing this writer life together. I could not be more grateful for the encouraging, inspiring women God has brought to our group. Lindsay Harrel, Sara Carrington, Jennifer Deibel, Sarah Popovich, Erin McFarland, Ruth Douthitt, Tari Faris, and Breana Johnson, thank you for speaking truth when the lies are easier for me to believe.

For my family, who encourages my love of theatre and tolerates my writing schedule. I'm glad I can always find someone to go to a show with me when I crawl out of my writing hole. The Johnson/Whitson clan is my favorite.

A special thanks to my niece Julia, who answered my drama-related questions while she was busy preparing to leave for college. You saved me more than once!

Finally, all my gratitude belongs to the One who speaks life over me every day. I'm eternally thankful for a Father who loves me so much.

Ready to head back to
Prince Edward Island for another
adventure? **Read an excerpt
from *The Red Door Inn*.**

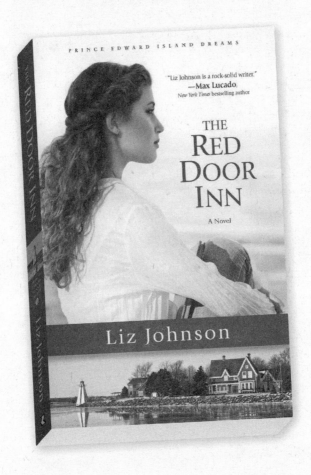

"The Red Door Inn took my breath away!
Highly recommended!"

—**Colleen Coble**, author of *The Inn at Ocean's Edge*
and the Hope Beach series

one

The change in Marie Carrington's pocket wouldn't pay for a ferry ride across the Northumberland Strait to Prince Edward Island, let alone a bus ticket to anywhere else in the world. As she cupped the Canadian dollar coins in her shaking hand, they clinked together, drawing the curious gaze of the man in the seat next to her.

Marie shifted on the painful plastic chair, putting her shoulder between all the money she had access to in the world and the gaze shrouded by bushy, white eyebrows.

Two. Four. Five. Six. Seven. Seven twenty-five.

The sign on the café attached to the ferry terminal announced a fish sandwich lunch special for $6.99, but tax would be more than a quarter. Besides, that would completely wipe her out. And then she'd be penniless in a strange town.

"Which color do you like better?" The man with the eyebrows and more wrinkles than she'd ever seen on one face leaned forward, holding out four paint swatches.

Marie rotated farther away from him, shoving her coins back in her pocket, but he didn't seem to notice.

"My wife liked the pale blue, but I think we need something brighter for the shutters of a bed-and-breakfast. Don't you?"

She couldn't fight the urge to survey the swatches, even if just out of the corner of her eye. With one finger she twisted the necklace at her throat, imagining each color on the front of a robust, two-story Maritime home.

He dipped his chin as though waiting for her answer. "Well? Don't you think it's too light?"

Finally she whispered, "Unless the house is a deep blue." Keeping an eye on him, she scooted to the far edge of her seat, the armrest digging into her side as she bent to scoop her backpack into the safety of her lap.

"What?" His eyebrows nearly reached his hairline. Pulling his glasses from his front shirt pocket and planting them on his face, he held the color swatch in question to within an inch of his nose, mumbling her words over and over. "Deep blue. The house could be deep blue."

After several seconds of peace, she decided he'd forgotten all about her until he flipped the same blue color swatch over her shoulder and pointed to the darkest hue on the row. "Is that dark enough?"

"No."

"Then what would be?"

Shoulder still in place, she pointed with her other hand to the blue of his pants. "Maybe with a hint of gray mixed in."

Holding the color card against a handful of jean fabric, he nodded slowly. "That might work. But not too much gray." He scratched his chin, his whiskers rasping beneath aged fingers. "What about the trim? Would you do the same color as the shutters?"

"It depends."

"On what?"

"Lots of things. What do the neighboring houses look like? Do you have other colors around the house?"

"Like what?"

She relaxed her back a fraction of an inch so that she didn't have to strain her neck to watch his reactions. "Maybe a flower garden or water feature. If you already have several other colors, keep the trim and shutters the same color or the house can look disjointed and unappealing."

"Never thought of having a flower garden." He poked his tongue into his cheek, staring at the color cards as though they'd failed him. "Suppose women might like that."

"Men too."

He raised one of his bushy brows at her.

"Really."

"Well, if I have to have flowers and a red door, I suppose the shutters and trim should be one color."

"Why a red door?" Marie hadn't asked a voluntary question in two months, but this one just slipped out before she could clamp her hand over her mouth.

The old man didn't seem to notice her surprise. Instead, lost in the colors in his hands, he cleared his throat. "We visited the island for the first time fifteen years ago, and the red doors captured her imagination. She said we had to have a red door. There was no argument. No discussion, only—"

"The nine thirty ferry will begin boarding shortly." The voice of the announcer echoed over the tinny intercom. "All passengers please make your way to the boarding area and have your ticket in hand."

The old man shuffled his cards and tucked them into his pocket before slipping one arm into his oversized coat. He reached for and missed the other arm twice before Marie set her bag back on the floor, stood, and held the jacket open for him. "Thank you."

She nodded and slipped back into her seat, fighting the urge to hug her knees to her chest and let the tears roll. She could sit here for hours, but it wouldn't make the money she needed appear. She'd never have enough for the ferry traveling north. She couldn't come up with the sixteen dollars to keep moving.

"Aren't you going on the boat?"

He wasn't from New England or the Canadian Maritimes. Any self-respecting man from that area would know it was a ship or a ferry, not a boat.

"No." Her fingers brushed over her pocket and the outline of her meager funds pressing through the black corduroy.

His eyebrows pulled into a V that looked like a single angry caterpillar. "Have some more ideas to ask you about."

She looked anywhere but into his ice-blue eyes, her gaze finally resting on the posted ferry schedule above the ticket counter. "I'm not going to Prince Edward Island today." If she was honest with herself, she probably wasn't ever going to make it to PEI. More than likely she'd have to call her father back in Boston and face him, no matter how much she hated that.

"Don't you want to go to the island?"

Her laugh was more stinging than humorous, even to her own ears. Of course she wanted to go to the island. Of course she wanted to keep putting more and more distance between her and her past.

She'd grown up reading books set on the island, dreaming of finding a home there. She'd even managed to squeeze one of her favorites by the island's beloved author into her backpack. Of course, the corners were bent and the edges worn, but she'd never loved the book or the dream of the island any more than she did sitting just a few miles away.

Of course she wanted to go to the island.

But wanting wouldn't get her more than a toe in the icy water.

"I don't have a ticket."

"That all? I'll get you a ticket."

She shook her head, swallowing the hint of hope that was quickly coupled with certain disappointment. "Thank you, no. I can't accept."

But he was halfway to the counter already, spreading the mouth of his cracked wallet and pulling a colorful bill from within. He said something to the raven-haired ticket agent, who tipped her head to shoot a curious glance around his arm.

Grabbing her bag, Marie jumped to her feet. If she were lucky, a wave would crash into the building, sweeping her away. Away from prying eyes and inquiring stares. Away from old men who asked too many questions. Away from that ever-present emptiness.

But luck wasn't on her side.

A familiar tightness rose in her chest, and she gasped for even the shallowest breath.

Oh, not again! Not with an audience and no place to lie down.

She tried to fill her lungs as a band squeezed around them. The ground shifted, her whole world tilting as she stumbled toward the chair she had just vacated. Squeezing her eyes shut against the black spots that danced in the edges of her line of sight, she leaned forward, fighting for a breath. Pain shot down the middle of her chest, but no amount of rubbing soothed the throbbing.

She was going to pass out in front of everyone.

A hand grabbed her forearm, and she jerked away from the searing touch. "You getting sick?"

The old man's now familiar voice made his hand on her shoulder barely tolerable, but she couldn't fight the blaze in her chest enough to get the air needed to reply. Finally she wiggled her head, her hair swiping across her shoulders.

"You sure?" His hands guided her all the way into the chair, his breath warm on her face as he sat beside her. "You look a little green. And we're not even on the water yet."

Shaking her head again, she gasped, this time rewarded with a loosening in her lungs. They weren't full, but the relief lessened the spinning in her head and the pain at her sternum. She arched her back and again managed a wheeze.

"Now boarding the nine thirty ferry to Wood Islands. All ticketed passengers should be in the boarding area." They both turned toward the girl in the fleece vest holding the microphone.

"Can you make it to the boat?"

Marie blinked into the wrinkled face, pinning her gaze on a particularly deep crevice between the corner of his eye and his jawline. "Going to miss . . ."

"Well then, let's get on there before they leave us behind." He held out a ticket, the white slip contrasting his tanned, weathered fingers. "Take this."

"Can't." The ticket didn't budge. Had he not heard? Or had the words not passed her lips?

Finally he squatted before her with an unusual agility for a man his age. "Why not?"

She couldn't possibly repay him. She had no money. At least none that she could access without drawing undue attention. But she wasn't so low that she had to accept charity.

Another pang seared her heart.

Well, maybe she was.

He shot a glance toward the entrance to the ferry boarding area. "If you don't use this ticket, it'll just go to waste."

"I don't even know your name."

The lines around his mouth grew deeper, his eyes catching a shimmer from the ceiling lights. "Jack Sloane from . . . well, I suppose I'm from North Rustico, PEI, now."

"Marie." Twisting her hands into the hem of her sweater, she continued, the words barely making it to her own ears. "I can't pay for it."

"Didn't ask you to, Marie." He winked at her, adding in a conspiratorial whisper, "I'll make you a trade. The ticket for your help in picking out paint colors."

The attack had left her too weak to argue, but the trade was certainly in her favor. "All right." She dismissed his outstretched hand, and they stood together, his knees creaking like the old screen door at her father's beach house.

When she slipped her fingers around the ticket, it fluttered like a flag caught in an ocean breeze, and she clutched it to her chest, finally catching a full breath.

But could he really expect so little in return?

⸺

"What color would you call that?" Jack gestured to the point where the open sea met the roiling gray clouds.

Marie squinted in the direction of his finger, hugging that silly pink bag to her chest but finally breathing normally. He'd been afraid she wouldn't make it onto the ferry, the way she'd been gasping for air, but she'd refused his arm as they boarded. And the salty sea air turned her pale cheeks pink like his wife's favorite flower.

After several long seconds, she shrugged one shoulder. "I don't know."

"Sure is pretty." She nodded slowly, thoughtfully, as she leaned back against the railing, tucking her chin again into her chest, nearly hidden behind the bag that was just about half her size. The pack wasn't so big, really. She was just a wisp of a creature. "You think I could paint the house that color?"

Without turning toward the sky again, she whispered, "I think it'd be perfect."

"Even with a red door."

"Especially with a red door." She offered him a tiny lift of the corner of her mouth, an obligatory smile. But she didn't mean it. He had a hunch she'd be a stunner if she really smiled, which she hadn't all morning. Not even when he pointed out the Caribou Lighthouse as they headed into open water. Rose had always smiled at the little lighthouse, delighted by the red roof.

"Maybe we should buy a lighthouse and become light keepers," his Rose would muse, leaning into his embrace.

"And give up on the bed-and-breakfast?" He only said it to watch her forehead wrinkle in distaste. "I'd be happy to take up light keeping, if you really want."

Rose had laughed and smacked his arm. "No so fast, Mr. Sloane. You aren't getting off the hook that easy."

Even after forty-one years, he'd loved it when she called him Mr. Sloane. Without fail it was accompanied by a twinkle in her eyes that reminded him of the day they'd met. The day he'd fallen in love with her.

But there wasn't a twinkle in Marie's eyes. They eclipsed her face, blue and haunted, as she gazed at the deck. Free of humor and good spirits, they made his heart ache.

What between here and heaven had caused such a pretty little thing to be so sad?

"So what brings you to the island?"

She turned those anxious eyes on him and without a hint of irony said, "You."

She may not have meant it to be funny, but he couldn't keep the laughter inside, letting the mirth roll from deep in his belly. Marie's eyes remained fixed on him, but she didn't say anything more. "You're quick, aren't you?" One bony shoulder poked up, and she wrapped a finger around the gold chain at her neck, twirling it. "I meant, why are you headed to PEI?"

She turned away from him, putting her shrugging

shoulder between them before whispering, "In the books I read as a child, it sounded like a magical place." Her head turned farther away from Jack, as though she were looking back at the gray horizon, but she'd closed her eyes, taking deep breaths through her nose and releasing them slowly through tight lips.

"Where are you staying?"

His gut flipped when she didn't answer him, and he knew. She didn't have sixteen dollars to buy a ferry ticket. She didn't have two pennies to rub together. She didn't have a soul to ask for help or anyplace to go.

As if sitting on his other side, Rose whispered in his ear, "It's a fine how-do-you-do when you can't help someone in need, Jack. Give the poor girl a place to stay."

Of course, Rose didn't bother with any particulars. She never had. Always a big-picture thinker, she wasn't concerned with the details. But Marie wasn't going to accept anything else for free. She'd fought him on the ferry ticket. What would she say about a room at his inn?

"They sure don't make these benches for seventy-two-year-old backsides." He shifted, relieving pressure from a sore spot and, in the meantime, leaning closer to her.

Marie nodded, but her shoulder dipped enough that he could see her whole face.

Apparently, if he wanted more of a response from her, he was going to have to ask direct questions. "How'd you get to know so much about colors and paint and stuff?"

Several seconds ticked by, the only sounds the hum of the ferry's motor and the squawking of a lone gull. "I took—" Her voice broke, and she had to clear her throat before she could continue. "I took a few art classes in college after a friend showed me a few things."

"You must have been pretty talented. Ever consider a career in it?"

"That wasn't really an option."

"Why not?" That barrier jumped into place again, and he tossed a less invasive question her way. "Do you know anything about decorating?"

"A bit."

He scrubbed his chin, rasping his fingernails over his whiskers, and let his eyes grow bigger as though just thinking of something. "Say, you wouldn't be available to help me with a project, would you?"

The girl could teach a college course in shrugging. One for every occasion, but this one most likely meant she wasn't going to commit to anything without more information. She might be broke, but she wasn't desperate.

Jack nodded slowly, rubbing his hands together, for the first time realizing that the kid didn't have more than a light jacket to ward off the damp chill of the late winter air. Maybe that's why she hugged that bag so tight.

"Don't know how long you're planning to stay in the area, but I need some help. I'm renovatin' a home in North Rustico, turning it into an inn along the harbor."

"Sounds beautiful."

"Oh, it is. The core renovations are almost done, but it's missing something."

Marie shot him a look and leaned in just enough to ask her question without having to speak.

"It's missing a woman's touch." He waved toward the sky. "That certain something from someone who knows what color the clouds are. It's missing the details that will make it a home."

Her forehead wrinkled. "I don't understand."

Over her shoulder, the green pine trees on the shoreline quickly approached. Soon they'd be on the island. Soon he'd miss his chance to help her. And to get her help.

"My inn opens in a couple months, and I need help getting it ready for guests. I have beds but no sheets. I have a little furniture but no decorations. I have rooms with no soul. And I could use a woman with an eye for color and details."

Marie's eyebrows lifted as she bit her lower lip. "Really?"

His hands jumped into the air, warding off too much hope. "I can't pay much, but you can stay in the basement apartment until we open the first of May."

A flicker of hope disappeared almost before he noticed it was there. "What's the catch?"

"No catch. I need help turning this house into a home." And as he said the words, he knew they were true. He did need help.

Rose would have called this meeting positively providential, and she'd have been right. The big guy upstairs clearly knew that Jack needed a hand before Jack even knew it.

Marie's eyelids drooped, and she turned away from him again. He had to do something to get her on board before the ferry landed and he was left with the ugliest bed-and-breakfast on the island.

"I could pay you four hundred dollars a month, and I'll cover all your living expenses."

The terse shake of her head made his stomach churn.

"Fine! Six hundred for the month, the best room in the house, and a bonus when the inn is done."

"I can't take your money."

"But you'll be earning it."

"Ladies and gentleman, please prepare for arrival at Wood Islands, Prince Edward Island." The disembodied voice sent both Jack and Marie turning toward the overhead speakers. The humming motor suddenly went silent as they floated to the dock, but Jack's heart revved. It was now or never.

"I've owned three auto shops, and I've always paid a fair wage. I won't start shorting employees now."

"Employee?" Chin still tucked, she looked up, her eyes glistening. It could be the wind making them water, but he had a feeling it was something else.

"Until the inn is ready."

"What's its name?"

"The inn?" She nodded, and he scratched at his hairline. "Well now, I haven't quite decided on that yet, but I'm thinking about the North Rustico Red Door."

Liz Johnson is the *New York Times* bestselling author of more than a dozen novels, including *Beyond the Tides* and *The Last Way Home*, as well as the Georgia Coast Romance and Prince Edward Island Dreams series. She works in marketing, makes her home in Phoenix, Arizona, and day-dreams of returning to PEI. Learn more at www.lizjohnson books.com.

Don't miss the rest of the
PRINCE EDWARD ISLAND SHORES SERIES!

"Love going back to PEI and meeting new characters mixed with those readers have already grown to love!"

—*Write-Read-Life*